'If only you could find a woman to marry who has no interest in actually being your wife, your problems would be solved.'

She spoke flippantly, more to divert his attention from her own tragic situation than anything else, but Innes, who had been in the act of taking another sip of whisky, stopped, the glass half-way to his lips, an arrested look in his eyes.

'Say that again.'

'What? That you need to marry…?'

'A woman who has no interest in being my wife,' he finished for her with a dawning smile. 'A woman who is in need of a home and has no fixed plans, who might actually be looking for a respite from her current life for a wee while. You're right—that's exactly what I need. And I know exactly the woman.'

'You do? You cannot possibly mean…'

His smile had a wicked light in it. 'I do,' Innes said. 'I mean you.'

AUTHOR NOTE

After I finished writing UNWED AND UNREPENTANT, which had a Clyde shipbuilder as its hero, I decided I wanted to stay close to home for my next story.

I started in Edinburgh, my favourite city second only to Paris, but the majority of Ainsley and Innes's story is set in Tighnabruaich, on the west coast of Argyll. I renamed it Strone Bridge, but anyone familiar with the area will recognise it. The view of the Kyles of Bute which Ainsley comes to love is one of my own favourites. Ostell Bay, with its golden sands and crystal-clear though icy sea, is a childhood haunt. And the weather—the wet, *driech*, grey west-coast weather—that's very true to life.

I hope that my love for the place where I was brought up, and where I now live and write, resonates in Ainsley and Innes's story. I hope it will inspire some of you to visit. More than anything, I hope that I've done justice to it, and that the romance of the place has enhanced the romance I've written.

Enormous thanks once again to all my Facebook and Twitter friends who have helped and encouraged me while writing this book. Thanks to all who suggested names for Ainsley's Agony Aunt alter ego, and in particular to Keira, who gave me Madame Hera, whose letters I had such fun dreaming up.

STRANGERS
AT THE ALTAR

Marguerite Kaye

First published in Great Brit
by Mills & Boon, an imprin   in (UK) Limited,
Large Print edition 2015
Harlequin (UK) Limited, Eton House, 18-24 Paradise Road,
Richmond, Surrey TW9 1SR

© 2014 Marguerite Kaye

ISBN: 978-0-263-25537-9

Harlequin (UK) Limited's policy is to use papers that are natural,
renewable and recyclable products and made from wood grown in
sustainable forests. The logging and manufacturing processes conform
to the legal environmental regulations of the country of origin.

Printed and bound in Great Britain
by CPI Antony Rowe, Chippenham, Wiltshire

Born and educated in Scotland, **Marguerite Kaye** originally qualified as a lawyer but chose not to practise. Instead, she carved out a career in IT and studied history part-time, gaining first-class honours and a master's degree. A few decades after winning a children's national poetry competition she decided to pursue her lifelong ambition to write, and submitted her first historical romance to Mills & Boon®. They accepted it, and she's been writing ever since.

You can contact Marguerite through her website at: www.margueritekaye.com

Previous novels by the same author:
THE WICKED LORD RASENBY
THE RAKE AND THE HEIRESS
INNOCENT IN THE SHEIKH'S HAREM†
  (part of *Summer Sheikhs* anthology)
THE GOVERNESS AND THE SHEIKH†
THE HIGHLANDER'S REDEMPTION*
THE HIGHLANDER'S RETURN*
RAKE WITH A FROZEN HEART
OUTRAGEOUS CONFESSIONS OF LADY DEBORAH
DUCHESS BY CHRISTMAS
  (part of *Gift-Wrapped Governesses* anthology)
THE BEAUTY WITHIN
RUMOURS THAT RUINED A LADY
UNWED AND UNREPENTANT
NEVER FORGET ME

and recent books in the Mills & Boon® Historical *Undone!* series:
CLAIMED BY THE WOLF PRINCE‡
BOUND TO THE WOLF PRINCE‡
THE HIGHLANDER AND THE WOLF PRINCESS‡
THE SHEIKH'S IMPETUOUS LOVE-SLAVE†
SPELLBOUND & SEDUCED
BEHIND THE COURTESAN'S MASK
FLIRTING WITH RUIN
AN INVITATION TO PLEASURE
LOST IN PLEASURE
HOW TO SEDUCE A SHEIKH
THE UNDOING OF DAISY EDWARDS◊
THE AWAKENING OF POPPY EDWARDS◊

In the Mills & Boon *Castonbury Park* Regency mini-series:
THE LADY WHO BROKE THE RULES

and in M&B eBooks:
TITANIC: A DATE WITH DESTINY

†linked by character
*Highland Brides
‡*Legend of the Faol*
◊*A Time for Scandal*

**Did you know that some of these novels
are also available as eBooks? Visit www.millsandboon.co.uk**

HISTORICAL NOTE

Paddle steamers and the railways brought tourism to the west coast of Scotland at around the time when Ainsley and Innes decided to set up their hotel. Though the original and most popular destinations 'doon the watter' on the Clyde were Rothesay, Largs and Dunoon, Tighnabruaich (aka Strone Bridge) had its share of excursionists. The engineer David Napier, whose Loch Eck tours inspired Ainsley, built a pier on the Holy Loch in the 1830s, not far from my own home.

Numerous versions of the *Rothesay Castle* paddle steamer made the journey from Glasgow, Gourock and eventually Wemyss Bay railway terminals to the Isle of Bute. Today, the last sea-going paddle steamer, the *Waverley*, makes the same journey from Glasgow to Bute and down the beautiful Kyles all the way to Tighnabruaich.

Strone Bridge Castle is actually based on Panmure House, the seat of the Maules near Dundee, which was demolished in 1955. The story which Innes tells Ainsley of the locked gates following the 1715 Jacobite rebellion belongs to Panmure, details and pictures of which are in Ian Gow's beautiful book *Scotland's Lost Houses*. The chapel attached to Strone Bridge Castle, though, is based on the one belonging to Mount Stuart in Rothesay.

Agony Aunts existed, astonishingly, as far back as the seventeenth century, though they reached their peak in the mid-Victorian era—a little after Madame Hera was writing. There are some fantastic examples of their letters in Tanith Carey's book *Never Kiss a Man in a Canoe*.

As to the traditions and customs in this book—well, I must admit that I've let my imagination loose a wee bit. All the Hogmanay customs are traditional, but the Rescinding ceremony is not. I actually invented it for an earlier book set in Argyll, THE HIGHLANDER'S REDEMPTION, and I liked it so much I thought I'd start a tradition of my own and re-use it.

Chapter One

Dear Madame Hera,

The other day, while taking a walk in the Cowgate district of Edinburgh, I was approached by a young man who gave me some assistance with my umbrella. Since he was very well dressed, seemed most polite, and the rain was coming down in torrents, it seemed churlish of me not to offer to share my shelter. He accepted with some alacrity, but the small circumference of my umbrella forced us into a somewhat compromising intimacy, of which the gentleman was not slow to take advantage. He stole a kiss from me, and I permitted him to take several more while we found respite from the downpour in the close of a nearby tenement. By the time the rain stopped, we were rather better acquainted than we ought to have been.

We parted without exchanging details. Alack, when he left me, the young man took not only my virtue but my umbrella. It was a gift from another gentleman, who is bound to question me most closely when he discovers its loss. I fear he will not understand the peculiar effect the combination of rain, a good-looking young man and a very small umbrella can have on a woman's willpower. What should I do?

Drookit Miss

Edinburgh—June 1840

'I am very sorry, Mrs McBrayne, but there is nothing to be done. Both your father's will and the law are perfectly clear upon the matter. Could not be clearer, in actual fact, though if you insist upon a second opinion, I believe my partner is now free.'

'You, Mr Thomson, *are* my second opinion,' the woman said scornfully. 'I have no intentions of spending more money I don't have, thanks to that spendthrift husband of mine and that trust of my father's, simply to hear what you have already made perfectly plain. The law is written by men for men and administered by men, too. Be damned to the law, Mr Thomson, for it seems to be forcing me to earn my living in a profession even older than your own, down in the Cowgate. I bid you good day.'

'Mrs McBrayne! Madam, I must beg you...'

The Fury merely tossed her head at the lawyer's outraged countenance and swept across the narrow reception hall of the office, heading for the door. Innes Drummond, who had just completed a similarly entirely unsatisfactory interview with Thomson's partner, watched her dramatic exit admiringly. The door slammed behind her with enough force to rattle the pane of glass on which the names Thomson & Ballard were etched. Innes could hear her footsteps descending the rackety stairs that led out into Parliament Square. She was as anxious to quit the place as he was himself. It struck him, as he flung the door behind him with equal and satisfying force, how ironic it was, that they both, he and the incandescent Mrs McBrayne, seemed to be victims of very similar circumstances.

He reached the bottom of the stairs and heaved open the heavy wooden door, only to collide with the person standing on the step. 'I am terribly sorry,' Innes said.

'No, it was my fault.'

She stood aside, and as she did so, he saw tears glistening on her lashes. Mortified, she saw him noticing, and scrubbed at her eyes with her glove, averting her face as she pushed past him.

'Wait!' Instinctively knowing she would not, Innes caught her arm. 'Madam, you are upset.'

She glared at him, shaking herself free of his reflexive grip. 'I am not upset. Not that it's any of your business, but I am very far beyond upset. I am…'

'Furious,' Innes finished for her with a wry smile. 'I know how you feel.'

'I doubt it.'

Her eyes were hazel, wide-spaced and fringed with very long lashes. She was not pretty, definitely not one of those soft, pliant females with rosebud mouths and doe-like gazes, but he was nonetheless drawn to her. She eyed him sceptically, a frown pulling her rather fierce brows together. She was not young either, perhaps in her late twenties, and there was intelligence as well as cynicism in her face. Then there was her mouth. No, not a rosebud, but soft all the same when it ought to be austere, with a hint of humour and more than a hint of sensuality. He noticed that, and with some surprise, noticed that he'd noticed, that his eyes had wandered down, over the slim figure in the drab grey coat, taking a rapid inventory of the limited view and wanting to see more, and that surprised him, too.

'Innes Drummond.' He introduced himself because he could think of nothing else to say, and because he didn't want her to go. Her brows lifted haughtily in response. For some reason, it made her look younger. 'A fellow victim of the law, of his father and of a trust,' he added. 'Though I'm not encumbered with a wife, spendthrift or otherwise.'

'You were listening in to a private conversation between myself and Mr Thomson.'

'Ought I to have pretended not to hear? The tone of your voice made that rather difficult.'

She gave a dry little laugh. 'A tone I feel sure Mr Thomson found most objectionable. Bloody lawyers. Damned law. You see, I can swear as well as shout, though I assure you, I am not usually the type who does either.'

Innes laughed. 'I really do know how you feel, you know.'

She smiled tightly. 'You are a man, Mr Drummond. It is simply not possible. Now, if you will excuse me?'

'Where are you going?' Once again, he had spoken without thinking, wanting only to detain her. Once again her brows rose, more sharply this time. 'I only meant that if you had no urgent business— But I spoke out of turn. Perhaps your husband is expecting you?'

'My husband is dead, Mr Drummond, and though his dying has left me quite without resources, still I cannot be sorry for it.'

'You don't mince your words, do you, Mrs McBrayne?'

Though he was rather shocked at this callous remark, Innes spoke flippantly. She did not smile, however, nor take umbrage, but instead paled slightly. 'I speak my mind. My opinions may be unpalatable, but at least in expressing them, there can be no pretending that I have none.'

Nor, Innes thought, could there be any denying that a wealth of bitter experience lay behind her words. He was intrigued. 'If you are in no rush, I'd very much like it if you would take a glass of something with me. I promise I don't mean anything in the least improper,' he added hurriedly,

'I merely thought it would be pleasant—cathartic, I don't know—to let off steam with a kindred spirit—' Her astonished expression forced him to break off. 'Forget it. It's been an awful day, an awful few weeks, but I shouldn't have asked.'

He made to tip his hat, but once again she surprised him, this time with a faint smile. 'Never mind weeks, *I've* had an awful few months. No, make that years. The only reason I've not taken to drink already is that I suspect I'd take to it rather too well.'

'I suspect that you do anything well that you set your mind to, Mrs McBrayne. You strike me as a most determined female.'

'Do I? I am now, though it is by far too late, for no matter how determined I am to get myself out of this mess, in truth I can see no solution.'

'Save to sell yourself down the Cowgate? I hope it doesn't come to that.'

She gave him what could only be described as a challenging look. 'Why, are you afraid I will not make sufficient to earn my keep?'

'What on earth do you know of such things?' Innes asked, torn between shock and laughter.

'Oh, I have my sources. And I have an umbrella,' she added confusingly.

She spoke primly, but there was devilment in her eyes, and the smile she was biting back was doing strange things to his guts. 'You are outrageous, Mrs McBrayne,' Innes said.

'Don't you believe me?'

'I have no idea what to make of you, and right at this moment, I don't really care. You made me laugh, and honestly, after what that lawyer told me, I didn't think that was possible.'

Her smile softened sympathetically. 'It sounds like I am not the only one in need of a dram,' she said. 'Why not! I've nothing at home waiting for me except final demands and most likely a few bailiffs. Buy me a drink, Mr Drummond, and we can compare our woes, though I warn you now that mine will far outweigh yours.'

Ainsley McBrayne wondered what on earth had come over her. There had been ample time in the short walk from Parliament Square over the North Bridge for her to change her mind, but she had not. Now here she was, in a secluded corner of the coffee room at the Waterloo Hotel, waiting while a complete stranger bribed one of the waiting staff to bring the pair of them something stronger than tea.

She had surrendered her coat at the door, and her bonnet, too, for they were both wet with that soft, mist-like mizzle that was not quite rain, in which Edinburgh specialised. Her hair, which even on the best of days was reluctant to succumb to the curling iron, was today bundled up into a careless chignon at her nape, and no doubt by now straggling equally carelessly out of it. On a good day, she would tell herself it was chestnut in colour, for it was not red enough to rate auburn, and she was fairly certain there was no such thing as mahogany hair. Today, it was brown, plain and simple and the colour of her mood. At least her gown was one of her better ones. Navy blue worked with silver-grey stylised flowers formed into a linking pattern, the full skirts contrasted with the tightly fitted bodice, with its long narrow sleeves and shawl neck. The narrow belt showed off her slender waist; the crossover pleating at the neck was cut just low enough to allow a daring glimpse of bosom. It had been designed to be worn with a demure white blouse, but this morning Ainsley hadn't been interested in looking demure. This morning she had not, however, intended to take off her coat. Now, she tugged self-consciously at the pleated shawl collar in an effort to pull it a little closer.

She had been angry when she left the lawyer's office, though she should not have been, but it seemed, despite all, that she'd not managed to lower her expectations quite enough. There had been a tiny modicum of hope left in her heart, and she'd been furious at herself for that. Hence the tears. Stupid tears. If Mr Innes Drummond had not seen those stupid tears, he'd more than likely have gone on his way and she wouldn't be here. Instead, she'd be at home. Alone. Or in the company of yet another bailiff. And it wasn't going to be her home for much longer. So she might as well be here. With a complete stranger. About to imbibe strong liquor, just like one of the loose women she'd claimed she would become.

Not that that was so far-fetched either, given the state of things, except one thing she was absolutely sure about was that she had no talents whatsoever for that sort of thing. In fact, she had not even the skill to interest a man if he didn't have to pay, if her husband was anything to go by.

Ainsley sighed. Second to tears, she hated self-pity. Giving her collar a final twitch, she forced herself to relax. Mr Drummond was still conferring with the waiter, so she took the chance to study him. His hair, which was cut unfashionably short, was glossily black. He was a good-looking man; there was no doubt about it, with a clean-shaven jaw, and none of the side whiskers gentlemen preferred these days. A high forehead spoke of intelligence, and lines fanning out from his eyes and forming a deep groove from nose to mouth spoke of experience. He looked to be in his mid-thirties, perhaps five years older than herself. A confident man, and well dressed in his dark coat and trousers, his linen impeccably white. Judging by appearances, money was not one of his worries. But then, if one could have judged John by appearances, money had not been one of his worries either. Not that her husband had ever been at all worried by money—or the lack of. No, that was not true. Those sullen silences of his spoke volumes. And latterly, so, too, did his habit of simply disappearing when she challenged him.

Ainsley sighed again, irked with herself. She was absolutely sick and tired of thinking about John. Across the room, Mr Drummond, having concluded his business with the waiter, glanced up and smiled at her. His eyes, under heavy dark brows, were a deep, vivid blue. She felt it then, what she had ignored before, a tug of something quite basic. Attraction. It made her stomach do a silly little flutter. It made her pulses skitter and it made her mouth dry, that smile of his, and the complicit look that accompanied it, as if the pair of them were in cahoots. It made her forget her anger at the injustice of her situation, and it reminded her that though she might well be a penniless widow with debts so terrifying they could not be counted, she was also a woman who had not known the touch of a man for a long time. And this man, this Mr Innes Drummond, who was seating himself opposite her, this man, she was pretty certain, would know exactly how to touch her.

'So, ladies first.'

Colour flooded her face. She stared at him blankly, horrified at the turn her mind had taken, praying that none of those shocking thoughts were visible on her countenance 'I beg your pardon?'

'Your tale of woe, Mrs McBrayne. You tell me yours, and then I'll tell you mine, and we can decide which of us is worst off.'

He had very long legs. They were stretched out to the side of the table that separated them. Well-made legs. Not at all spindly. And really rather broad shoulders. *Well built,* that was the phrase she was looking for. Athletic, even. And yes, his face and hands were rather tanned, as if he spent a deal of his life out of doors. 'What is it you do?' she asked. 'I mean—do you—are you a resident here in Edinburgh? Only, you do have an accent, but I cannot place it.'

Instead of taking offence, or pointing out that she had changed the subject, Innes Drummond gave a little shrug. 'I'm originally from the High-lands, Argyll on the west coast, though I've lived in England most of my adult life. I'm an engineer, Mrs McBrayne.'

'A practical man.'

He smiled. 'You approve.'

'I do. It is none of my business, but—yes.' She smiled back. 'What do you build?'

'Railway lines. Tunnels. Canals. Bridges and aqueducts. There is a very high demand for all these things, thanks to the steam locomotive. Though I don't actually build the things my-self, I design them. And even that— Business is very good, Mrs McBrayne. I am afraid I employ a rather large number of men to do most of the real work while I spend too much of my time in the boardroom, though I still like to think of myself as an engineer.'

'A very successful one, by the sounds of it. I did not think that money could be an issue with you.'

He gave her an enigmatic look before turning his attention to pouring them both a glass of whisky from the decanter that the waiter had deposited. *'Slàinte!'* he said, touching her glass with his.

'Slàinte!' Ainsley took a sip. It was a good malt, peaty and smoky, warming. She took another sip.

'I take it, then, that money *is* an issue for you,' Innes Drummond said.

She nodded. He waited, watching her, turning his glass round and round in his hand. One of the many things she'd learned from her marriage had been how to keep her own counsel—and how to keep her own secrets. Her failures, and the trusting, timid nature that had contributed to them, made her ashamed. She confided in no one, not even Felicity, and Felicity was the best friend she had. But confiding in this stranger, what harm could it do? Whatever had brought him to Edinburgh, he wasn't likely to be stopping long. If—however—he judged her, she'd be spared the pain of seeing it. Who knew, perhaps articulating her problems might even help her see a path to re-solving them.

Catching sight of her wedding band, Ainsley tucked her left hand into the folds of her gown. 'It is money,' she said, 'it comes down to money, and though I tell myself it's not fair, for I did not spend the money, I know at heart it's just as much my fault as his.'

Mrs McBrayne took another sip of whisky. 'Dutch courage,' she said, recklessly finishing the amber liquid and replacing the glass on the table before straightening her back and taking an audible breath. Innes wondered what on earth was to come, and wondered if he should stop her confidences, but dismissed this idea immediately. She was steeling herself, which meant she wanted to talk. Besides, he was interested, and it was good to have his mind concentrate on someone else's woes rather than his own for a while. He took a cautious sip of his own whisky and waited.

'I will need to go back a bit,' she said. 'Are you sure you want to hear this?' When he nodded, she smiled an on-your-head-be-it kind of smile. 'So,' she said, 'I met my husband, John McBrayne, when I was twenty. Nearly a decade ago. He was very much the gentleman, respectable, handsome, presentable, popular.' She counted her husband's assets off on her fingers. 'He was also what they call a charmer, and I was charmed. I met him at the Assembly Rooms. He was the friend of a friend. He seemed to be a man of means. Within six months, he had proposed, and I was delighted. I was happy. I was in love.' Another smile, only this one was a bitter little twist. 'John spoke to my father. My father asked me if I was sure, he told me there was no hurry, that if I wanted to change my mind—but I didn't, and I didn't think—I thought Papa was just being his usual cautious self, that's all. He was always polite to John, never said a word against him to me, and— But I'm getting ahead of myself.'

Innes swallowed the rest of his malt. 'Do you want another?' he asked, indicating her glass, and when Mrs McBrayne shook her head, resisted the urge to pour one for himself. 'Go on.'

'We were happy. I find I have to remind myself of that, but for a year or so we were happy. Then the bills started to go unpaid, and when I asked John, he told me not to worry. But I did, and when I eventually looked into matters properly, I discovered we owed a monstrous amount.

My husband was furious when he found out that I knew, he told me it was a temporary situation, he told me—ach, he told me all sorts, and I believed some of it, because I wanted to. I'd never enquired about his income until then, I had assumed my father—but there, you see, I'm putting the blame on others when it was my own fault. I should have asked right at the start. I should have made it my business, but by the time I did, it was too late.'

'You mean that by that time, your husband's debts were unmanageable?'

'I mean it was too late for me to persuade my husband that his debts were not only his business but mine, too,' Mrs McBrayne responded wryly. 'I think I will have another, if you don't mind.'

She was pale despite the whisky, her mouth thinned, her eyes focused inwards. When she sipped her drink, her hand trembled. Noticing that, she placed the glass carefully down. It was a common enough tale, but the way she told it was not at all common. Her feelings ran very deep. Innes was struggling to understand why.

'I told you you wouldn't understand,' she said, taking him aback by seeming to read his thoughts.

He made no attempt to deny it. 'Explain it, then,' Innes said.

'Imagine how you would feel if someone else was given control of your business. Imagine how you'd feel if they could make decisions about it over your head, without consulting you. Decisions that had consequences for you, but that you had no say in. Now imagine that at first you don't realise this is going on. Then when you do realise, and you challenge this person, they tell you that they're only doing what is expected of them. Then they tell you that you've no right to challenge them. And then they simply turn a cold shoulder. As a businessman, you can do something about it. You can even take action in court, if that person's been fraudulent. As a wife...' Mrs McBrayne spread her hands and gave him another of those bitter smiles. 'As a wife, you can choose to make both your lives a misery with constant nagging, or you can put up and shut up. What you can't do is change a thing. Not a single damn thing.'

Innes felt slightly sick. Having sworn all those years ago never to marry, he had never actually considered the state of matrimony from any point of view. Mrs McBrayne's perspective was horrible, and all the more so for the almost cool way she described it. Almost cool—for he was willing to bet that her fist was tightly clenched in the folds of her gown, and there was hurt in those hazel eyes as well as anger. He felt angry on her behalf, though he knew her husband had done nothing that society would condemn. In fact, more likely society would condone, for a man was expected to take care of his wife, and a wife—was it true, that a woman was expected simply to *put up and shut up*, as Mrs McBrayne so succinctly put it?

Innes put his glass down, and ran an agitated hand through his hair. 'You're right, if I were in such a situation— It sounds intolerable.'

'And yet I bore it,' she said bitterly. 'I wonder if things would have been different had I not. I thought of leaving him, but lack of funds made that impractical, and I would not go to my father. Edinburgh might appear to be a large town, but in practice it is not much more than a village. My leaving my husband's protection would have caused quite a scandal. Besides, I was— I was ashamed.' She glared at him as she said this. 'I was under the misapprehension that if I'd behaved differently I could have changed my husband,' she said. 'It took me some time to realise that since he would never change, then I must.'

She concluded with a small, satisfied smile that made Innes wonder how, exactly, she had changed and what, exactly, the effect had been on her spendthrift husband, but before he could ask, her smile had faded. She took a sip of whisky. Her hand was quite steady now. 'I remained with my husband, but matters between us were extremely strained. John devoted himself to myriad schemes he found to lose money, and I—I pursued a new interest of my own which was distracting and made me feel not quite so useless, but ultimately, I was burying my head in the sand. And then my father died, and his will dealt our marriage a death blow.'

'The trust?'

She nodded. 'I discovered later that John had asked him for money. Neither of them saw fit to inform me of that fact.' Her eyes blazed. 'My own father! I thought he trusted me. I thought— But there, I was wrong. Money is a matter for the man of the house, apparently.' The fire disappeared from her eyes as quickly as it had come. 'To cut a long and tedious story short, my father changed his will so that my entire inheritance was put into trust for my first child. He did not specify the sex, so at least I should be grateful for that—not that it makes any difference, since there is no child. When John found out, he…' Her voice wavered, but she quickly got it back under control. 'He was furious. He wanted to break the trust. He wanted *me* to find a way to break the trust, to use the law to go against my own father's wishes. It was not exactly conducive to marital harmony. Not that there was much of that by then. When I wouldn't cooperate—well, it seems I didn't have to, for what was mine was actually my husband's. Fortunately for my father's wishes, though not so fortunately for my husband and his creditors, the trust could not be broken. And then my husband died.'

Her voice was hard. Obviously, the love she'd felt for the man she had married was long gone. 'How?' Innes asked, wondering fleetingly if she was about to confess to killing him. There was a bit of him that would not have been surprised. A bit of him that would have approved.

'Pleurisy,' she replied. 'They found him dead drunk down in the Cowgate, out cold in a puddle. Heaven knows how long he'd been there or where he'd been before. He had not been home for three days.'

Was that what she'd meant when she implied she knew more than any respectable woman ought, about the women who plied their business in that scurrilous area? He wanted to ask, but he didn't want to distract her. Despite the sorry tale she'd told him, she was defiant, and he couldn't help but admire her for that. 'I take it then, that your husband left you with nothing?' Innes said.

'Nothing but debts. Not even my jointure, for it was to be sourced from investments that are now worthless. There is a mortgage on our house that becomes due in a month, a year after his death, and my father's trust is so watertight that, as Mr Thomson confirmed this morning, not even my utter ruin can break it. But you know, it's not even the money that bothers me. It's the extent to which I have been kept in the dark—allowed myself to be kept in the dark—not just by John, but by my father. It makes me feel about this size.' Mrs McBrayne held her thumb and index finger about an inch apart. 'That's how much of a say they gave me in my own life.'

'I am sure your father meant only to protect you.'

'Because I'm nothing but a frail female without a mind of my own?' she snapped. 'It made me wonder how many hundreds, thousands more of us poor wee souls there are out there, living life blindfolded.'

'You make it sound like a conspiracy.'

'That's because it feels like one, and not even Madame He...'

'Madame He?'

'Never mind.' Mrs McBrayne shook her head and picked up her glass, swirled the contents, then replaced it without drinking. 'I beg your pardon. I did not mean to become so emotional. I have made my bed, as they say, and now I must lie on it. Or not, for it is to be sold.' She smiled tightly. 'Like all sorry tales, this one comes with a moral. Whatever happens, I shall never again allow anyone to make my decisions for me. For good or ill, my fate will be of my own determination in the future. And now that is quite enough of me. It is your turn.'

He had a hundred questions, but she had folded her hands and her lips together, and was making a great show of listening. Innes was not fooled. Her eyes were overbright, her fingers too tightly clasped. She had taken quite a battering, one way or another. A lesser woman would have cried, or flung herself on some man's mercy. He could not imagine Mrs McBrayne doing either. He wanted to cheer her. He wanted to tell her she would be fine, absolutely fine. He was very tempted to offer her money, but she would be mortified, to say nothing of the fact that he was pretty certain she'd also see it merely as a transfer of obligation, and he didn't want her to feel beholden. What he wanted was for her to be free. It wasn't so much that he felt sorry for her, though he railed at the injustice of it all, but he felt—yes, that was it—an affinity.

'What have I said to make you smile?'

'Your situation, Mrs McBrayne, has struck a great many chords.'

'I do not see how. I don't know you, but you have told me yourself you're a self-made man and a success. Men such as you will never brook any interference in your life.'

'Actually, that's not true. Unfortunately, I know very well indeed what it's like to have someone else try to bind you to their rules, to dictate your life without you having a say.'

He was pleased to see that he had surprised her. 'What do you mean?' she asked.

'Did I not say at the outset that we are both the victims of fathers and trusts?' Innes replied. 'It's a strange coincidence, but I while you were consulting Thomson on the finer points of your father's will, I was consulting Ballard on the very same thing. I too have been left the victim of a trust fund, only my father's intention was not to protect me but to call me to heel, and unlike your trust, mine can be broken, though only in a very particular way.'

'What way, Mr Drummond?'

Innes smiled thinly. 'Marriage, Mrs McBrayne. An institution that I assure you, I abhor every bit as much as you do yourself.'

Chapter Two

Ainsley stared at him in astonishment. 'Your father's will sets up a trust that requires you to marry?'

'No, it establishes a trust to control the family lands that will remain in effect *until* I marry,' Innes replied.

'Lands?' She only just managed to prevent her jaw dropping. 'As in—what, a country estate?'

'A little more than that. I'm not sure what the total acreage is, but there are about twenty tenanted farms as well as the home farm and the castle.'

'Good heavens, Mr Drummond—a castle! And *about* twenty farms. Is there a title, too?'

He shook his head. 'My father was known as the laird of Strone Bridge, but it was just a courtesy.'

Laird. The title conjured up a fierce Highland

patriarch. Ainsley eyed the impeccably dressed gentleman opposite her and discovered it was surprisingly easy to imagine him in a plaid, carrying a claymore. Though without the customary beard. She didn't like beards. 'And these lands, they are in Argyll, did you say?'

When he nodded Ainsley frowned in puzzlement. 'Forgive me, Mr Drummond, but did you not tell me you had spent most of your life in England? Surely as the heir to such a substantial property—I know nothing of such things, mind you—but I thought it would have been customary for you to have lived on the estate?'

His countenance hardened. 'I was not the heir.'

'Oh?'

She waited, unwilling to prompt him further, for he looked quite forbidding. Innes Drummond took a sip of whisky, grimaced and put the glass back down on the table. 'Dutch courage,' he said, with a shadow of her own words and her own grim little smile. 'I had a brother. Malcolm. He was the heir. It is as you said—he lived on the estate. Lived and breathed it, more like, for he loved the place. Strone Bridge was his world.'

He stared down at his glass, his mouth turned

down in sorrow. 'But it was not your world?' Ainsley asked gently.

'It was never meant for me. I was the second son. As far as my father was concerned, that meant second best, and while Malcolm was alive, next to useless, Mrs McBrayne.'

He stared down at his glass, such a bleak look on his face that she leaned over to press his hand. 'My name is Ainsley.'

'I don't think I've heard that before.'

'An old family name,' she said.

He gave her a very fleeting smile as his fingers curled around hers. 'Then you must call me Innes,' he said. 'Another old family name, though it is not usually that of the laird. One condition I have been spared. My father did not specify that I change my name to Malcolm. Even he must have realised that would have been a step too far. Though, then again, it may simply have been that he thought me as unworthy of the name as the lands.'

He spoke viciously enough to make Ainsley recoil. 'You sound as though you hate him.'

'Rather, the boot was on the other foot.' He said it jeeringly. She wondered what hurt lay behind those words, but Innes was already retreating, patently regretting what he had revealed. 'We did not see eye to eye,' he tempered. 'Some would call him a traditionalist. Everyone had a place in his world. I did not take to the one he allotted me. When I finally decided to forge my own way, we fell out.'

Ainsley could well imagine it. Innes was obviously a man with a very strong will, a modern man and an independent one who clearly thrived in the industrial world. It would be like two stags clashing. She wondered what the circumstances had been that had caused what was obviously a split, but curious as she was, she had no wish to rile him further. 'Tell me about the trust,' she said. 'Why must you marry, and what happens if you do not?'

Innes stared down at his hand, the one she had so abruptly released, his eyes still dark with pain. 'As to why, that is obvious. The Strone Bridge estate has been passed through the direct line back as far as records exist, and I am the last of the line. He wanted an heir.'

'But he only specified that you must take a wife? That seems rather odd.'

'We Drummonds have proved ourselves potent over the generations. My father no doubt assumed that even such an undeserving son as I would not fail in that most basic of tasks,' Innes said sarcastically.

'You don't want children?'

'I don't want a wife, and in my book, one must necessarily precede the other.'

This time Ainsley's curiosity overcame her caution. 'Why are you so against marriage?' she asked. 'You don't strike me as a man who hates my sex.'

'You don't strike me as a woman who hates men, yet you don't want to get married again.'

'It is a case of once bitten with me.'

'While I have no intentions of being bitten for a first time,' Innes retorted. 'I don't need anyone other than myself to order my life, and I certainly don't want to rely on anyone else to make me happy.'

He spoke with some vehemence. He spoke as if there was bitter experience behind his words. As there was, too, behind hers. 'Your father's will has put you in an impossible situation, then,' Ainsley said.

'As has yours,' Innes replied tersely. 'What happens to your trust if you have no children?'

'It reverts to me when I am forty and presumably deemed to be saying my prayers.' She could not keep the bitterness from her voice. She had loved her father, but his unwitting condemnation of her was still difficult to take. 'I have only to discover a way of avoiding my husband's creditors and surviving without either a roof over my head or food in my belly for the next ten years in order to inherit, since I have no intentions of marrying again.'

'Nor any intention of producing a child out of wedlock, I take it? No need to look so shocked,' Innes said, 'it was a joke.'

'A poor one.'

'I'm sorry.'

She forced a smile. 'I do not really intend to sell myself down the Cowgate, you know.'

Innes covered her hand. 'Are your debts really so bad?'

'There will certainly still be sufficient of them to pay off when I finally do come into my inheritance,' she said.

His fingers tightened around hers. 'I wish I could be of some help to you.'

'You have been, simply by listening,' Ainsley replied, flustered by the sympathy in his look. She no longer expected sympathy. She had come to believe she did not deserve it. 'A problem shared and all that,' she said with a small smile.

'It's a damnable situation.'

He seemed much bigger, this close. There was something terribly comforting in those broad shoulders, in the way his hand enveloped hers, in the way he was looking at her, not with pity at all but with understanding. Close-up, his irises were ringed with a very dark blue. She had never seen eyes quite that colour.

Realising her thoughts were once more straying down a most inappropriate path, Ainsley dropped her gaze. 'If my father had not left my money in trust, my husband would have spent it by now, and I'd have nothing to look forward to in what he clearly thought of as my forty-year-old dotage. The money might have postponed my husband's demise, but I doubt very much it would have been for more than a few years, and frankly I don't think I could have borne a few more years married to him.'

'I confess, at one point I thought you were going to tell me you had killed him yourself,' Innes said.

Ainsley laughed. 'I may not be the timid wee mouse he married, but I don't think I've become a monster.'

'I think you are a wonder.' She looked up, surprised by the warmth in his tone, and her pulses began to race as he lifted her hand to his mouth, pressing a kiss to her knuckles. There was no mistaking it for one of those polite, social, nothing kisses. His mouth lingered on her skin, his lips warm, his eyes looking deep into hers for long, long seconds. 'You are a most remarkable woman, Ainsley McBrayne.'

'Thank you. I— Thank you.'

'I really do wish there was some way that I could help you, but I know better than to offer you money.'

'I really do wish there was a way I could accept it, but—well, there we are, I cannot, so there is no point in discussing it. In fact, we have talked far more about me than you. I'm still not clear about what happens to your lands if you remain unmarried. What does this trust entail?'

She was pleased with how she sounded. Not a tremor to betray the quickening of desire his lips had stirred, and she hoped the flush she could feel blooming had not reached her cheeks.

However Innes Drummond felt, and she would have dearly liked to have known, he took his cue from her. 'A trustee appointed by that lawyer, Ballard, to manage them, and all monies associated with them banked. I can't touch a penny of it without a wife,' he replied, 'and even with a wife, I must also commit to living for a year on Strone Bridge.'

'Is it a great deal of money?'

Innes shook his head. 'I've no idea, since I'm not even entitled to see the accounts, but the money isn't the point, I have plenty of my own. I haven't a clue what state the place is in at all. It could be flourishing, it could have gone to rack and ruin, for all I know.'

'So the fall out between yourself and your father then, it was…'

'More like a complete break. I told you, he was an old-fashioned man. Do as I say, or get out of my sight.'

Innes spoke lightly enough, but she was not fooled. 'How long is it since you were there?'

'Almost fourteen years. Since Malcolm—since I lost my brother.' Innes shuddered, but recovered quickly. 'You're wondering why I'm so upset about the trust when I've spent most of my adult life away from the place,' he said.

'I think this has all been much more of a shock than you realise,' Ainsley answered cautiously.

'Aye, mayhap you're right.' His accent had softened, the Highland lilt much more obvious. 'I had no inkling the old man was ill, and he'd no time to let me know. Not that I think he would have. Far better for me to be called to heel through that will of his from beyond the grave. I don't doubt he's looking down—or maybe up—and laughing at the mess he's put me in,' Innes said. 'He knew just how it would stick in my craw, having to choose between relying on someone else to run what is mine or to take up the reins myself under such conditions. Be damned to him! I must find a way to break this trust. I will not let him issue decrees from beyond the grave.'

He thumped his fist on the table, making his glass and Ainsley jump. 'I'm beginning to think that your situation is worse than mine after all.'

'Ach, that's nonsense, for I at least don't have to worry about where my next meal is coming from. It's a sick coincidence, the way the pair of us are being punished by our parents, though,' Innes said. 'What will you do?'

'Oh, I'm beyond worrying right now.' Ainsley waved her hand in the air dismissively. 'The question is, what will you do? If only you could find a woman to marry who has no interest in actually being your wife, your problems would be solved.'

She spoke flippantly, more to divert his attention from her own tragic situation than anything, but Innes, who had been in the act of taking another sip of whisky, stopped, the glass halfway to his lips, an arrested look in his eyes. 'Say that again.'

'What? That you need to marry...'

'A woman who has no interest in being my wife,' he finished for her with a dawning smile. 'A woman who is in need of a home, and has no fixed plans, who might actually be looking for a respite from her current life for a wee while. You're right, that's exactly what I need, and I know exactly the woman.'

'You do? You cannot possible mean...'

His smile had a wicked light in it. 'I do,' Innes said. 'I mean you.'

Ainsley was staring at him open-mouthed. Innes laughed. 'Think about it, it's the ideal solution. In fact, it could almost be said that we are perfectly matched, since you have as little desire for a husband as I have for a wife.'

She blinked at him owlishly. 'Are you drunk?'

'Certainly not.'

'Then I must be, for you cannot possibly be proposing marriage. Apart from the fact that we've only just met, I thought I had made it plain that I will never—absolutely *never* again—surrender my independence.'

'I'm not asking you to. I'm actually making it easier for you to retain it, because if we get married, I can pay off all those debts that bastard of a husband of yours acquired and then you really will be free.'

'But I'd be married to you.'

'In name only.'

'I owe a small fortune. I couldn't take it from you just for the price of putting my name on a bit of paper.'

'You'd have to come with me to Strone Bridge. The clause that specified my spending a year there doesn't actually include my wife, but all the same, I think you'd have to come with me for a wee while, at least.'

'That would not be a problem since, as you have already deduced, I'm going to be homeless very shortly, and would appreciate a change of scene, but I simply couldn't think of accepting such a huge amount of money and give so little in return.'

'What if you saw it as a wage?' Innes asked, frowning.

'For what?'

'A fee, paid for professional services,' he said, 'and a retainer to be paid in addition each year until you are forty, which you could pay me back if you wish, when you eventually inherit, though there is no need.'

'But I'm not a professional.' Her eyes widened. 'You cannot possibly mean— I told you, I was joking about the Cowgate.'

Innes laughed. 'Not that! I meant a business professional.' She was now looking utterly bewildered. Innes grinned. 'The more I think about it, the more I see how perfect it is. No, wait.' He caught her as she made to get up. 'I promise you, I'm neither drunk nor mad. Listen.'

Ainsley sat down, folding her arms, a sceptical look on her face. 'Five minutes.'

He nodded. 'Think about it as a business proposal,' he said. 'First of all, think of the common ground. To begin with, you need to pay off your debts and I am rich enough to be able to do so easily. Second, you are a widow, and I need a wife. Since we are neither of us in the least bit interested, now or ever, in marrying someone else...'

'How can you be so sure of that?'

'How can you?' He waited, but she made no answer, so he gave a satisfied nod. 'You see? We are of one mind on that. And we are of one mind on another thing, which is our determination to make our own way in life. If you let me pay off your debts, I can give you the freedom to do that, and if you marry me, you'll be freeing me to make up my own mind on what to do—or not—about my inheritance.'

'But we'll be tied to one another.'

'In name only, Ainsley. Tied by a bit of paper, which is no more than a contract.'

'Contracts require payment. What *professional* services can you possibly imagine I can provide?'

'An objective eye. An unbiased opinion. I need both.' Innes shifted uncomfortably. 'Not advice, precisely,' he said.

'Because you do not like to take advice, do you?'

'Are you mocking me?'

'Another thing you're not used to, obviously.' Ainsley smiled. 'Not mocking, teasing. I'm a little rusty. What is it, then, that involves my giving you my unbiased and objective opinion without advising you?'

'When you put it like that!' He was forced to

smile. 'What I'm trying to say is, I'd like you to come to Strone Bridge with me. Not to make my decisions, but to make sure when I do make them, I'm doing so without prejudice.'

'Is that possible? It's your birthright, Innes.'

He shook his head vehemently. 'That's the point. It's not. It pains me to admit it, but I don't know much about it, and I haven't a clue what I want to do with it. Live there. Sell it. Put in a manager. I don't know, and I won't know until I go there, and even when I do—what do you say?'

'That's the price? That's the professional services I'm to render in order to have my life back?'

'You think it's too great a cost?' Innes said, deflated.

Ainsley smiled. Then she laughed. 'I think it's a bargain.'

'You do? You understand, Strone Bridge is like to be—well, very different from Edinburgh.'

'A change from Edinburgh, a place to take stock, is, as you pointed out, exactly what I need.'

'I'm not asking you to stay the full year. A few months, until I've seen my way clear, that's all. And though I'm asking you to—to consult with me, that does not mean I'll necessarily take your advice,' Innes cautioned.

'I'm used to that.' Ainsley's smile faded momentarily, but then brightened. 'Though being asked is a step in the right direction, and I will at least have the opportunity of putting my point across.'

Glancing at the decanter of whisky, the level of which had unmistakably fallen by more than a couple of drams, Innes wondered if he was drunk after all. He'd just proposed marriage to a complete stranger. A stranger with a sorry tale, whose courage and strength of mind he admired, but he had met her only a couple of hours ago all the same. Yet it didn't seem to matter. He was drawn to her, had been drawn to her from that first moment when she'd stormed out of the lawyer's office, and it wasn't just the bizarre coincidence of their situations. He liked what he saw of her, and admired what he heard. That he also found her desirable was entirely beside the point. His instincts told him that they'd fare well together, and his instincts were never wrong. 'So we are agreed?' Innes asked.

Ainsley tapped her index fingers together, frowning. 'We're complete strangers,' she said, reflecting his own thoughts. 'Do you think we'll be able to put on enough of a show to persuade your people that this isn't a marriage of convenience?'

'I'm not in the habit of concerning myself with what other people think.'

'Don't be daft. You'll be the—their—laird, Innes. Of course they'll be concerned.'

She was in the right of it, but he had no intentions of accepting that fact. He was not the laird. The laird was dead, and so, too, was his heir. Innes would not be branded. 'They must take me—us—as they find us,' he said. Ainsley was still frowning. 'Strone Bridge Castle is huge. If it's having to rub shoulders with me on a daily basis you're worried about, I assure you, we could go for weeks without seeing each other if we wanted.'

'That is hardly likely to persuade people we're living in domestic bliss.'

'I doubt domestic bliss is a concept that any laird of Strone Bridge is familiar with. My ancestors married for the getting of wealth and the getting of bairns.'

'Then that puts an end to our discussion.' Ainsley got to her feet and began to head for the door of the coffee room.

Innes threw down some money on the table and followed her, pulling her into a little alcove in the main reception area of the hotel. 'I don't want either of those things from you. I don't want to be like them,' he said earnestly. 'Can't you see, that's the point?'

'This is madness.'

He gave her arm a little shake, forcing her eyes to meet his. 'Madness would be to do what you're doing, and that's walking away from the perfect solution. Stop thinking about what could go wrong, think about what it will put right. Freedom, Ainsley. Think about that.'

Her mouth trembled on the brink of a smile. 'I confess, it's a very attractive idea.'

'So you'll do it?'

Her smile broadened. The light had come back into her eyes. 'I feel sure there are a hundred reasons why I should walk very quickly in the other direction.'

'But you will not?' He was just close enough for her skirts to brush his trousers, to smell the scent of her soap, of the rain in her hair. She made no attempt to free herself, holding his gaze, that smile just hovering, tempting, challenging. Tension quivered between them. 'You would regret it if you did,' Innes said.

'Do you know, Mr Innes Drummond, I think you may well be right.'

Her voice was soft, there was a tiny shiver in

it, and a shiver, too, when he slid his hands from her shoulders down her arms, closing the space between them and lowering his mouth to hers. It was the softest of kisses, the briefest of kisses, but it was a kiss. A very adult kiss, which could easily have become so much more. Lips, tongues, caressed, tasted. Heat flared and they both instinctively recoiled, for it was the kind of heat that could burn.

Ainsley put her hand to her mouth, staring wide-eyed at him. Innes looked, he suspected, every bit as shocked as she. 'I'm sorry,' he said.

'Are you?'

'Not really, but I promise *that* was not in any way part of the bargain I'm proposing.'

She slanted him a look he could not interpret as she disentangled herself from his loose embrace. '*That* was merely the product of too much whisky on top of too much emotional upheaval. It was like a—a valve to release the steam pressure on one of those steam engines you build bridges and tunnels for, nothing more.'

He laughed. He couldn't help it, because she was right in a way, and she was quite wrong in another, but in every way she was wholly unexpected and a breath of much-needed fresh air. 'I'm thinking that my return to Strone Bridge is going to be a source of constant emotional up-heaval,' Innes said. 'We might need to do a lot of kissing.'

'You're an engineer,' Ainsley replied primly, though her eyes were sparkling. 'I suggest you invent a different kind of safety valve for yourself.'

'Ainsley, what a nice surprise.' Felicity Blair, editor of the *Scottish Ladies Companion*, greeted her friend with a warm smile, waving her into the shabby chair on the other side of the huge desk that dominated her tiny office. 'I've just been reading Madame Hera's latest advice. I am not at all sure we can publish this reply, not least because it's rather long.'

'Which one is that?' Ainsley asked.

In response, Felicity picked up a piece of paper from the collection that Ainsley recognised she'd handed in to the office a week ago, and began to read:

'Dear Anxious Miss,
Simply because you are more mature than the average bride-to-be—and I do not consider

two-and-thirty to be so old—does not mean
that you are exempt from the trepidation natural to one in your position. You are, when all
is said and done, setting sail into unchartered
waters. To put it plainly, no matter how well
you think you might know your intended, you
should be prepared for the state of matrimony
to alter him significantly, for he will have se-
cured his prize, and will no longer be required
to woo you. This might mean calm, tranquil
seas. But it might prove to be a stormy passage.

My advice is to start the way you mean to
go on and take charge of the rudder! Give no
quarter, Anxious Miss; let your husband see
that he cannot set the course of the matrimonial vessel to suit only himself. Do not allow
yourself to be subsumed by his nature nor his
dictates simply because you have assumed his
name. Do not allow your nerves, your maid-
enly modesty or your sex to intimidate you.
Speak up for yourself from the first, and set a
precedent that, if not immediately, will, I am
sure, eventually earn your husband's respect.

As to the more intimate matters with which
you are concerned. You say your intended
has indicated a lack of experience, and you

are worried that this might—once again, I will revert to the seafaring metaphor—result in the becalming of the good ship wedlock. First, I would strongly advise you to muster your courage and have a frank chat about the mechanics of your wedding night with a married lady friend, thus eliminating the shock of the complete unknown. Second, I would advise you equally strongly to give your husband no inclination that you come to the wedding night armed with such information, lest he find it emasculating. Third, remember, if he really is as innocent as he claims, he will be as nervous as you. But he is a man, Anxious Miss, and thus a little flattery, some feminine admiration and a pliant female body, will ensure the success of your maiden voyage.
Good luck!
Madame Hera'

Ainsley smiled doubtfully. 'I admit, the sailing metaphor is rather trite, but if I had not used it, I would have been forced to invent something else equally silly, else you would have deemed it too vulgar to print.'

'At least you did not surrender to the obvious

temptation to talk about dry docks in the context of the wedding night,' Felicity replied acerbically.

'No, because such a shocking thing did not occur to me,' Ainsley replied, laughing. 'Though to be serious for a moment, it is becoming quite a challenge for Madame Hera to advise without entirely hiding her meaning behind the veil of polite euphemisms. The whole point of the column is to provide practical help.'

Felicity set the letter down. 'I've been pondering that very issue myself. You know how limited the space is for Madame's column each month, yet we are now receiving enough correspondence to fill the entire magazine.'

'Aren't you pleased? I know I am. It is proof that I was absolutely right about the need for such a thing, and you were absolutely right to take the chance to publish it.'

'Yes, the volume of mail is a true testament to the quality of Madame's advice but, Ainsley, the problem is we can't publish most of it, for our readers would consider the subjects far too warm. Even with your shipping metaphor, that reply to Anxious Miss is sailing close to the wind. Oh, good grief, you've got me at it now!' Felicity adjusted the long ink-stained cuffs that protected her blouse. 'I'm glad you stopped by, because I've got an idea I'd like to discuss. You know it will be exactly two years since we launched Madame Hera's column next month?'

'Of course I do.' It had been the first step away from self-pity towards self-sufficiency Ainsley had taken. She remembered it vividly—the thrill of dreaming up the idea after one particularly dispiriting evening with her husband. 'It's funny,' she said to Felicity, 'at first it was the secret of Madame's existence that I enjoyed most, knowing I had something all mine that John knew nothing about. But these days, it is the hope that some of Madame Hera's advice actually helps the women who write to her that I relish. Though of course, one can never really know if one has helped.'

'You do,' Felicity said firmly. 'You know you do, just by providing an ear. Now, as I said, there are a great deal more people asking for Madame's advice than we can cover in our column, which brings me to my idea. A more personal service.'

'What on earth do you mean by that?' Ainsley wondered, for a startled moment, if her friend had somehow heard of her remark about earning a living in the Cowgate the other day.

Felicity gave a gurgle of laughter. 'Your face! I

do not mean anything immoral, never fear. I mean a personal *letter* service. For a price, of course, for matters of a more sensitive nature, we can offer a personal response from Madame. We'll split the fee between the journal and yourself, naturally. Depending on how many you can answer in a month I'd say your earnings from the journal could triple at least. What do you say?'

'I'm getting married,' Ainsley blurted out.

Felicity's dark brown eyes opened so wide as to appear quite round. 'You're doing what?'

'I know, it's a shock, but it's not what you think. I can explain,' Ainsley said, wondering now if she could. She'd hardly slept a wink these past few nights wondering if she had been an idiot, and coming here this morning had been a test she'd set herself, for if practical, outspoken, radical Felicity thought it was a good idea...

Half an hour and what seemed like a hundred questions later, her friend sat back at her desk, rummaging absent-mindedly for the pencil she had, as usual, lost in her heavy chignon of hair. 'And you're absolutely sure that this Mr Drummond has no ulterior motives?'

'As sure as I can be. He's started the process of paying all of John's debts.'

'At least you'd no longer be obliged to call yourself by that man's name. Does he include the mortgage on Wemyss Place in the debts?'

Ainsley shook her head. 'Innes wanted to pay it, but as far as I'm concerned, the creditors can have the house. It has nothing but unhappy memories for me. Besides, I have every intention of repaying it all when I inherit my trust fund, and that mortgage would take up nearly all of it.'

'So, you are going to be a Highland lady. The chatelaine of a real Scottish castle.' Felicity chuckled. 'How will you like that, I wonder? You've never been out of Edinburgh.'

'It's only a temporary thing, until Innes decides what he wants to do with the place.'

'And how long will that take?'

'I don't know. Weeks. Months? No more, though he must remain there for a year. I'm looking forward to the change of scenery. And to feeling useful.'

'It all sounds too good to be true. Sadly, in my experience, things that are too good to be true almost always are,' Felicity said drily.

'Do you think it's a mistake?'

'I don't know. I think you're half-mad, but you've had a raw deal of it these past few years, and I've not seen you this animated for a long time. Perhaps getting away from Edinburgh will be good for you.' Felicity finally located her pencil and pulled it out of her coiffure, along with a handful of bright copper hair. 'What is he like, this laird? Are you sure he'll not turn into some sort of savage Highlander who'll drag you off to his lair and have his wicked way with you the minute you arrive on his lands?'

'There is no question of him having his wicked way,' Ainsley said, trying to ignore the vision of Innes in a plaid. The same one she'd had the first day she'd met him. With a claymore. And no beard.

'You're blushing,' Felicity exclaimed. 'How very interesting. Ainsley McBrayne, I do believe you would not be averse to your Highlander being very wicked indeed.'

'Stop it! I haven't the first idea what you mean by wicked, but...'

Felicity laughed. 'I know you don't,' she said, 'and frankly, it's been the thing that's worried me most about this idea of mine for Madame Hera's personal letter service, but now I think you've solved the problem. I suppose you've already kissed him? Don't deny it, that guilty look is a complete giveaway. Did you like it?'

'Felicity!'

'Well?'

'Yes.' Ainsley laughed. 'Yes, I did.'

'Was it a good kiss? The kind of kiss to give you confidence that your Mr Drummond would know what he was doing? The kind of kiss that made you want him to do more than kiss you?'

Ainsley put her hands to her heated cheeks. 'Yes. If you must know, yes, it was! Goodness, the things you say. We did not— Our marriage is not— That sort of thing is not...'

'You're going to be out in the wilds. You've already said that you're attracted to each other. It's bound to come up, if you'll forgive the dreadful *double entendre.* And when it does—provided you take care there are no consequences—then why not?' Felicity said. 'Do you want me to be blunt?'

'What, even more than you've been already?'

'Ainsley, from what you've told me—or not told me—about your marriage, it was not physically satisfying.'

'I can't talk about it.'

'No, and you know I won't push you, but you also know enough, surely, to realise that with the right man, lovemaking can be fun.'

'Fun?' Ainsley tried to imagine this, but her own experience, which was ultimately simply embarrassing, at times shameful, made this impossible.

'Fun,' Felicity repeated, 'and pleasurable, too. It should not be an ordeal.'

Which was exactly how it had been, latterly, Ainsley thought, flushing, realising that Felicity had perceived a great deal more than she had ever revealed. 'Is it fun and pleasurable for you, with your mystery man?'

'If it were not, I would not be his mistress.'

It was only because she knew her so well that Ainsley noticed the faint withdrawal, the very slight tightening of her lips that betrayed her. Felicity claimed that being a mistress gave her the satisfaction of a lover without curtailing her freedom, but there were times when Ainsley wondered. She suspected the man was married, and loved her friend too much to pain her by asking. They both had their shameful secrets.

Ainsley picked up the latest stack of letters from the desk and began to flick through them. What

Felicity said was absolutely true. As Madame Hera's reputation spread, her post contained ever more intimate queries, and as things stood, Ainsley would be hard-pressed to answer some of them save in the vaguest of terms. She replaced the letters with a sigh. 'No. Even if Innes was interested...'

'You know perfectly well that he would be,' Felicity interjected drily. 'He's a man, and, despite the fact that John McBrayne stripped you of every ounce of self-esteem, you're an attractive woman. What else will you do to while away the dark nights in that godforsaken place?'

'Regardless,' Ainsley persisted, 'it would be quite wrong of me to use Innes merely to acquire the experience that would allow Madame Hera to dispense better advice.'

'Advice that would make such a difference to all these poor, tormented women,' Felicity said, patting the pile of letters. 'Wasn't that exactly what you set out to do?'

'Stop it. You cannot make me feel guilty enough to— Just stop it, Felicity. You know, sometimes I think you really are as ruthless an editor as you pretend.'

'Trust me, I have to be, since I, too, am a mere

woman. But we were talking about you, Ainsley. I agree, it would be wrong if you were only lying back and thinking of Scotland for the sake of Madame Hera and her clients. Though I hope you've more in mind than lying back and thinking of Scotland.'

'Felicity!'

'Fun and pleasure, my dear, require participation,' her friend said with another of her mischievous smiles. 'You see, now you are intrigued, and now you can admit it would not only be for Madame Hera, but yourself. Confess, you want him.'

'Yes. No. I told you, it...'

'Has no part in your arrangement. I heard you. Methinks you protest just a little too much.'

'But do you approve?' Ainsley said anxiously.

Felicity picked up her pencil again and began to twist it into her hair. 'I approve of anything that will make you happy. When does the ceremony take place?'

'The banns are being called on Sunday for the first time. The ceremony will be immediately after the last calling, in three weeks. Will you come, Felicity? I'd like to have you by my side.'

'Will you promise me that if you change your mind before then, you will speak up? And if you are unhappy at this Strone Bridge place, you will come straight back here, regardless of whether you feel your obligations have been met?'

'I promise.'

Felicity got to her feet. 'Then I will be your attendant, if that's what you want.' She picked up the bundle of letters and held them out. 'Make a start on these. I will draw up the advertisement, we'll run it beside Madame's column for this month and I will send you a note of the terms once I have them agreed. Will you be disclosing your alter ego to the laird?'

'Absolutely not! Good grief, no, especially not if I am to— He will think…'

Felicity chuckled gleefully. 'I see I've given you food for thought, at the least. I look forward to reading the results—in the form of Madame's letters, I mean.' She hugged Ainsley tightly. 'I wish you luck. You will write to me, once you are there?'

Ainsley sniffed, kissing her friend on the cheek. 'You'll get sick of hearing from me.' She tucked the letters into the folder, which was already stuffed with the bills she was to hand over to Mr Ballard, Innes's lawyer.

'Just one thing,' Felicity called after her. 'I'll

wager you five pounds that if your Highlander ever discovers that you are Madame Hera, he'll be far more interested in finding problems for the pair of you to resolve together than taking umbrage.'

'Since I shall take very good care that he never finds out, you will lose,' Ainsley said, laughing as she closed the door behind her.

Chapter Three

Dear Madame Hera,

I have been married for three months to a man whose station in life is very superior to my own. Having moved from a small house with only two servants to a very large manor with a butler and a housekeeper, I find myself in a perfect tizzy some mornings, trying to understand who I should be asking to do what. My husband has suggested turning to his mother for advice, but she obviously thinks he has married beneath him and would see my need for guidance as evidence of this. As it is, I am sure the housekeeper is reporting my every failure in the domestic sphere to my mother-in-law. Only last week, when I committed the cardinal sin of asking the second housemaid to bring me a pot of tea, the woman actually chastised me as if I were a child. Apparently, such requests should be relayed through the footman, and I should not desire to take tea outside the usual hours, whatever these might be.

I love my husband, but I am being made to feel like an upstart in my new home, and I dare not tell him for fear he will start to take on his mother's opinion of me. Is there some sort of school for new wives I can attend? Please advise me, for I am beginning to wonder if my housekeeper would have made a better wife to my husband than I can.

Timid Mouse

Argyll, July 1840

It was cold here on the west coast. Despite the watery sunshine, a stiff breeze had blown up in the bay at Rhubodach. Innes shivered inside his heavy greatcoat. He'd forgotten how much colder it was here, and it would be colder still in the boat. Sitting on a bandbox a few feet away, Ainsley was reading a letter, clutching the folds of her travelling cloak tightly around her and staring out over the Kyles of Bute. These past three weeks there had been so much business to attend to they'd barely had time to exchange more than a few words. Standing before the altar beside him just a few days ago, she had been almost as complete a stranger to him as the day he'd proposed. Yet in a very short while, they'd be on Strone Bridge, playing the part of a happily married couple.

The dread had been taking a slow hold of him. It had settled inside him with the news of his father's death. It had grown when he learned the terms of his inheritance, then became subdued when Ainsley agreed to marry him, and even suppressed as they made their arrangements and their vows. But on the coach from Edinburgh to Glasgow it had made itself known again. Then on the paddle steamer *Rothesay Castle* as they sailed from the Broomilaw docks to the Isle of Bute it took root, and by this afternoon's journey from Rothesay town to the north part of the Isle of Bute where they now stood waiting, it had manifested itself in this horrible sick feeling, in this illogical but incredibly strong desire to turn tail and run, and to keep running, just as he had done fourteen years before.

He was Innes Drummond, self-made man of fortune and some fame in the business he called

his own. He was a man who made his living building bridges, engineering solutions to problems,
turning the impossible into reality. Yet standing
here on the pebbled shores of Rhubodach bay, he
felt as if none of this mattered. He was the second son, his father's runt, the upstart who had
no right to be coming back to Strone Bridge to
claim a dead man's property. The memories of his
brother he had worked so long to suppress were
lurking just across the water to claim him. On
Strone Bridge, Malcolm's absence would make
his death impossible to deny. Guilt was that sick
feeling eating away at his stomach. Fear was the
hard, cold lump growing inside of him. He had
no right to be here. He was afraid that when he
arrived, he'd be subsumed, that all he thought he
was would be peeled ruthlessly back to expose
the pretender beneath.

Innes swore under his breath, long and viciously.
And in Gaelic. He noticed that too late, and then
swore again in the harsher, more familiar language of his construction workers. Picking up a
handful of pebbles, he began to launch them one
after the other into the water, noting with faint
satisfaction that they fell far out.

'Impressive.'

He hadn't heard her moving. How long had she been standing there, watching him? 'The boat is late.' Innes made a show of shading his eyes to squint out at the Kyles.

'You must be nervous,' Ainsley said. 'I know I would be, returning after such a long period of time. I expect you'll be wondering how much has changed.'

Her tone was light, almost indifferent. She was studiously avoiding his gaze, looking out at the water, but he was not fooled. She was an astute observer. One of those people who studied faces, who seemed to have the knack of reading the thoughts of complete strangers. 'Nothing will have changed,' Innes said with heavy certainty. 'My father prided himself on maintaining traditions that were hundreds of years old. You'll feel as if you've stepped back into the eighteenth century.'

Her brows lifted in surprise. He could see the wheels turning in her clever brain, but she chose merely to nod, and perversely, though he knew he would not like it, he wanted to know what she was thinking. 'Go on. Say it.'

'It is nothing. Only—you are very much a man of the nineteenth century.'

'You mean you're not surprised I left such a backward place.'

'Such a backward place must be crying out for a man like you.' Ainsley pushed her windswept hair out of her eyes. 'I meant that I am not surprised you and your father could not see eye to eye.'

She slipped her gloved hand into his, in the folds of his greatcoat. He twined his fingers around hers, glad of the contact. Ainsley Drummond, his wife. A stranger she might be, but he was glad of her presence, and when she smiled up at him like that, the dread contracted just a little. 'I think that's the boat,' she said, pointing.

It was, and he could see already that Eoin was at the helm. With a determined effort, Innes threw off his black mood. 'Are you ready?' he asked, sliding his arm around Ainsley to anchor her to his side.

'You sound like you're standing under the gallows, if you don't mind my saying.'

Innes managed a rigid smile. 'Judgement Day is what it feels like,' he said wryly, 'and I suspect it will be a harsh one.'

Looking out over the bay, Ainsley's nerves made themselves known in the form of a fluttering stomach as she watched the little boat approaching. Until now, she had lost herself in the bustle of arrangements, the thrill of the journey. Her first time on a paddle steamer, her first time on the west coast and now her first time in a sailing boat was looming. Then would be her arrival at Strone Bridge with the man who was her husband. She worried at the plain gold band on her finger, inside her glove. She still couldn't quite believe it. It did not feel at all real. She was now Mrs Drummond, wife of the laird of Strone Bridge, this stranger by her side whose dawning black mood had quite thrown her.

Innes didn't want to be here, though he was now doing a good job of covering it up. There was a lot going on below the surface of that handsome countenance. Secrets? Or was it merely that he had left his past behind and didn't want to be faced with it again? She could understand that. It was one of the reasons she'd been happy to leave Edinburgh for a while. Perhaps it was resentment, which was more than understandable, for unlike her, the life Innes was leaving behind was one he loved.

As he hefted their luggage down to the edge of the shoreline, Ainsley watched, distracted by the fluidity of his movements, the long stride over the pebbles, the smooth strength in the way he lifted even the heaviest pieces so effortlessly. She recalled Felicity's joke about him being a wild Highlander, and wondered if he would wear a plaid when he was back at Strone Bridge. He had the legs for it. A prickle of heat low in her belly made her shiver.

'*Feasgar math.*' The bump of the boat against the tiny jetty made her jump.

Ainsley stared blankly at the man. 'Good day to you, Mrs Drummond,' he repeated in a softly lilting accent, at odds with the curt nod he gave her before starting to heave the luggage Innes was handing him into the boat.

'Oh, good day,' Ainsley replied.

'This is Eoin Ferguson,' Innes told her, 'an old friend of mine. Eoin, this is my wife.'

'I'm afraid I don't speak any Gaelic,' Ainsley said to the boatman.

'Have the Gaelic,' he said to her. 'We don't say speak it, we say have it.'

'And there's no need to worry, almost everyone on Strone Bridge *speaks* English,' Innes said, frowning at the man he claimed for a friend, though Ainsley could see no trace of warmth between the two men.

'I have never been to the Highlands,' she said with a bright smile.

'Strone Bridge is not far north of Glasgow as the crow flies,' Eoin replied. 'If you're expecting us all to be wandering around in plaid and waving claymores, you'll be disappointed. Are you getting in or not?'

'Oh, right. Yes.' She could feel herself flushing, mortified as if he had read her earlier thoughts. He made no move to help her. Seeing Innes's frown deepen, Ainsley gave him a slight shake of the head, clambering awkwardly and with too much show of leg into the boat. Eoin watched impassively, indicating that she sit on the narrow bench at the front of the dinghy, making a point of folding his arms as she then proceeded to clamber over the luggage stacked mid-ship.

She tried not to feel either slighted or crushed, reminding herself she was a stranger, a Sassenach, a lowlander, who spoke—no, *had*—no Gaelic and knew nothing of their ways. Innes, his mouth drawn into a tight line, had leaped into the boat, and was deftly untying the rope from the jetty as Eoin tended the sail. She watched the pair of them working silently together as they set out into the water, the contrast between the harmony of their movements stark against the undercurrent of tension that ran between them. It spiked as Innes made to take the tiller.

'The tide is against us, and I know the currents,' Eoin said, keeping his hand on the polished wood.

'I know them every bit as well as you.'

'You used to.' Eoin made no attempt to hide his enmity, but glared at Innes, his eyes, the same deep blue as Innes's own, bright with challenge. 'It's been a long time.'

Innes's fists clenched and unclenched. 'I know exactly how long it's been.'

A gust of wind took Eoin's words away. When Innes spoke again, it was in a soft, menacing tone that made the hairs on the back of Ainsley's neck stand on end. And it was in Gaelic. Eoin flinched and made to hand over the tiller, but Innes shook his head, joining Ainsley in the prow, turning away from her to stare out at the white wake, his face unreadable.

The wind that filled the sail blew in her face, whipping her hair from under her bonnet, making her eyes stream. Innes had not worn a hat today, a wise move, for it would surely have blown into the sea. Though he was, as ever, conservatively dressed, his trousers and coat dark blue, his linen pristine white; compared to Eoin's rough tweed trews and heavy fisherman's jumper, Innes looked like a dandy. She had watched the other man noticing this when he docked, but couldn't decide whether the twitch of his mouth was contempt or envy.

The boat scudded along, the keel bumping over the waves of the outgoing tide. While the paddle steamer had felt—and smelled—rather like a train that ran on water instead of rails, in this dinghy, Ainsley was acutely conscious that only a few planks of wood and some tar separated her from the icy-cold strait. Spray made her lips salty. The sail snapped noisily. She began to feel nauseous, and looking up, catching a cold smile on Eoin's face as the boat lifted out of the water and then slapped down again, began to suspect that he was making their voyage deliberately rough.

'You're from the city, I hear. You'll not be used to the sea,' he shouted.

Ainsley gripped the wooden seat with both hands, determined to hold on to the contents of her breakfast. She wished she hadn't had the eggs.

She mustn't think about the eggs. 'How did you know that?' she asked.

'Himself told Mhairi McIntosh, the house-keeper, in the letter he sent.'

Innes snapped his head round. 'Well, it wouldn't have done me any good to write to you.'

Eoin, to Ainsley's surprise, turned a dull shade of red, and looked away. Innes swallowed whatever else he had been about to say and resumed his staring out at the sea. The undercurrent of emotion that ran between the two men was as strong as the ebb of the tide that was making their entrance into the bay a battle.

The pier was old and crumbling, extending far out into the bay. The low tide forced them to berth right at the very end of the structure, where Innes threw the rope neatly over a post to make fast. It was only as he put one foot on the first rung of the ladder that Eoin spoke, putting a hand on his shoulder, making him freeze.

'You'll find the place much changed.'

'If you tell me once again that it's been fourteen years...' he said through gritted teeth.

'It's not that.' Eoin pulled his hand away, a bleak look in his eyes. 'You know Mhairi's got the Home Farm ready for you? The big house—ach, you'll see for yourself soon enough. Give Angus a shout; I can see he's there with the cart. I'll see to the luggage.'

Innes ascended the worn ladder quickly, then turned to help Ainsley. She was eyeing the gap between boat and pier with a trepidation she was trying—and failing—to disguise. Her cheeks were bright with the wind, her hair a tangle. She looked endearing. She was most likely wondering what the hell she'd let herself in for, with the enmity between himself and Eoin almost palpable. He swore under his breath. Whatever was going on in Eoin's head, there would be time enough to sort it out. Right now, he needed to get poor Ainsley, who might well be his only ally, out of that boat before she fell out of it. 'Put one foot on the bottom rung and give me your hand,' he said, leaning down over the end of the pier.

She looked at the seaweed-slimed lower struts of the ladder pier dubiously. 'I can't swim.'

Innes went down on his knees and leaned over. 'I can. If you fall, I promise I'll dive in right behind you.'

'And walk up the beach with me in your arms, dripping seawater and seaweed.'

'Just like a mermaid.'

Ainsley chuckled. 'More like a sea monster. Not the grand entrance that the laird and his lady are expected to make. It's as well we've no audience.'

'I told Mhairi—that's the housekeeper—that we did not want a formal welcome until we were settled. I must admit, I'm surprised she listened, though,' Innes said, looking about him. Save for Angus, making his lumbering way down the pier, there was not a soul in sight. Perhaps he'd maligned his friend after all. Eoin knew how much he hated the pomp and ceremony of the old ways that his father had gone to such pains to preserve. He looked over Ainsley's shoulder to thank him, but Eoin was busying himself with the ropes.

Shrugging inwardly, Innes held out his hand to Ainsley, pulling her up without a hitch and catching her in his arms. 'Welcome to Strone Bridge.'

She smiled weakly, clutching tight to him, her legs trembling on the wooden planking. 'I'm sorry, I think my legs have turned to jelly.'

'You don't mean your heart? I'm not sure what you've let yourself in for here, but I am pretty certain things are in a bad way. I'll understand if you want to go back to Edinburgh.'

'Your people are expecting you to arrive with

a wife. A fine impression it would make if she turned tail before she'd even stepped off the pier—or more accurately, judging by the state of it, stepped through it. Besides, we made a bargain, and I plan to stick to my part of it.' Ainsley tilted her head up at him, her eyes narrowed, though she was smiling. 'Are you having cold feet?'

'Not about you.' He hadn't meant it to sound the way it did, like the words of a lover, but it was too late to retract. He pulled her roughly against him, and he kissed her, forgetting all about his resolution to do no such thing. Her lips were freezing. She tasted of salt. The thump of luggage being tossed with no regard for its contents from the boat to the pier made them spring apart.

Ainsley flushed. 'It is a shame we don't have more of an audience, for I feel sure that was quite convincing.'

Innes laughed. 'I won't pretend that had anything to do with acting the part of your husband. The truth is, you have a very kissable mouth, and I've been thinking about kissing you again since the first time all those weeks ago. And before you say it, it's got nothing to do with my needing an emotional safety valve either, and everything to do with the fact that I thoroughly enjoyed it, though I know perfectly well it's not part of our bargain.'

'Save that it can do no harm to put on a show, now and then,' Ainsley said with a teasing smile.

'Does that mean you'll only kiss me in public? I know there are men who like that sort of thing, but I confess I prefer to do my lovemaking in private.'

'Innes! I am sure we can persuade the people of Strone Bridge we are husband and wife without resorting to—to engaging in public marital relations.'

He gave a shout of laughter. 'Good grief, I hope not. That makes it sound like a meeting of foreign ministers.'

'It does? Really?' They began to make their way slowly to the head of the pier.

'Really,' Innes said.

'Oh. What is your opinion on *undergoing a husband's ministrations*?'

'That it sounds as if the husband is to carry out some sort of unsavoury medical procedure. You may as well talk about performing hymeneal duties, which is the sort of mealy-mouthed and utterly uninformative phrase I imagine any number of poor girls hear from their mothers on the eve of their wedding. They probably think they're going to be sacrificed on the matrimonial altar. Whatever they imagine, you can be damned sure they won't be looking forward to it.'

'Oh, I couldn't agree more. The belief that innocence and ignorance must go hand in hand seems to me quite perverse. I wonder sometimes if there is a conspiracy by society to keep young girls uninformed in order to encourage them into marriages they would not otherwise make.'

The sparkle had returned to her hazel eyes, but it was no longer teasing. Rather, Innes thought, studying her in some surprise, it was martial. 'Are you speaking from experience?'

'My mother died when I was twelve, and I had no other female relative close enough to divulge the pertinent facts before my wedding night. It was a—a shock.'

He was appalled, but she was bristling like a porcupine. 'Perhaps there should be some sort of guidebook. An introduction to married life; or something of that sort.'

He meant it as a joke, but Ainsley seemed much struck. 'That is an excellent idea.'

'Though if what you say about the conspiracy is true, then mothers will surely forbid their daughters from reading it.'

'More likely fathers would.'

Most definitely martial. Intrigued, he could not resist pushing her. 'Since the shops that would sell such a thing are the kind frequented by men and not women, then your plan is defeated by the outset,' Innes said.

'That shows how little you know,' Ainsley said with a superior smile. 'Shops are not the only outlet for such information.'

Above them the white clouds had given way to iron-grey. The wind was picking up as the tide turned, making white crests on the water, which was turning the same colour as the sky. While they'd been talking, the luggage had been loaded onto the cart, where Angus was now waiting patiently. Of Eoin there was no sign. Reluctantly, Innes abandoned this intriguing conversation. 'Whatever else has changed,' he said, 'the weather is still as reliably fickle as ever. Come on, let's get out of this wind before you catch a cold.'

Ainsley woke with a start and sat up, staring around her at the unfamiliar surroundings. The room was panelled and sparsely furnished. It had the look of a place hastily put together, and it felt as if the fires had not been lit for some time. Shivering as she threw back the covers and stepped onto the bare floorboards, she could feel the cold begin to seep into her bones.

Though it was July, it felt more like April. She made haste with her ablutions. Without the help of a maid, she laced her corsets loosely and tied her hair into a simple knot before pulling a woollen dress from her trunk. The colours, broad stripes of cream and turquoise, made her think of a summer sky that bore no resemblance to the one she could see through the window. The narrow sleeves were long, the tight-fitting bodice made doubly warm with the overlapping kerchief-style collar that came to a point at her waist. Woollen stockings and boots completed her *toilette* in record time. Reluctantly, she abandoned the idea of wrapping her cloak around her, telling herself that a lesson in hardiness was in order.

The corridor outside was dark and windowless. The fading daylight darkened by the deluge that had erupted as she arrived yesterday had prevented her from gaining any perspective of her new residence. Exhaustion had set in once she had eaten, and Ainsley had retired almost immediately afterwards.

Start the way you mean to go on. Muttering

Madame Hera's own advice like a charm, she stumbled her way towards the door where she had dined last night, cheered by the faint smell of coffee. The room looked much more attractive in the daylight, and the fire, which last evening had smouldered, today was burning brightly. 'Good morning,' she said.

Innes was seated at the table, staring moodily at his empty plate, but he stood when she came into the room. His jaw looked raw. Most likely he'd shaved in water as cold as she'd used to wash. Perhaps he simply wasn't a morning person. Ainsley hovered at the door.

'Are you staying or going?' Innes asked, and she gave herself a little shake.

'Staying,' she said, seating herself opposite.

'I didn't know if you'd want tea or coffee, so I had Mhairi bring both.'

'Coffee, thank you.'

He sat down and poured her a cup. 'There's crowdie and oatcakes, but if you'd prefer a kipper, or some ham or porridge?'

'No, that will be fine—at least— What is crowdie?'

'Cheese.'

'Thank you.' She took the oatcakes and creamy

cheese. 'This looks delicious.' Innes poured himself a cup of tea. 'Have you eaten?' she asked, cringing as she spoke, for she had already noticed his empty plate, and she sounded as if she was making polite conversation over the tinkling of teaspoons in an Edinburgh drawing room.

'Yes,' Innes said.

Ainsley bit into an oatcake. The crunch was embarrassingly loud. She took a sip of coffee. It sounded like a slurp. This was ridiculous. 'Innes, would you prefer…?'

'Ainsley, if you would prefer…?'

He stopped. She stopped. Then he laughed. 'I'm not used to having company at breakfast. I don't know whether you'd prefer to be left in peace, or— What?'

'I don't know. I'm not any more accustomed to it than you. It's silly, I know it's silly, but it feels strange.'

'Would you rather I went?'

'No. Unless you'd rather—' She broke off, laughing. 'For goodness' sake, I'd like you to stay, and I'd like to talk, but not if we're going to make polite chit-chat for the sake of it.'

Innes grinned. 'I am more than happy to promise never to make polite chit-chat, though I would like to know if your bedchamber was comfortable—and please, give me the real answer, and not the drawing-room one.'

Ainsley chuckled. 'One does not mention a lady's bedchamber in the drawing room.'

'Actually, that very much depends on the drawing room,' Innes said, smiling. 'Let me put it another way then—did you manage to sleep, or were you frozen to death?'

'I slept, but I confess I dressed very quickly.'

'I'm sorry about that. It seems that my father had the main part of the castle shut up and took to living in just two or three rooms. This place is sound and dry enough, but it's been empty awhile, and Mhairi had little notice of our arrival, as you know. She gave you that bedchamber because it was the best of a bad bunch.'

'She apologised for the fact it was several rooms away from your own,' Ainsley said, flushing. 'I got the impression she was worried the effort it would take to walk the distance would put you off. I confess, it did not do my ego much good to think my husband would be so easily deterred.'

'If I thought I would be welcomed into your bedchamber for a bout of debauchery, not even a chastity belt would deter me,' Innes said wickedly.

''Tis a shame I cannot lay my hands on such an item, else I would be tempted to test your resolve.'

'Don't be too sure, there are all sorts of things in the armoury,' Innes replied. 'Debauchery and chastity belts—who'd have thought that conversation over the breakfast cups could be so interesting?'

'*I* did not introduce the topic of debauchery,' Ainsley said, spluttering coffee.

'No, but you did say you didn't want to make polite chit-chat.'

'Innes Drummond, you should have considered entering the legal profession, for you can twist an argument better than any lawyer I've dealt with— and believe me, I've dealt with a few.'

He gave a theatrical sigh. 'Very well, we will change the topic, though it is your own fault, you know.'

She eyed him warily. 'I am very sure I should not ask what you mean by that.'

'Then do not.'

Ainsley took a sip of coffee. Innes folded his mouth primly. She took another sip, trying not to laugh, then finally cast her cup down in the saucer with a clatter. 'Oh, for goodness' sake, you win. Tell me what you meant.'

'No, for it is not true, it's not debauchery I think of when I look at that mouth of yours, it's kissing.'

'Just kissing.'

'Not *just* kissing.' Innes leaned forward over the table and took her hand. *'Kissing.* There's a difference.'

He was teasing. Or was it flirting? She wasn't sure. She didn't think she was the kind of woman that men flirted with. Did she amuse or arouse? Was it possible to combine the two? Ainsley had no idea, but she knew he was not laughing at her. There was complicity in the way he was looking at her, and something in those beguiling blue eyes of his that made her tingle. 'What difference?' she asked, knowing she ought not, sure that if she did not she would regret it.

Innes lifted her hand to his mouth, just barely brushing the back of it with his lips. 'That,' he said, 'was *just* a kiss.' He turned her hand over. *'This,'* he said softly, 'is the difference.'

His lips were warm on her palm. His tongue flicked over the pad of her thumb, giving her the most delicious little shiver. When he enveloped her thumb with his mouth and sucked, she inhaled sharply. 'You see,' he said, his voice husky. 'There is only one problem with those kinds of kisses.'

She knew exactly what he meant. She was experiencing that very problem. 'More?' Ainsley said, meaning it as an answer, though it sounded like a request.

'More,' Innes said, taking it as a request, pushing back his chair, leaning across the table, doing just as she asked.

He hadn't intended to kiss her, but he couldn't resist, and when she did not either, when she opened her mouth to him and twined her arms around his neck with the most delightful little sigh, his teasing kiss became something deeper. She kissed him back. The tip of her tongue touched his, triggering the rush of blood, the clenching of his muscles, the shiver of arousal. He slid his hand down to her breast under the shawl that formed part of her bodice, only to find himself frustrated by the bones of her corset, by the layers of clothes. A knife clattered to the ground, and they both jumped.

He was hard. He was very glad that the table lay between them. Ainsley's face was flushed, her lips soft, eyes dark with their kisses. The urge to pull her across the table and ravage that sinful mouth of hers was unbearably tempting. What the devil was wrong with him that he couldn't seem to keep his hands off her! Sitting carefully back down in his chair, Innes thought ruefully that it had been the same right from their first meeting. Why hadn't he realised it would be a problem? Was it a problem?

'Mhairi could have come into the room at any moment,' Ainsley said.

Innes ran his fingers through his hair. 'Is that why you kissed me?'

She picked up a teaspoon and began to trace a pattern on the table. 'Actually, you kissed me, though I cannot deny that I kissed you back,' she said, looking at him fleetingly from under her lashes. 'I don't know why, save that I wanted to, and I haven't wanted to for... And ever since I met you I have and—and so I did.'

'I can't tell you how relieved I am to hear that, because it's been exactly the same for me.' Innes swallowed a mouthful of cold coffee and grimaced. 'I never was one to toe the line, you know. Maybe it's because our bargain precludes it that I'm so tempted.'

'You mean you want to kiss me because it is illicit?'

'Oh, no, I want to kiss you because you have a

mouth that makes me think of kissing. But perhaps it's so difficult not to because I know it's not permitted, even though we're married.' Innes shook his head and jumped to his feet. 'I don't know. Maybe we should check the armoury for a chastity belt.'

'Maybe we should stop worrying about it, and discussing it and analysing it,' Ainsley said. 'We are adults. We are neither of us interested in becoming attached. There is no harm in us having some—some fun.'

'Fun? You say that as if you are taking a dose of Mr Rush's patented pills for biliousness.'

'I am sure that they too are healthful.'

Innes burst out laughing. 'You say the strangest things. Healthful! It's the first time I've heard it referred to in that way.'

'You think it's an inaccurate term to use?'

She was frowning, looking genuinely puzzled, just as she had yesterday, now he thought about it, when she'd mentioned—what was it—marital relations? 'I think it's best if we think about something else entirely,' Innes said. 'Delightful as this breakfast has been, the day is getting away from us. First things first, we'll start with a tour of the castle. I warn you, it's a great barrack of a place and like to be as cold as an icehouse.'

Ainsley got to her feet. 'I'll go and fetch a shawl.'

The door closed behind her. Innes gazed out of the window, though the view was almost entirely obscured by an overgrown hedge. It looked as if it had not been cut for a good many years. Like everything he'd seen at Strone Bridge so far, from the jetty to the stables, it was neglected. Eoin had warned him that things had changed. He wondered, if the state of the house and grounds were anything to go by, what had happened to the lands. He was surprised, for though his father had been old-fashioned, archaic even in his practices, he had never been negligent. He was also angry, though guiltily aware he had little right to be so. These were Malcolm's lands. If Malcolm was here, he would be appalled at the state of them. Yet if Malcolm were here, Innes would not be. If Malcolm was here, he would not have allowed the place to fall into decline, and Innes...

He cursed. He could go round in circles for ever with that logic. He was not looking forward to this tour of the castle. It wasn't so much the state of disrepair he was now certain he'd find in the rooms, it was the history in those rooms, all *his* history. He didn't want anyone to see him coping—or not coping—with that history, and Ainsley was a very astute observer. It had been fourteen years. Surely that was long enough for him to at least put on a show of disaffection. Yet here he was, feeling distinctly edgy and wondering how to explain it away.

The castle was just a building. A heap of stones and wood of dubious aesthetic value. There was no ancient law that said he must live there if he chose to remain on Strone Bridge after a year, which was highly unlikely. No, he would have the Home Farm made more comfortable, because nothing would persuade him to play the laird in the castle, not even for a few weeks.

The vehemence of this thought took Innes so aback he did not notice Ainsley had returned until she spoke his name. 'Right,' Innes said, sounding appropriately businesslike. 'Let's get on with it.'

Chapter Four

The sun shone weakly from a pale blue sky dotted with puffy clouds, the kind a child would paint. Following in Innes's wake along the narrow path of damp paving slabs, Ainsley could see that the gloom inside the Home Farm's lower rooms was largely due to the height of the untended hedge. Emerging through an extremely overgrown arch, she came face-to-face with Strone Bridge Castle for the first time.

They were standing at the side of a long sweep of carriageway with what must have been a huge lawn on either side, though at present it was more like the remnants of a hayfield, part long yellowed grass falling over, part fresh green pushing through. The building loomed over them, such an imposing structure she could not imagine how she had missed its hulk yesterday, though the stone was indeed the grey colour the sky had been.

Ainsley walked backwards to gain some perspective. 'This is the rear of the house,' Innes said. 'The drive meets the main overland road, which cuts over to the other side of the peninsula and Loch Fyne, though to call it a road… It's far easier to travel by boat in this neck of the woods.'

'We did not come this way yesterday?'

He shook his head. 'The front of the house faces down to the shore. We came up that way. I'll show you, we'll go in by the main entrance, but I wanted you to see the scale of this damned monstrosity first.'

Strone Bridge Castle was indeed enormous, and though it was not precisely charming, Ainsley would not have called it a monstrosity. An imposing construction with a large tower at each corner, and another central turret projecting from the middle of the main building, it was like a castle from a Gothic novel. The sturdy turrets had unexpected ogee roofs, adding a hint of the east into the architectural mix, each roof topped with tall spires and embellished with slit windows. The turrets looked, with their rugged masonry walls and stolid, defensive air, quite at odds with the central part of the building, which was considerably more elegant, mostly Jacobean in style, with four storeys of tall French-style windows, a low Palladian roof ornamented with a stone balustrade and a huge portico that looked as if it had been added on as an afterthought. The overall effect was certainly not of beauty, but it was striking.

'It looks,' Ainsley said, studying it with bemusement, 'as if someone has jumbled up three or four different houses, or taken samples from a book of architectural styles through the ages.'

'You're not far off,' Innes said. 'The main house was built about 1700. The roof and that central tower were added about fifty or sixty years after that, and my own father put those corner towers up. There's no rhyme nor reason to it. As I said, it's a monstrosity.'

'That's not what I meant at all. It is like nothing I have ever seen.'

'One of a kind. That, thank heavens, is certainly true,' Innes said grimly.

'You are not fond of it, then?' Ainsley asked. 'Though there must be some interesting stories attached to a building so old. And perhaps even a few ghosts.'

He had taken her arm as they made their way over the untended lawn around the building, and now slanted her a curious look. 'Do you believe in such things?'

'Honestly, I've never considered the question before, but looking at this place, I could easily be persuaded.'

'There is a tale of one of the lairds who went off to fight in the 1715 Jacobite uprising. He was for the Old Pretender. There's a set of gates, right at the end of the carriageway, which he had locked, so they say, and made his wife promise never to unlock them until his return.'

'What happened?'

'He died in the Battle of Sheriffmuir. His wife had the gates unlocked for his corpse to pass through in its coffin, but—' Innes broke off, shaking his head. 'No, there's enough here already to give you nightmares without adding a walking, wailing, clanking ghost to the mix.'

Ainsley stopped in her tracks, looking up at him in horror. 'Walking and wailing and clanking?'

He bent down to whisper in her ear. 'He rattles the chain that should have been kept around the gates. He walks just over there, on the carriageway. He wails for the treachery of his lady wife, who married his enemy less than a year after he was slain.'

She shuddered, looked over to where he was pointing, then looked back at him. 'Have you actually seen him?' Innes made a noncommittal noise. Ainsley narrowed her eyes suspiciously. 'Has anyone ever seen him?'

'None who have lived to tell the tale,' he answered sorrowfully.

She punched him on the arm. 'Then how can the tale be told! You made that up.'

He laughed, rubbing his arm. 'Not all of it. The first part was true. The laird at the time did fight, he did die at Sheriffmuir and he did have the gates locked.'

'Are there any real ghosts?'

His laughter faded as he took her arm and urged her on. 'Plenty, believe me, though none that you will see, I hope.'

His expression was one she recognised. *Don't ask.* Not because she wouldn't like the answers, but because *he* would not. This was his home, this place that he was mocking and deriding, this place that he called a monstrosity. She wondered, then, if he really meant the bricks and mortar. Yesterday it was obvious that Innes had not wanted to come back to Strone Bridge. It was equally obvious from this morning that he'd not expected the place to be in such a state of disrepair, but now she wondered what else there was to disturb him here. What was at the heart of the quarrel that had so completely estranged him from his father?

How little of Innes she knew. His formative years had been spent here, yet he had left all of it behind without, it seemed, a backward glance, to make a new and very different life for himself. Why? It was all very well to tell herself it was none of her business, but—no, there was no *but*. It was absolutely none of her business, Ainsley told herself rather unconvincingly. Yet it was strange, and very distractingly intriguing, like the man himself.

'You were a million miles away. I was only teasing you about the ghosts. I didn't mean to give you the jitters,' Innes said, cutting in on her thoughts.

'You didn't.' Ainsley looked around her with slight surprise. They had reached the front of the house, and the prospect was stunning, for it sat on a hill directly above the bay where they had landed yesterday. 'My goodness, this is absolutely beautiful.'

'That's the Kyles of Bute over there, the stretch

of water with all the small islands that you sailed yesterday,' Innes said. 'And over there, the crescent of sand you can see, that's Ettrick Bay on Bute, the other side of the island from which we set sail. And that bigger island you can just see in the distance, that's Arran.'

'I don't think I've ever seen such a wonderful prospect. It is exactly the sort of view that one conjures up, all misty-eyed, when one thinks of the Highlands. Like something from one of Mr Walter Scott's novels.'

'Aye, well, strictly speaking Eoin was right in what he said yesterday, though. We're only a wee bit farther north than Glasgow here, and Arran is south.'

'As the crow flies,' Ainsley said. 'It doesn't matter, it feels like another world, and it really is quite spectacular. There must be a magnificent view from the castle.' She looked back at the house, where a set of long French-style windows opened out on the first floor to what must have once been a beautiful terrace at the top of a flight of stairs.

'That's the drawing room,' Innes said, following her gaze.

'How lovely to take tea there on a summer's

day. I can just imagine the ladies of old with their hoops and their wigs,' she said dreamily.

'The hoops and wigs are like as not still packed away up in the attics somewhere. My family never throws anything away. Do you really like this place?'

'It's entrancing. Do you really *not* like it?'

Innes shrugged. 'I can see it's a lovely view. I'd forgotten.'

Without waiting on her, he turned on his heel and began to walk quickly up the slope towards the central staircase. 'Like someone determined to swallow their medicine as quickly as they can and get it over with,' Ainsley muttered, stalking after him.

'What was that?'

'This may be a monstrosity to you, Innes, but to someone accustomed to a terraced house in Edinburgh, it's magical.'

Innes stopped abruptly. 'Ach, I'm like a beast with a sore head. I'm sorry. It's not your fault.'

No, it was most definitely this place. Curious as she was, and with a hundred questions to boot, Ainsley had no desire to see him suffer. 'We could leave it for today. Or I could look around myself.'

'No,' Innes said firmly, 'it has to be done.' He

took her hand, forcing a smile. 'Besides, you came here thinking you'd be lady of the manor—you've a right to see over your domain. I'm only sorry that it's bound to be a disappointment.'

'I did not come here with any such expectations. Aside from the fact that I know absolutely nothing about the management of a place this size, I am perfectly well aware that your people will regard a destitute Edinburgh widow without a hint of anything close to blue in her blood as nothing more than an upstart.'

Innes gave a startled laugh. 'You're not seriously worried that people here will look down their noses at you, Ainsley?'

'A little,' she confessed, embarrassed. 'I hadn't really thought about it until I arrived here yesterday. Then your boatman...'

'Ach! Blasted Eoin. Listen to me. First, if there's an upstart here, then it's me. Second, for better or worse, I'll be the laird while I'm here, and while you're here, I will not tolerate anyone looking down their noses at you. Third, the state of your finances are nobody's business but our own.' He pulled her closer, pushing a strand of her hair out of her eyes. 'Finally, though I have no intention of playing the laird and therefore there's no need for you to play lady of the manor, if I did, and you did, then I think you'd play it very well. And on the off chance you couldn't quite follow me,' he added, 'that was me saying you've not a thing to worry about.'

She felt a stupid desire to cry. 'Thank you, I will try not to let you down.'

'Wheesht, now,' he said, kissing her cheek. 'You'll do your best, and that's all I ask. Anyway, it's not as if *you* are stepping into a dead person's shoes. My mother died when I was eight years old.'

'And your father never remarried?'

Innes gave a crack of laughter. 'What for, he'd already produced an heir and a spare.'

'What about your brother. Did he…?'

'No.'

Another of those 'do not dare ask' faces accompanied this stark denial. And Innes would not be married either, were it not for the terms of the old laird's will. Were the Drummond men all misogynists? Or perhaps there was some sort of dreadful hereditary disease? But Innes seemed perfectly healthy. A curse, then? Now she was being utterly fanciful. It was this place. Ainsley gave herself a little shake. 'Well, then, let us go and inspect this castle of yours, and see what needs to be done to make it habitable.'

Everything inside Strone Bridge Castle was done on a grand scale. The formal salons opened out one after the other around the central court-yard with the Great Hall forming the centrepiece, heavy with geometric panelling, topped with rich fretwork ceilings like icing on a cake, or one of those elaborate sugar constructions that deco-rates the table at a banquet. Massive fireplaces and overmantels rose to merge the two, and every-where, it seemed to Ainsley, every opportunity had been taken to incorporate heraldic devices and crests. Dragons and lions poked and pawed from pilasters, banisters and pediments. Shields and swords augmented the cornicing, were carved into the marble fireplaces and fanned out above the windows. It was beautiful, in an oppressive and overwhelming way.

The turrets that marked each corner were dank places with treacherous-looking staircases wind-ing their way steeply up, and which Ainsley decided she did not need to climb. 'They serve no real purpose,' Innes told her. 'A whim of my father's, nothing more.'

After two hours and only a fraction of the hundred and thirty rooms, she had seen enough for one day. Back in the courtyard, she gazed up at the central tower, which was square and not round, and faced directly out over the Kyles of Bute. Bigger than the others, it seemed to contain proper rooms, judging from the wide windows that took up most of the sea-facing wall on each of the four stories. Ainsley wrestled with the heavy latch, but it would not budge.

'It's locked.' Innes made no attempt to help her. 'Has been for years. Most likely the key is long gone, for it's not on here,' he said, waving the heavy bunch of keys he carried.

Ainsley frowned at the lock, which seemed surprisingly new, and showed no sign of rust, wondering how Innes would know such a thing when he himself had not been here for years. 'The view from up there must be spectacular,' she said, looking back up at the battlements.

Innes had already turned away. 'We'll take a look at the kitchens.'

'There must be a door from inside the castle,'

Ainsley said, frowning at the tower in frustration, trying to recall the exact layout of rooms that lay behind it. 'Is that the dining room? I don't recall a door, but...'

'The door isn't in the dining room.' Innes was holding open another door. 'Do you want to see the kitchens? I was hoping to get out to some of the farms this afternoon.'

He sounded impatient. Though this was all new to her, for him it was different. 'I can come back myself another time,' Ainsley said, joining him.

'I don't want you going up there,' Innes said sharply. 'It's not safe.'

She cast a dubious look at the tower, thinking that it looked, like the rest of the castle, neglected though sound, but Innes was already heading down the narrow corridor, so she picked up her skirts and walked quickly after him.

A few moments later she forgot all about the locked tower, gazing in astonishment at the table that ran almost the full length of the servants' hall. It looked as if it would sit at least fifty. 'Good grief, how many staff does it take to keep this place running?'

Innes shook his head. 'I've no idea. Even in my youth, most of the rooms were closed up, save for formal occasions, and there were few of those. My father was not the most sociable of men.'

They exited the servants' hall and entered the main kitchen, which had two bread ovens, a row of charcoal braziers, a stove the size of a hay cart and the biggest fireplace Ainsley had ever seen. Out through another door, they wended their way through the warren of the basement, past linen rooms and still rooms, pantries and empty wine cellars, and then back up a steep flight of stairs to another door that took them out to the kitchen gardens.

Innes turned the lock and turned his back on the castle. 'As you can see, the place is uninhabitable,' he said.

He sounded relieved. She couldn't understand his reaction to it. 'Is the building itself in such a poor state of repair, is it the cost of restoring it you're worried about?'

'It's sound enough, I reckon. There's no smell of damp and no sign that the roof is anything but watertight, though I'd need to get one of my surveyors to take a look. But what would be the point?'

'I have no idea, but—you would surely not wish to let it simply fall into ruin?'

'I could knock it down and get it over with.'

Innes tucked the weight of keys into his coat pocket with a despondent shrug. 'I don't know,' he said heavily, 'and I think I've more pressing matters to consider, to be honest. Maybe it was a mistake to start with the castle. For now, I think it would be best if you concentrated on the immediate issue of making the Home Farm a bit more comfortable. Speak to Mhairi, she'll help you. I'll need to spend some time out on the lands.'

Ainsley watched him walk away, feeling slightly put out. He was right, their living quarters left a lot to be desired, and it made sense for her to sort them out. 'Whatever that means,' she muttered. The idea of consulting the rather forbidding Mhairi McIntosh did not appeal to her. Madame Hera had suggested that Timid Mouse appeal to her housekeeper's softer side. Ainsley was not so sure that Mhairi McIntosh had one.

Besides, that wasn't the point. She had not come here to set up Innes's home for him, but to provide him with objective advice. How was she to do that if she was hanging curtains and making up beds while he was out inspecting his lands? Excluding her, in other words, and she had not protested. 'Same old Ainsley,' she said to herself in disgust. 'You should be ashamed of yourself!'

* * *

Dear Madame Hera,

My husband's mother gave me a household manual on my wedding day that she wrote herself. It is extremely comprehensive, and at first I was pleased to know the foods my husband prefers, and how he likes them served. However, I must say that right from the start I was a bit worried when I read what his mother calls 'The Order of the Day'—and there is one for every day. I do try to follow it, but I confess I see no reason why I must do the washing on a Wednesday and polish the silver on a Saturday, any more than I see why we have to have shin of beef every single Tuesday, and kippers only on a Thursday. And as to her recipe for sheep's-head soup—I will not!

I tried to tell my husband that his mother's way is not the only way. I have many excellent recipes from my own mother that I am sure he would enjoy. I tried, with all my wifely wiles, to persuade him that I could run the household without following his mother's manual to the letter. He spurned my wifely wiles, Madame, and now he is threatening to have his mother, who has a perfectly good house of her own, to

come and live with us. I love my husband, but I do not love his mother. What should I do?
Desperate Wife

Ainsley pulled a fresh sheet of paper on to the blotting pad. It was tempting to suggest that Desperate Wife invite her own mother to stay, and even more tempting to suggest that she simply swap abodes herself with her husband's mother, but she doubted Felicity would print either solution. Instead, she would advise Desperate Wife to put her foot down, throw away the manual and claim the hearth and home as her own domain. It was Madame Hera's standard response to this sort of letter, of which she received a great many. Mothers-in-law, if the readers of the *Scottish Ladies Companion* were to be believed, were an interfering lot, and their sons seemed to be singularly lacking in gumption.

Claiming this hearth and home as her own had turned out to be relatively easy. Yet looking around the room, which in the past ten days, like the rest of the Home Farm, had been made both warm and comfortable, Ainsley felt little satisfaction. Mhairi McIntosh had proved cooperative but reserved. She had not looked down her nose at Ainsley, nor had she mocked or derided a single one of her suggestions, which had made the task Innes had given her relatively easy, but it was not the challenge she had been looking forward to. She had, in essence, been relegated to the domestic sphere when he had promised her a different role.

Irked with herself, Ainsley tucked Madame Hera's correspondence into her leather folder and pushed it to one side of the desk, covering it with the latest copy of the *Scottish Ladies Companion*, which Felicity had sent to her. There could be no doubt that Innes needed help, but he had made no attempt to ask her for it. Though she rationalised that he most likely thought he'd fare better with his tenants alone, as the days passed, she felt more excluded and more uncomfortable with trying to address this fact. She was not unhappy, she was not regretting her decision to come here, but she felt overlooked and rather useless.

Standing on her tiptoes at the window, she could see the sky was an inviting bright blue above the monstrous hedge. Ainsley made her way outside, making for her favourite view out over the Kyles of Bute. Tiny puffs of clouds scudded overhead, like the steam from a train or a paddle steamer.

It was a shame that the dilapidated jetty down in the bay was not big enough to allow a steamer to dock, for it would make it a great deal easier to get supplies.

She had to speak to Innes. She had a perfect right to demand that he allow her to do the task he had brought her here for. The fact that he was obviously floundering made it even more important. Yes, it also made him distant and unapproachable, but that was even more reason for her to tackle him. Besides, she couldn't in all conscience remain here without actually doing what she'd already been paid to do. She owed it to herself to speak to him. She had no option but to speak to him.

Mentally rehearsing various ways of introducing the subject, Ainsley wandered through the castle's neglected grounds, finding a path she had not taken before, which wended its way above the coastline before heading inwards to a small copse of trees. The chapel was built of the same grey granite as the castle, but it was warmed by the red sandstone that formed the arched windows, four on each side, and the heavy, worn door. It was a delightful church, simple and functional, with a small belfry on each gable end, a stark contrast to the castle it served.

The door was not locked. Inside, it was equally simple and charming, with wooden pews, the ones nearest the altar covered, the altar itself pink marble, a matching font beside it. It was clean swept. The tall candles were only half-burned. Sunlight, filtered through the leaves of the sheltering trees and the thick panes of glass in the arched windows, had warmed the air. Various Drummonds and their families were commemorated in plaques of brass and polished stone set into the walls. Presumably their bones were interred in the crypt under the altar, but Ainsley could find none more recent than nearly a hundred years ago.

Outside, she discovered the graveyard on the far side of the church. Servants, tenants, fishermen, infants. Some of the stones were so worn she could not read the inscription. The most recent of the lairds were segregated from the rest of the graveyard's inhabitants by a low iron railing.

Ainsley read the short list on the large Celtic cross.

Marjorie Mary Caldwell
1787-1813, spouse of
Malcolm Fraser Drummond

This must be Innes's mother. Below her, the last name, the lettering much brighter, his father:

Malcolm Fraser Drummond
Laird of Strone Bridge
1782-1840

The laird had married early. His wife must have been very young when she had Innes. Ainsley frowned, trying to work out the dates. Seventeen or eighteen? Even younger when she had her first son. Her frown deepened as she read the lettering on the cross again. Above Marjorie was the previous laird. Nothing between her and Innes's father. Innes's brother was not here, and she was certain he was not mentioned in the church. Perhaps he was buried elsewhere? What had Innes said? His brother's death had been the trigger for the split between Innes and his father, she remembered that.

She could ask him. Taking a seat on the stone bench by the main door, Ainsley knew she would not risk antagonising him. She began to pick at the thick rolls of moss, which were growing on the curved arm of the seat. Theirs was a marriage of convenience. Her role as Innes's wife was a public one—to appear on his arm at church on Sunday—and not a private one. She had no right to probe into his past, and she would not like it if he questioned her on hers.

Which did not alter the fact that he was preventing her from helping, and he quite patently needed help. She was bored, and she felt not only useless but rather like an outcast. What would Madame Hera say?

Wandering back along the path, with the sky, not surprisingly, now an ominous grey, Ainsley was thankful that Madame Hera had never been consulted on such a complex problem. There were a score of letters Madame Hera still had to answer, including the one to Desperate Wife. Was there an argument to defend the mother-in-law's precious household manual? Perhaps there were traditions, comforting customs, that Desperate Wife's husband valued or enjoyed, which he feared would be lost if the manual were ignored? Perhaps these very traditions were helping the husband adjust to his new life. Madame Hera rarely concerned herself with the men at the root of her correspondents' problems, but it must be supposed that some of them had feelings, too. Perhaps Desperate Wife might have better success with what she called her wifely wiles if she put them to a more positive use, to discover what parts of the dratted manual actually mattered to him? Though of course, there was always a chance it was simply the case that he simply did like to have kippers on a Thursday.

'I am glad one of us has something to smile about.' Innes was approaching the front door from the direction of the stables. His leather riding breeches and his long boots were spattered with mud, as were the skirts of his black coat. He had not worn a hat since he'd arrived at Strone Bridge, and his hair was windswept. 'What is so amusing, assuming it's not my appearance?' he asked, waiting for her on the path.

'Kippers,' Ainsley replied, smiling. He looked tired. There were shadows under his eyes. She had missed him at breakfast these past few days. 'You do look a bit as if you've been dragged through a hedge backwards. A very muddy hedge,' Ainsley said. 'I'll speak to Mhairi when we get in, I'll have her heat the water so you can have a bath. The chimney has been swept, so it shouldn't take long.'

Innes followed her down the hallway to the sitting room that doubled as their study. 'Thank you, that sounds good. Where have you been?'

'I came across the chapel. I saw your father's grave.'

He was sifting through the pile of mail that Mhairi had left on the desk and did not look up. 'Right.'

She wondered, surprised that it had not occurred to her until now, whether Innes himself had seen it. If so, he had made no mention of it. Another thing he would not talk about. 'I'll go and speak to Mhairi,' Ainsley said, irritated, knowing she had no right to be, and even more irritated by that fact.

When she returned, bearing a tea tray, Innes was sitting at the desk reading a letter, but he put it down as she entered and took the tray from her. 'I think half the population of Strone Bridge must now be in Canada or America,' he said. 'We've more empty farms than tenanted ones.'

She handed him a cup of tea. 'Why is it, do you think?'

'High rents. Poor maintenance—or more accurately, no maintenance. Better prospects elsewhere.' Innes sighed heavily.

'I know nothing about such matters, but even I can see from the weeds growing that some of the fields have not been tilled for years,' Ainsley said carefully. 'Is the land too poor?'

'It's sure as hell in bad heart now,' Innes said wretchedly, 'though whether that's through neglect or lack of innovation, new methods, whatever they might be. There are cotter families who have lived in the tied cottages for decades who have moved on. I'm sick of hearing the words, "I mentioned it to the laird but nothing happened". My father's factor apparently left Strone Bridge not long after I did, and he did not employ another, though no one will tell me why. In fact, no one will tell me anything. They treat me like a stranger.'

'What about Eoin?' Ainsley asked tentatively.

'What about him?'

'You said he was your friend. Couldn't you talk to him?'

'Eoin is as bad as the rest. It doesn't matter, it's not your problem.'

Innes picked up another letter. As far as he was concerned, the conversation was over. *It's not your problem.* Ainsley sat perfectly still. The words were a horrible echo from the past. How many times had she been rebuffed by John with exactly that phrase, until she stopped asking any questions at all?

'Don't say that.'

Her tone made Innes look up in surprise. 'Don't say what?'

Ainsley stared down at her tea. 'It is my problem. At least it's supposed to be. It's what you brought me here for, to help you.'

'This place is beyond help. I can see that for myself.'

'So that's it? You've already decided—what? To sell? To walk away and let it continue to crumble? What?'

'I don't know.'

'So you haven't decided, but you're not going to ask me because my opinion counts for nothing.'

'No! Ainsley, what the devil is the matter with you?'

'What is the matter?' She jumped to her feet, unable to keep still. 'You brought me here to *help*! You have paid me a considerable sum of money, a sum I would not have dreamed of accepting if I thought all I was to do was sit about here and—and fluff cushions.'

'You've done a great deal more than that. I'm sorry if I have seemed unappreciative, but—'

'I have done nothing more than Mhairi McIntosh could have done. Oh, granted, I married you, and in doing so allowed you to claim this place, which seems to me to have been a completely pointless exercise, if all you're going to do is say that it's past help, and walk away.'

'I didn't say I was going to do that. Stop haranguing me like a fishwife.'

'Stop treating me like a child! I have a brain. I have opinions. I know I'm a Sassenach and a commoner to boot, but I'm not a parasite. I may know nothing about farming, but neither do you! Only you're so blooming well ashamed of the fact, though you've no reason to be, because why should you know anything about it when you told me yourself your father did not allow you to know anything, and—and...'

'Ainsley!' Innes wrested the teaspoon she was still clutching from her clenched hand and set it down on the tea tray. 'What on earth has come over you? You're shaking.'

'I'm not,' she said, doing just that. 'Now you've made me lose track of what I was saying.'

'You were saying that I'm an ignoramus not fit to own the lands.'

'No, that's what you think.' She sniffed loudly.

'If I could have got by without asking Mhairi for advice on this house, I would have, but I couldn't, Innes.'

'Why should you, you know nothing of the place.'

'Exactly.' She sniffed again, and drew him a meaningful look. Innes handed her a neatly folded handkerchief. 'I'm not crying,' Ainsley said.

'No.'

She blew her nose. 'I've never known a wetter July. I've likely got a cold.'

'It wouldn't surprise me.'

'I hate women who resort to tears to get their way.'

'I'm not sure it ever works. From what I've seen, what usually happens is that she cries, he runs away, and whatever it was gets swept under the carpet until the next time,' Innes said wryly.

'You know, for a man who has never been married before, you have an uncanny insight into the workings of matrimony.'

'I take it I've struck a chord?'

It was gently said, but she couldn't help prickling. 'Sometimes tears are not a weapon, but merely an expression of emotion,' Ainsley said, handing him his kerchief. 'Such as anger.'

'Stop glowering at me, and stop assuming that all men are tarred with the same brush as the man you married.'

The gentleness had gone from his voice. Ainsley sat, or rather slumped, feeling suddenly deflated. 'I don't.'

'You do, and I'm not like him.'

'I know. I wouldn't be here if I thought you were. But you are shutting me out, Innes, and it's making me feel as if I'm here under false pretences. If you won't talk to me, why not talk to Eoin? There's nothing shameful in asking for help.'

Her tea was cold, but she drank it anyway. The silence was uncomfortable, but she could think of no way of breaking it. She finished her tea.

'I'm not used to consulting anyone,' Innes said. 'You knew that.'

'But it was your idea to have me come along here. An objective eye.'

'I didn't realise things would be so bad. As I said, it's obvious that it's too late.'

'So you're giving up?'

'No! I'm saving you the effort of getting involved in something that is next to useless.'

'Giving up, in other words,' Ainsley said.

His face was quite white. The handle of his teacup snapped. He stared at it, then put it carefully down. 'I don't give up,' he said.

She bit her tongue.

'I'm not accustomed to— It's been difficult. Seeing it. Not having answers. That's been hard.'

Ainsley nodded.

'They are all judging me.'

She sighed in exasperation. 'Innes, you've been gone a long time. They don't know you.'

'I don't see how you can help.'

'I won't know if I can, if you don't talk to me.' Ainsley tried a tentative smile. 'At the very least, I would be on your side.'

'Aye, that would be something more than I have right now.' Innes smiled back. 'I'll think about it.'

'Please do. I have plenty of time on my hands.'

He tucked a strand of hair behind her ear, looking at her ruefully. 'You might want to use some of it to partition this place off into his and her domains. I'm like a bear with a sore head these days, though contrary to what you might think, I quite like having you around. And that's your cue, in case you missed it, to tell me you feel the same.'

Ainsley laughed. 'Would I have suggested helping you if I had wanted to avoid you?'

'True.'

'Perhaps you should consider having some sort of welcoming party.'

'Even though I'm not welcome.' He shook his head. 'No, I'm sorry, don't bite my head off.'

Ainsley frowned, thinking back to the letter she had been reading that morning from Desperate Wife. 'Sometimes traditions can be a comfort. Sometimes they can even help heal wounds,' she said, making a mental note to include that phrase in Madame Hera's reply.

'Sometimes you sound like one of those self-help manuals, do you know that?'

'Do I?'

'"Engaging in marital relations,"' he quoted, smiling. '"Undergoing a husband's ministrations." No, don't get on your high horse, it's endearing.'

'It is?'

'It is. What were you suggesting?'

'Didn't you say that there ought to have been a ceremony when we arrived?' There was a smut of mud on his cheek. She reached up to brush it away.

'A ceremony. I'm not very keen on ceremonies.' Innes caught her hand between his and pressed a kiss on to her knuckles.

Was it just a kiss, or a *kiss*? It felt like more

than just a kiss, for it made her heart do a silly little flip. But his mouth did not linger, and surely knuckles could not be—what was the word, *stimulating*? She wanted to ask him, but that would give too much away, and he might not have been at all stimulated. 'A celebration, then,' Ainsley said. 'Lots of food and drink. Something to mark the changes. You know, out with the old and in with the new.'

'Mmm.' He kissed her hand again. 'I like that,' he said, smiling at her.

'Do you?' She had no idea whether he meant her idea or the kiss.

'Mmm,' he said, pulling her towards him and wrapping his arms around her. 'I like that very much,' he said. And then he kissed her on the mouth.

It was definitely not *just* a kiss. He tasted of spring. Of outdoors. A little of sweat. And of something she could not name. Something sinful. Something that made her heat and tense and clench, and made her dig her fingers into the shoulders of his coat and tilt her body against his. And that made him groan, a guttural noise that seemed to vibrate inside her.

One hand roamed up her back, his fingers delving into her hair, the other roamed down to cup her bottom and pull her closer. She could feel the hard ridge of his arousal through his trousers, through her skirts. She touched her tongue to his and felt his shudder, and shuddered with him, pressing her thighs against his, wanting more, wanting to rid herself of the layers of cloth between them, wanting his flesh, and then thinking about her flesh, exposed, thinking about him looking at her. Or looking at her and then turning his head away. Then not wanting to look at her. Like John. And then...

'Ainsley?'

'Your bath,' she said, clutching at the first thing she could think of. 'Your bath will be ready.'

'Is something wrong?'

'No,' she said, managing a smile, forcing herself to meet his concerned gaze, hating herself for being the cause of that concern, frustrated at having started something she had not the nerve to finish, frustrated at how much she wished she could. 'No, I just don't want the water to get cold.'

'The state I'm in, I think cold is what I need. What happened? Did I do something wrong?'

She flushed. Men were not supposed to ask such questions. Men hated discussing anything intimate. She knew that it was not just John who had been like that, because Madame Hera's correspondence was full of women saying that their husbands were exactly the same. Why did Innes have to be different!

'Nothing. I changed my mind,' Ainsley said, mortified, not only for the lie, but for knowing she was relying on Innes being the kind of man who would always allow a woman to do so. And she was right.

'A lady's prerogative,' he said, making an ironic little bow. 'I'll see you at dinner.'

Chapter Five

'Come and sit by the fire.' Innes handed Ainsley a glass of sherry.

'I thought it was warm enough to wear this without shivering,' she answered him with a constrained smile, 'but now I'm not so sure.'

Her dress was cream patterned with dark blue, with a belt the same colour around her waist. Though it was long-sleeved, the little frill around the *décolleté* revealed her shoulders, the hollows at her collarbone, the most tantalising hint of the smooth slope of her breasts. She sat opposite him and began to twirl her glass about in her hand, a habit she had, Innes had noticed, when she was trying to work up to saying something uncomfortable.

Her face had that pinched look that leached the life from it. Earlier, he'd suspected that she had pulled away from him because of her memories connected to McBrayne. Lying in the cooling bath water in front of the feeble fire in his bedchamber, Innes had begun to wonder what, exactly, the man had done to her. It was more than the debts, or even the fact that they were incurred without her knowing. He couldn't understand how she could be kissing him with abandon one minute and then turning to ice the next, and he was fairly certain it wasn't anything he'd done—or not done. When she forgot herself, she was a different person from the one opposite him now, twisting away nervously at her glass and slanting him timid looks.

Innes threw another log on the fire. 'I think I've solved one problem, at least,' he said, picking up the magazine that he'd been flicking through while he waited on her. 'This thing, the *Scottish Ladies Companion*. There's a woman who doles out spurious advice to females in here, and she uses that very same phrase of yours.' He opened the periodical and ruffled through the pages. 'Aye, here it is. "Make a point of extinguishing the light before engaging in marital relations"—you see, your very phrase—"and your husband will likely not notice your having so unwittingly misled him.

Better still, retain your modesty and your night-gown, and your little deceit will never have to be explained." This Madame Hera is either a virgin or a fool,' he said scathingly.

'What do you mean?'

'The lass has been stuffing her corsets with—What was it?'

'Stockings.'

'I see you have read it, then.' Innes shook his head.

'It was her mother's idea.'

'And a damned stupid one. Pitch dark or broad daylight, you can be certain the husband will know the difference. And as for the idea of keeping her nightgown on...'

'For modesty's sake. I am sure many women do.'

'Really? I've never come across a single one.'

'I doubt very much that the women you have—experienced—are—are— I mean— You know what I mean.'

'The women I've *experienced*, as you put it, have certainly not been married to another man at the time, but nor have they been harlots, if that is what you're implying.' She was blushing. She was unduly flustered, considering she was neither a virgin herself, nor as strait-laced as she now sounded. 'I'm finding you a puzzle,' Innes said, 'for the day I met you, I recall you were threatening to join the harlots on the Cowgate.'

'You know very well I was joking.' Ainsley set her glass of sherry down. 'Do you really think Madame Hera's advice misguided?'

'Does it matter?'

She bit her lip, then nodded.

Innes picked up the magazine and read the letter again. 'This woman, she's not exactly lied to the man she's betrothed to, but she's misled him, and it seems to me that Madame Hera is encouraging her to continue to mislead him. It's that I don't like. The lass is likely nervous enough about the wedding night without having to worry about subterfuge. Hardly a frame of mind conducive to her enjoying what you would call her husband's ministrations.'

'What would you call it?'

Innes grinned. 'Something that doesn't sound as if the pleasure is entirely one-sided. There's a dictionary worth of terms depending on what takes your fancy, but lovemaking will do.'

'You might think that innocuous enough, but I

assure you, the *Scottish Ladies Companion* will not publish it,' Ainsley said.

'You are a subscriber to this magazine, then?'

She shrugged. 'But—this woman, Innes. Don't you think her husband will be angry if he discovers her deception? And anger is no more conducive to—to lovemaking than fraud.'

'In the grand scheme of things, I doubt it. Chances are he's not any more experienced than she, and like to be just as nervous. I'd say he's going to be more concerned about his own performance than anything else, something your Madame Hera doesn't seem to take any account of.'

'It is a column of advice for women.'

'And most of the letters in this issue seem to be about men. Anyway, Madame Hera is completely missing the main point.'

'Which is?'

'The lass thinks she's not well enough endowed, and Madame Hera is by implication agreeing by telling her to cover up. If she goes to her wedding night ashamed, thinking she's not got enough to offer, you can be sure that soon enough her husband will think the same.'

'So it's her fault?' Ainsley said.

'Don't be daft. If anyone's at fault it's that blasted Madame Hera—and the mother.' Innes threw the magazine down on the table. 'I don't know why we're wasting our time with this nonsense.'

Ainsley picked the magazine up, her face set. 'Because I wrote it,' she said. 'I'm Madame Hera.'

Innes laughed. Then, when she continued to look at him without joining in, his laughter stopped abruptly. 'I'll be damned. You mean it? You really do write this stuff?'

'It is not *stuff*. It is a very well-respected column. I'll have you know that in the past month, Madame Hera has received no less than fifty letters. In fact, such is the demand for Madame's advice that the magazine will from next month offer a personal reply service. Felicity has agreed a fee with the board, and I shall receive fifty per cent of it.'

'Felicity?'

'Blair. The editor, and my friend.'

'So all that correspondence you receive, they are letters to this Madame Hera.' Innes looked quite stunned. 'Why didn't you tell me?'

'Because it was none of your business.' Ainsley flushed. 'And because I knew you would most likely react exactly as you have. Though I am not ashamed, if that's what you're thinking. Madame Hera provides a much-needed service.'

'So why tell me now?'

Ainsley reached for her sherry and took a large gulp. She had not meant to tell him. She had been so caught up in worrying about how to explain away her earlier behaviour that Madame Hera had been far from her mind, though her advice would have been straightforward. *'Il faut me chercher'* was one of Madame's axioms. Men must hunt and women must avoid capture. Kissing, not even *just* kissing, without the benefit of a wedding band, was quite wrong. And though Ainsley did have the benefit of a wedding band, she was not really married, so it was still wrong. Kissing gave a man all sorts of immoral ideas. Such ideas were, in Madame Hera's world, the province only of men. That Ainsley herself had had *ideas*—her mind boggled, trying to imagine what Madame would say to that.

In fact, those very *ideas* cropped up in several of the letters Felicity had forwarded to her, variously referred to as 'unnatural desires', 'longing', 'carnal stirrings', 'fever of the blood', 'indecent

thoughts' and even, memorably, 'an irrepress-
ible need to scratch an itch'. On the one hand, it
was consoling to know that she was not unusual,
but on the other, she was utterly defeated when
it came to even contemplating a reply. Felicity
had been right—Ainsley knew very little of such
matters. She'd been right, too, in suggesting that
Ainsley would do well to learn. But Felicity had
no idea of the hurdles Ainsley would have to overcome in order to do so.

She had concluded that her only option was to
return the letters to Felicity until Innes had read
out Madame Hera's letter, and she saw what she
had suspected: that her advice wasn't only skewed
but perhaps even hypocritical. Madame Hera existed to liberate women from ignorance, not to re-
flect Ainsley's own insecurities.

Her stomach had tied itself in knots in her bedroom earlier as she'd contemplated that kiss. Now
she was aware of Innes studying her, waiting patiently for an explanation, and she had never felt
more inarticulate in her life. Seeing with some
surprise that her sherry glass was empty, Ainsley
reached for the decanter and topped it up, taking
another fortifying gulp. 'Felicity said that—
Felicity suggested that— She said...' She took

another sip of sherry. 'Felicity was concerned that I had not the experience to answer some of the more intimate queries made of Madame Hera. I agreed with her, but I thought—I was certain that in all other instances, my advice was sound.'

Ainsley took another sip of sherry. It was really rather good sherry. She took another sip. 'Then earlier today, when I was mulling over the contents of another letter, I began to wonder if perhaps I had been a little biased. Failing to take account the other side of the problem. A little. And then, when you read that letter out I realised that—that perhaps you were right. To a degree.'

Innes looked as confused by this rambling explanation as she felt. 'I'm sorry, but I still don't understand why this led you to confess your secret identity.'

Ainsley tried to sort out the tangle of threads in her head into some sort of logical order. 'These letters are written by real women with real problems. They are not printed in the journal to titillate, nor to provide some sort of vicarious enjoyment to readers who can congratulate themselves on their own superior, problem-free lives. The letters that are printed are chosen because the problems posed are sadly commonplace.' She swallowed the remainder of her sherry and topped her glass up once more, grimacing. 'I didn't mean Madame Hera to sound like a shrew.'

'Well, I didn't mean to sound like a pompous git when I criticised your advice,' Innes said ruefully. 'You've quite thrown me.'

His honesty disarmed her. That, and the sherry. And that smile of his, which was really just as warming as the sherry. Ainsley took another sip of her drink. 'Do you really want to know why I told you?'

'Yes.'

'Even if it is embarrassing?'

'Now I'm intrigued.'

'Really?' Ainsley eyed him warily. 'You're not angry?'

'I'm not sure what I am, but I'm definitely not angry.'

'I wonder if Felicity was right,' Ainsley said, raising her glass, her mood lightening considerably.

'Felicity again. I think I would like to meet her.'

'Then you must find an excuse to invite her here. A party. The welcoming thing. If you deign to listen to my advice. Oh, dear, now I sound like a shrew again.'

'Not a shrew, but you can be extremely prickly.'

'Like a hedgehog, you mean?'

'More like a porcupine. I am rather fond of porcupines.'

'That is downright perverse.' Ainsley helped herself to more sherry and topped up Innes's glass, even though it was virtually untouched. 'Do you really mean to invite Felicity? She is most keen to meet you.'

'No doubt she wishes to make sure I am being a good husband.'

'Well, you couldn't be worse than the last one, that is for sure,' Ainsley said. 'Sorry. Actually, I'm not really.' She sipped her sherry contemplatively. 'Anyway, she's not so much interested in your husbandly qualities, since she knows this is a business arrangement.' She wriggled back in her chair, because despite the thin calico of her gown, the heat from the fire was making her face flush. 'Now I suppose you want to know what she *is* interested in.'

Innes, who had been inspecting the sherry decanter, which seemed to have almost emptied itself, put it rather selfishly down on the table out of her reach. 'I do,' he said, 'but first I'd like to know why you confessed to being Madame Hera. You still haven't yet told me, in case you'd forgotten.'

'Aha! That's where you're wrong,' Ainsley exclaimed with a triumphant wave of her hand, 'because the two things are inexpressibly—no, inex—inextricably linked.' She picked up her glass, remembered it was empty and placed it very carefully back down again, because the side table had developed a wobble. Then, realising she had slumped unbecomingly back in her chair, she struggled upright, leaning forward confidentially. 'Those letters. The intimate ones to Madame Hera. They are all about marital—no, lovemaking. And—and the acquisition of womanly wiles. Felicity fears that I do not know enough about such things to be of any value, and I fear she is right. Are you perfectly well? Only your face has gone sort of fuzzy.'

Innes leaned forward. 'Better?'

Ainsley nodded. 'Do you know you have a charming smile?'

'Only because I am charmed by you.'

She giggled. 'Felicity said I should let you have your wicked way with me, and that you sounded like the kind of man who would not expect me to—to lie back and think of Scotland. And she said that we needed something to while away the long dark nights in this godforsaken place—though I don't think it is godforsaken, actually—and she said that I needed some lessons in—in fun. And pleasure. Do you have a kilt?'

'I do. Does Felicity's idea of fun and pleasure involve dressing up?'

Ainsley giggled. 'Not Felicity's idea—that was mine. I think you have a fine pair of legs, Innes Drummond. I would like to see you in Highland dress. But we are straying from the point, you know. Is there any more sherry?'

'No.'

Ainsley frowned over at the decanter. It seemed to her that it was not completely empty. Then she shrugged. 'Oh, well. What was I— Oh, yes, what Felicity said. She said that you would be well placed to teach me about womanly wiles and such—though I don't think she called it that, zactly—*ex*actly—and I don't know how she knew this, for she has not met you, and all I told her was that you kissed very nicely, which you know you do…'

'Only because you kiss me so very nicely back.'

'Really?' Ainsley smiled beatifically. 'What a lovely thing to say.'

'And true, into the bargain.' Innes took her hand. 'So this Felicity of yours believes that you need to be inducted into the palace of pleasure.'

'Palace of pleasure. I like that. Would you mind if Madame Hera borrowed it?'

'I would be honoured.'

'What would you say if I told you that Felicity also suggested I use you to assist me in finding answers to some of Madame Hera's problems?'

'You mean, provide you with practical experience of the solutions?'

Ainsley nodded sagely. 'You would be insulted, wouldn't you? That's what I told Felicity, that you would be insulted.'

'Would you be taking part in this experiment merely for the sake of obtaining better advice?'

'No.' She stared down at her hands. Despite the tingling, and the fuzziness and the warmth induced by the sherry, this was still proving surprisingly difficult, but she was determined to bring this embarrassing conversation to an end, one way or another. 'The reason I told you,' she said, 'about Madame Hera, I mean. It wasn't only that you were right about the advice I was dispensing, it was—it was—it was earlier. Me. When you kissed me. It was because I— Felicity says that

he took away all my self-respect. John. My husband. Self-respect, that's what she called it. I don't
know what to call it. I don't want to talk about
it. But when you kissed me, it made me feel— I
liked it. I liked it a lot. But then I remembered,
you see. Him. What happened. Didn't happen.
And it made me stop liking what you were doing
and thinking about then, and him, and it wasn't
that I think you're the same, you're so different,
and he never, but— Well, that was it. That's what
happened. Are you angry?'

She looked up. His eyes were stormy. 'No,'
Innes said quickly. 'I'm not angry with you.'

She nodded several times.

'You don't have to say any more, Ainsley.'

'I want to finish telling you or I might not— I
want to.' She clutched at his hand. 'I don't want to
feel like this. I don't want to feel the way he made
me feel. I want to feel what Felicity said, and what
you made me feel before I thought about him. And
that's why I told you about Madame Hera,' she
finished in a rush. 'Because when you kiss me, I
want to—and because you know, we're not really
married and it can't ever mean anything, so it's
sort of *safe*. You can help me, and then I can be
better at helping other women. That's why I told

you. Because I want you, and I really want to be able to— If you do? So now you know.'

'Now I know,' Innes said, looking rather stunned.

'You can say no.'

'I'm not going to say anything right now. You've given me a lot to think about.'

'And you're not angry about Madame Hera?'

Innes laughed. 'Absolutely not. I am more than happy to discuss these intimate problems that Madame Hera has to answer. In fact, if you ever run short of problems then I'm sure I will be able to think up a few for us to discuss.'

'No!' Ainsley exclaimed. 'That's what Felicity said you would say. Now I owe her five pounds.'

Innes laughed. 'I am looking forward to meeting Felicity.'

Ainsley yawned, frowning at the clock. 'It's past dinner time. I shall go and find Mhairi.'

She got to her feet, swaying, and Innes caught her. 'I think maybe you'd be better in your bed.'

Ainsley yawned again. 'I think maybe you're right.'

'Thank you for telling me what you did. I'm honoured,' Innes said. 'I mean it.'

'I didn't want you to think I was a cock tease.'

Ainsley grinned. 'Proof that I am not always so mealy-mouthed.'

Innes kissed her cheek. 'What you are is…'

'A porcupine.'

'A wee darling.'

She smiled. 'I like that,' she murmured. Then she closed her eyes, sank gracefully back onto the chair and passed out.

'The laird said that you'd be hungry, seeing as you missed dinner, so I made you some eggs, and I've cut you a slice of ham.' Mhairi laid the plateful down in front of Ainsley.

'Thank you. It smells delicious,' Ainsley said, repressing a shudder.

'Himself had to go out, but he said to tell you he'd be back by mid-morn at the latest. Here, I'll do that.' Mhairi took the coffee pot from Ainsley's shaking hand and poured her a cup. 'Do you want me to put a hair of the dog in it?'

'Is it so obvious?' Lifting the cup in both hands, Ainsley took a grateful sip, shaking her head, flushing. 'I don't normally— I hope you don't think I usually overindulge.'

'Oh, I'm not one to judge,' Mhairi said with a toss of her head. 'Unlike the rest of them.'

Sensing that the housekeeper was offering her an opening, and feeling that she had nothing much to lose, as she sat nursing her hangover, Ainsley smiled at her. 'Why don't you join me? It's about time we got to know each other a bit better. Please,' she added when the other woman demurred.

Mhairi studied her with pursed lips for a few seconds, then took a seat and poured herself a coffee, adding two lumps of sugar, though no cream. 'You're not at all what we expected when we heard Himself had wedded an Edinburgh widow woman,' she said.

'What were you expecting?'

'Someone fancier. You know, more up on her high horse, with more frills to her.'

'You mean not so plain?'

Mhairi shook her head. 'I mean not so nice,' she said with a wry smile. 'And you're not plain. Leastwise, you're not when you've some life in that face of yours. If you don't mind my saying.'

'I don't mind at all,' Ainsley said, buttering an oatcake, and deciding to brave a forkful of eggs. 'Am I a disappointment, then?'

'No one knows enough about you to judge.'

'Yet you said that people do judge—or that is what you implied just a minute ago.'

Across from her, the housekeeper folded her arms. Ainsley ate another forkful of eggs and cut into the ham. Mhairi McIntosh was younger than she had thought at first, not much over forty, with a curvaceous figure hidden under her apron and heavy tweed skirt. Though she had a forbidding expression, her features were attractive, with high cheekbones and a mouth that curved sensually when it was not pulled into a grim line. Her eyes were grey and deep-set, and she had the kind of sallow skin that made the hollows beneath them look darkly shadowed. But she was what would be called a handsome woman, nevertheless. She wore no ring.

'No, I was never married,' Mhairi said, noticing the direction of Ainsley's gaze. 'I've worked here at the castle since I was ten years old, starting in the kitchens—the big kitchens—back in Mrs Drummond's day.'

'So you've known Innes since he was a boy?'

Mhairi nodded.

'And his brother?'

'Him, too.'

'Is it because of him that people judge Innes so

harshly? Do they resent the fact that he is here and not Malcolm?'

Mhairi shook her head sadly. 'Himself should not have stayed away so long.'

'But surely people understand he had his own life to lead. And it's not as if— I mean, the state of the lands, the way things have been allowed to deteriorate… That was his father's fault, it was nothing to do with Innes.'

'He should not have stayed away,' Mhairi said implacably.

'Oh, for goodness' sake! It's not his fault.' Realising that recriminations were getting her nowhere, Ainsley reined in her temper. 'He's here now, and so am I, and what matters is the future of Strone Bridge.'

'It seems to many of us that Strone Bridge hasn't much of a future,' Mhairi said.

'What do you mean?'

'Himself has obviously decided that this place is not worth wasting his time on.'

'He hasn't decided anything. He's not even been here a month.'

'And not a single sign has there been that he's going to be remaining here another. He forbade the formal welcoming at the pier, and there's been no word of the Rescinding. Not that the castle is in any fit state to be used. And that's another thing. He's the laird, and he's living here at the Home Farm. It's obvious he has no plans to stay here. He'll be off as soon as he can decently go, back to building his bridges.'

There was no doubting the belligerence in the woman's voice now. 'Innes hasn't made any decisions about the castle. He's been spending his time looking at the land, because—'

'Because he plans to do what all the landlords are doing, break up the crofts and put sheep on them. Does he think we're daft? Sheep. That's what he'll do, that's what they all do. Get rid of the tenants. Bring in a bailiff. Out with the old, and in with the new. That's what Himself is doing, and then it will be back to Edinburgh or London or wherever he's been hiding these last fourteen years, and you with him, and he'll go back to pretending Strone Bridge doesn't exist because it's too hard for him to—' Mhairi broke off suddenly. 'Never mind.'

Ainsley stared at her in shock. 'He has made no mention of sheep, and he has no intentions of going anywhere for at least—for some time,' she amended, for she did not imagine that Innes would like the terms of his father's will made public.

A shrug greeted this remark. Ainsley risked pouring the pair of them another cup of coffee. 'What is this thing you mentioned? A restitution?'

'Rescinding.' Mhairi took a sip of her coffee. 'A forgiving and forgetting. After the burial of the old laird, a feast is held for all to welcome in the new laird. It is a wiping clean of the slate, of debts and grudges and disputes, a sign that they have been buried with the old. But since Himself was not here for the burial...'

'Can it not be held on another day?' Ainsley asked.

'To my knowledge it never has been.'

'Yes, but if it is held on another day would this Rescinding be invalid?'

Mhairi shook her head slowly. 'It's never been done. You'd have to consult the book. *The Customs and Ways of the Family Drummond of Strone Bridge,*' she said when Ainsley looked at her enquiringly. 'It's in the castle library.'

'Then I will do so, but do you think it's a good idea?' Ainsley persisted.

'It would mean using the Great Hall. I'd need

a lot of help and good bit of supplies, and as to the food...'

'Yes, yes, we can see to that, but what do you think?'

The housekeeper smiled reluctantly. 'I think if you can persuade Himself, that it's an excellent idea.'

'A Rescinding?' Innes frowned. Ainsley had accosted him immediately when he had returned in the early afternoon. He had expected her to be sheepish, or reserved, or even defensive. He had not expected her to launch enthusiastically into some wild plan for a party. 'I'm not even sure that I know what's involved,' he said cautiously.

'It's a forgiving and forgetting, Mhairi says. She says that all debts and grudges are buried with the old laird to give the new one a clean start. She says that though it's customary to have it the day after the funeral, there is no reason why we cannot hold it on another day and combine it with a welcoming feast. She says that the chair that the laird uses for the ceremony is in the Great Hall. And there is a book in the library. *The Customs and Ways of the Family Drummond of Strone Bridge,* it's called.' Ainsley was looking at him anxiously. 'What do you think?'

'I think Mhairi has quite a lot to say all of a sudden. I wonder how she knows so much about it, for she cannot have seen one herself.'

'She has worked in the castle since she was ten years old. I suppose, these past few years while your father was alone here, he must have confided in her.'

'I can't imagine my father confiding in anyone,' Innes said drily. 'To be honest, I can't imagine him forgiving or forgetting either, Rescinding or no. He was not a man who liked to be crossed, and he bore a long grudge.'

'Were you always at outs with him, even before—before your brother died?'

'Yes.'

Ainsley was watching him. Innes could feel her eyes on him, even though he was studiously looking down at a letter from his chief surveyor. He wondered what else Mhairi had said. She was as closed as a fist, and always had been. It surprised him that Ainsley had managed to have any sort of conversation with her. He pushed the letter to one side. 'The old ways were the only ways, as far as my father was concerned,' he said, 'and for my brother, too.'

'Sometimes the old ways can be a comfort.'

'You mean the Rescinding?'

Ainsley nodded.

'A—what did you call it—healing of wounds?' He smiled. 'There can be no denying the need for that.'

'So you agree, it's a good idea?'

'It sounds like a lot of work.'

'I will handle that. With Mhairi. I am not too proud to ask for help.'

'Is that a dig at me?'

Ainsley hesitated only fractionally. 'Yes.'

Innes sighed. 'If I speak to Eoin, will it make you happy?'

'It would be a start. A forgiving and forgetting, that's what the Rescinding is. Perhaps you could do some of that before the ceremony.'

Innes threw his hands up in surrender. 'Enough. You've made your point. I will even write to your Miss Blair and invite her to attend. Unless you've changed your mind. Or perhaps forgotten that conversation entirely?'

'I was half-cut, not stotious!' Ainsley said stiffly.

'Ach, I didn't mean to bite your head off. At

least I did, but don't take it personally. You make too good a case, and I don't want to hear it.' Innes got up from the desk and took her hand. He took her hand, pressing it between his own. 'Forgive me.'

Her fingers twined round his. 'It is I who should be begging your forgiveness. Last night, I propositioned you. In fact, I practically threw myself at you,' Ainsley said, flushing. 'You must not feel awkward at turning me down.'

'I have no intentions of turning you down, if you are not retracting your offer. I thought I'd made it clear, from almost the first moment I met you, that I find you very desirable.'

'You do?'

'I do.'

'I don't want to. Retract, I mean.'

'Are you sure? Yesterday, you turned to ice while I was kissing you.'

'It won't happen again.'

'I think maybe it will. I think, in fact, we should expect it. I wonder what Madame Hera would advise?'

'As you pointed out last night, Madame Hera would most likely provide quite unwise advice,' Ainsley said drily.

'I offended you. I'm sorry.'

'No,' she said, quite unconvincingly, and then she laughed. 'Yes, you did. I was upset.'

'If I had known that you and she were one and the same person...'

'I am glad you did not. It was a difficult lesson, but I hope that I have learned from it. I want Madame Hera to be helpful.' Ainsley opened the thick leather folder on the desk that contained her correspondence. 'These women are desperate enough to write to a complete stranger for help. They deserve honesty.' She replaced the folder and wandered over to her favourite chair by the fire, though she did not sit down. 'When John died, one of the things I promised myself was always to speak my mind, and that's what Madame Hera has done. I didn't realise, though, that my opinions were so coloured.'

'I think that you're being very hard on yourself, but if it would help, I'd be happy to provide you with a counterpoint when you're writing your replies.'

'Would you?'

'I think I might even enjoy it.'

'What if we disagree?'

Innes pulled her round to face him, sliding his arms around her waist. 'Madame Hera has the final say, naturally.'

'And as to the—the other thing?'

Innes smiled. 'Your introduction into the palace of pleasures? I was thinking that it would be best if we started first with some theory.'

Her eyes widened. 'You have textbooks?'

'Good lord, no. I meant Madame Hera's correspondence. We could discuss it. I could explain anything you are not sure of. That way, you will be able to start answering some of your letters, and at the same time, you can accustom yourself to—to—before you have to—if you do. You might decide not to.' Innes stopped, at a loss for words, wondering if what he was suggesting was idiotic, or even repugnant.

But Ainsley smiled at him. 'You mean that I become accustomed to what to expect?' she asked.

'And you can accustom me to what you want, too.'

'I don't know what I want.'

'Save that I must wear a kilt?'

Her cheeks flamed. 'I had forgotten that.'

'Do you dream of a wild Highlander?'

'No. Yes.'

'What does he do?'

'I don't know.' Ainsley's mouth trembled on the brink of a smile. 'He—he wants me.'

'You know I already do.'

'No, I mean he—he really wants me. He— No, it's silly.'

'He finds you irresistible,' Innes said, charmed and aroused. 'He wants you so much,' he whispered into her ear, 'that he carries you off, right in the middle of the day, and has his wicked way with you on the moor. Or would you prefer a cave?'

'A cave. In the firelight.'

He was hard. Innes cursed under his breath. He hadn't meant this to happen. He edged away from her carefully. 'You are a very apt pupil,' he said.

'Oh. I didn't realise— Is that what that was, a lesson?'

'It's all it was meant to be,' Innes said, 'but you are a little too good at this. Another minute and I'd be rushing off to find a kilt.'

'Oh.'

It was a different kind of 'oh' this time. She looked at him with the most delightful, pleased little smile on her face, and Innes simply could not resist her. He kissed her, briefly but deeply. 'I am already looking forward to the next lesson,' he said.

Chapter Six

A week later, Innes stared down at the Celtic cross, at the bright lettering of the new inscription and the long empty space below that was left to fill. His own name would be next, but after that, it would be a distant cousin, if anyone. He dug his hands into the pockets of his leather breeches and hunched his shoulders against the squally breeze, steeling himself against the wall of emotions that threatened to engulf him. Until now, he'd been able to ignore what had happened, tell himself that this was a temporary thing, that he was not really the laird, that his life was not inextricably tangled up in Strone Bridge. He'd been able to contain and control whatever it was that was building inside him, fence it in with resentment and anger, let the waste and destruction he saw every day tack it down, the hurt and the suffering gnaw at his conscience and prevent him from thinking about the reason he was here at all.

He'd arranged to meet Eoin here, but had arrived early, wanting some time alone. He'd come here telling himself that fourteen years had bred indifference, but he was wrong. It was like one of those seventh waves, building from the swell, scooping up memories and guilt and remorse, hurtling them at him with an implacable force. Innes screwed his eyes so tightly shut he saw stars behind his lids.

'It was all done properly, if that's bothering you at all.' He opened his eyes to find Eoin standing a few feet away. 'Your father's funeral. It was all done as he would have wanted it,' he said. 'Mhairi made sure of that.'

His father's housekeeper had been the one to arrange his father's funeral. Innes refused to feel guilty.

'She had me play the chief mourner.' Eoin came a few steps closer. 'I didn't want to, but she said someone with Drummond blood had to bear the laird's standard, and bastard blood from two generations back was better than none.'

It had been a joke between them when they were boys, that bastard blood. Malcolm had traced the

line once, working out that Eoin was their half
cousin twice removed, or some such thing. Their
father had a coat of arms made for Eoin, with
the baton sinister prominently displayed. Malcolm had dreamed up a ceremony to hand it over,
Innes remembered. The laird had given them all
their first taste of whisky. They'd have been ten,
maybe eleven. He had forgotten that there were
days like those.

'I didn't get the letter in time to attend,' Innes
said tersely.

'Would it have made any difference?' Eoin demanded, and when Innes said nothing, he shook
his head impatiently and turned away. 'I meant it
to be a comfort to you, knowing that all had been
done as it ought. I wasn't casting it up.'

'Wait.' Innes covered the short distance between
them, grabbing the thick fisherman's jumper Eoin
wore. His friend shrugged him off, but made no
further move to go. Blue eyes, the same colour
as Innes's, the same colour as Malcolm's, the
same colour as the dead laird's, glowered at him.
'I wrote to you,' Innes said. 'After—I wrote to
you, and you did not reply.'

'I live here, Innes, and unlike you, I've never
wanted to leave. It was not only that I owed a

duty to your father as the laird, I respected him. When you left, the way you left, you forced me to choose. What else was I to do?'

'I was your friend.'

'You were his son,' Eoin said, nodding at the Celtic cross. 'When Malcolm died, it broke his heart.'

'What do you think it did to me?' Innes struggled, eyes smarting, the sick feeling that had been lurking inside him since he'd arrived here growing, acrid, clogging his throat. He turned away, fists clenched, taking painful breaths, fighting for control, forcing back the images, the guilt, waiting desperately for the sound of Eoin's footsteps disappearing, leaving him alone to deal with it, to make it go away.

Eoin didn't move. When he spoke, his voice was raw, grating. 'I could hardly look at you the other day. All these years, I've told myself it was the right thing to hold my peace. All these years, with the laird letting things go, letting the place wither, I've told myself that if that was what he wanted and— No, not just that. I've told myself you deserved it. If you did not care enough to look after your heritage…'

Innes had intended this as a reconciliation. It

felt as though he was being tried, and found wanting, by the one person here on Strone Bridge he
had thought might be on his side. The disappointment was crushing. 'It was never meant for me,'
he roared. 'It was never mine.'

His words echoed around the enclosed space,
but still Eoin stood his ground, his face grim,
his own fists clenched. 'It is yours now. You've
known for fourteen years that it would be yours.'

'And by the looks of it, for fourteen years my
father has done his damnedest to run the place
into the ground. Don't tell me I could have stopped
him, Eoin. You of all people know he would never
listen to me.'

There was silence. The two men glared at each
other. Finally, as Innes was about to turn away,
Eoin spoke. 'It's true,' he said grudgingly. 'I did
blame you, and it was wrong of me. You've every
bit as much right to choose your life as the next
man, and it's obvious from the look of you that
the life you've chosen suits you well. You're a rich
man. A successful one.'

'Much good my successes will do me here.
I know nothing about sheep, and certainly not
enough to go clearing my lands to bring them in.'

'So you've heard that rumour, then?'

'And I'd be happy if you'd deny it for me.'

'I'll be delighted to, if it's the truth.' Eoin kicked at the ground. 'They do blame you, as I did. It's not fair, but that's how it is. Your father never got over Malcolm, and you're right, it was as if he was deliberately letting the place go to spite you. They think you should have put Strone Bridge first. They think if you'd have come back, you could have stopped him, so the longer you stayed away, and the worse it got, the more they blamed you.'

'Eoin, he wouldn't have listened to me. If I'd come back while he was alive I'd have ended up murdering him. Or more likely, he'd have murdered me.' Innes looked grimly at the cross. 'You know what he was like. I was the second son. He wanted me to study the law in Edinburgh, for goodness' sake! I was to be the family lackey.'

Eoin gave a bark of laughter. 'I'll admit, that was never on the cards.'

'No, but you know how hard I tried to do things his way—or more precisely, how hard I tried to make him see things my way. He couldn't care less about me. All he cared about was shaping my brother for the next laird in his own image, but he would not let me shape myself. I tried, but I was always going to leave. And when Malcolm—

When it happened— How can you seriously think that would make me more likely to stay here?'

Eoin shook his head. 'But you could have come back, at least to visit,' he said stubbornly. 'You would have seen how things were going. Gradual it was. I didn't notice at first. And then— Well, like I said, I thought you deserved it. That was wrong of me. It's why I've been avoiding you. You're not the only one who feels guilty, Innes. I should have done something. I'm sorry. I should have done something, and now it's far too late. I truly am sorry.'

He held out his hand. Hesitating only a moment, Innes gripped it. 'I'm here now,' he said, 'and I need your help.'

Eoin nodded, returning the grip equally painfully. They sat together in silence on the stone bench. 'I did write,' Innes said eventually. 'Only once, but I did write to my father.'

'I didn't know that,' Eoin said. 'Mhairi would surely have told me, so she can't have known, either.'

'Why should she?'

Eoin looked surprised. 'She was his wife in all but name.' He laughed. 'You did not know?'

'No— I— No.' Innes shook his head in astonishment. 'He left no provision for her in his will.'

'Oh, he took care of that years ago. There's an annuity, you'll probably not have noticed it yet unless you've gone through the accounts, and she owns the farm over at Cairndow.'

'Then what the devil is she doing working for me when she does not have to?'

'Innes, for someone so far-sighted, you can be awfully blind. She's looking out for you. She's about the only one who is. She was ever on your side, you know, it's the one thing she and the laird had words about, but even she thinks you should have come back. I'm not saying it's right, I'm saying that's how it is.'

'I'm here now. Why can't they see that as a step in the right direction?'

'Maybe because they're wondering how long it will be before you go again.' Eoin got to his feet. 'Think about it from their point of view, Innes. The laird obviously believed he would be the last, else he would not have been so destructive.'

'He obviously thought I'd come back here simply to rid myself of the place. His will specifies I must remain here a year,' Innes conceded.

'The auld bugger obviously hoped being here would change your mind. Will you?'

Innes shook his head. 'I haven't a clue what I'm going to do,' he admitted ruefully, 'but I don't want to sell. I've spent every day, since I got off that boat of yours, going round the lands, making endless lists of things that need to be done.'

Eoin laughed. 'People think you've been sizing up the assets to sell.'

'For heaven's sake, why did no one tell me that?'

'Why didn't you say anything yourself, tell people your plans?'

Innes shook his head. 'Because I don't know what they are yet.'

'This is not one of your projects, where you have to have your blueprints and your costs and—I don't know—your list of materials all sorted out before you make your bid, Innes. Plans change, we all know that, but people would like to hear that they exist. They'd like to know you're not going to sell the roof over their heads.' Eoin got to his feet. 'I'm glad we talked. It's been eating away at me, the way we were when you arrived.'

This time it was Innes who held out his hand. 'It is good to see you, Eoin. I've not missed this place, but I've missed you. I would value your input to what needs done.'

'You know you have only to ask.'

'I wouldn't have, if it were not for Ainsley. She is the one who pushed me into this.'

Eoin smiled. 'Then I owe her. I look forward to meeting her properly.'

'You will do soon. She's planning a Rescinding.' Innes shook his head. 'Don't ask, because I'm not quite sure what it is myself, save that it will involve everyone.'

'Then I hope you will make sure not to let the water of life run dry. I must go, but we'll talk again.'

Innes watched his friend walk away. He felt as if his mind had been put through a washtub and then a mangle. Striding along the path that led round the front of the castle, he spotted the ramshackle pier and came to a sudden halt. Here was something he could do, and it was something, moreover, that Strone Bridge urgently needed, for it would allow paddle steamers to dock. He couldn't understand why he hadn't thought of it before. Vastly relieved to be able to focus on a project that was entirely within his control, Innes made his way down to the bay and began a survey of the jetty with the critical eye of the engineer it had cost him and, it seemed, the people of Strone Bridge, so much to become.

Dear Madame Hera,
I am a twenty-eight-year-old woman, married with two small children and absolutely bored stiff. My husband is a wealthy man and insists that our house is taken care of by servants and our children by a nanny, but this leaves me with nothing to do. I try to count my blessings, but even that occupation has become tedious. One of my friends suggested taking a lover would amply occupy my free afternoons, but lying convincingly is not one of my accomplishments. What shall I do?
Yours sincerely, Mrs A

Ainsley smiled to herself as she read this missive. Many of Madame Hera's correspondents complained of boredom, though none had suggested this novel answer. 'Take charge,' Ainsley wrote, 'of your children, of your housework, of your life!' She put the pen down, frowning. Mrs A's husband was doing exactly what was expected of him. More, in fact, than many could or would.

Mrs A's friends might well even envy her. If Mrs A were to dismiss the nanny, or take over the housework, her husband would most likely be insulted. Or offended.

Ainsley looked at the clock. It was gone two. Innes had left before breakfast this morning, and she had not seen him since. Was he avoiding her? In the days since he had agreed to hold the Rescinding ceremony, he had continued with his visits to various farms and tenants, his poring over documents late into the night. True, she too had been very busy—too busy, in fact, to have any time to devote to anything else, but still, the niggling feeling that she was being pushed to one side would not go away.

With a sigh of frustration, Ainsley pushed Madame Hera's half-finished letter to one side and picked up the heavy bunch of castle keys from the desk, intending to consult the tome she had now christened the *Drummond Self-Help Manual* in the library once more, before taking another look at the Great Hall. Outside, as ever, it was blowy. There were several fishing boats in the bay. She paused to drink in her favourite view and spotted a figure down on the pier. Black coat with long skirts birling in the breeze. Long boots. All the

Strone Bridge men wore trews and fishing jumpers or short tweed jackets. Tucking the keys into her pocket beside the notebook and pencil she had brought, Ainsley began to pick her way carefully down the steep path.

The tide was far enough out for Innes to have clambered down underneath the pier when she arrived. 'What on earth are you doing?' she asked, peering through one of the planks down at him.

'I was inspecting the struts,' he said, looking up at her, 'but now that you're here, there's a much nicer view.'

'Innes!' Scandalised, laughing, she clutched her skirts tightly around her.

Laughing, he appeared a few moments later on the beach, climbing up the ancient wooden supports of the pier fluidly. 'Do you always match your garters to your gown?'

'What kind of question is that?'

'One you needn't answer if you don't want to, I'm happy to imagine.' Innes picked a long strand of seaweed from the skirts of his coat and threw it on to the beach. 'I'm going to have this thing rebuilt.'

'Of course you are! I wonder you didn't think of it before.'

'Couldn't see the wood for the trees,' Innes said wryly. 'I don't suppose you've got a pencil and a bit of paper with you?'

Ainsley delved into her pocket and pulled out the notebook and pencil. 'Here, I was on my way to the castle when I saw you.'

'How are the arrangements progressing?'

She was about to launch into a stream of detail, but stopped herself, giving Innes a dismissive shrug instead. 'Nothing for you to worry about,' she said.

He had been scribbling something in her notebook, but he looked up at the change in her tone. 'I thought you wanted to take this on—have you changed your mind?'

'No.'

'Is it too much? Do you need help?'

'No, I told you, there's nothing for you to worry about. It's not your problem.'

Frowning, Innes stuck her pencil behind his ear. 'Aye, that was it. *It's not your problem.* I remember now, that's what set you off before.'

'I don't know what you're implying, but...'

'Actually, it's what you're implying, Ainsley,' he

exclaimed. 'I'm not shutting you out deliberately. I thought we were dividing and conquering, not just dividing, for heaven's sake. Once and for all, I'm not the man you married, so stop judging me as if I am.'

She wrapped her arms tightly around herself. 'I know you're not.'

'Then what are you accusing me of?'

'Nothing.' She bit her lip. 'You don't talk to me. You don't value my opinion.'

'Well, that's where you're wrong. Do you know what I was doing this morning? No, of course you don't, for I didn't tell you—and before you berate me for that, I didn't tell you because I wasn't sure he'd come.'

'Who?'

'Eoin.'

Her latent anger left her. Ainsley smiled. 'You've spoken to Eoin?'

'I have. I met him at the chapel.'

'And?'

Innes laughed nervously. 'And it was difficult.'

He was clearly uncomfortable. If she did not press him, he would leave it at that. She was pleased, no, more than pleased, that he had taken her advice, though it would most likely result in her further exclusion from matters of the lands. 'Has Eoin agreed to help you?' Ainsley asked carefully.

'He has.'

Innes was staring down at his notes, but she was not fooled. 'And you've made your peace?' Ainsley persisted.

'We've agreed to disagree.' Finally, Innes met her gaze. 'He thinks I should have come back sooner. Though he understands why I left, he doesn't understand why I stayed away. Though he knows fine that if I'd come back, my father and I would have done nothing but argue, and my father would have carried on down whatever path he'd chosen regardless, still Eoin thinks I should have tried.'

'That's ridiculous. Then you would have both been miserable. Besides, you had no cause to think that your father would choose this path of destruction,' Ainsley said fiercely. 'You told me yourself, he was a good laird.'

'Aye, well, it seems you're the only person to see it my way,' Innes said despondently.

She put her hand on his arm. 'You brought me here so you'd have someone on your side.'

'And I've done my damnedest to push you away

since we arrived.' He smiled ruefully down at her. 'I'm sorry. I did warn you. You need to speak up more.'

She flinched. 'I know.'

Innes cursed under his breath. 'That was unfair of me.' He kissed her fingertips. 'This marriage business, I'm not very good at it, I'm afraid. I'm too used to being on my own.'

'That's one thing you need to remember. You're not alone. May I see?' she asked, pointing at the notebook.

Innes had made several small sketches. He began to talk as he showed them to her, of tides, about the advantages of wood over stone, of angles and reinforcing. She nodded and listened, though she understood about a quarter of what he said, content to hear his voice full of enthusiasm, to watch the way he ran the pencil through his hair, reminded of the way Felicity did something very similar.

'That's quite enough,' he said eventually, closing the notebook. 'You're probably bored to death.'

'No. I didn't follow much of it, but it wasn't boring.'

Innes laughed, putting his arm around her.

'Do you think you'll be ready to announce the

new pier after the Rescinding?' she asked. 'Perhaps you could show them a drawing. There's three weeks, would there be time?'

'I don't see why not. I could do the preliminary survey myself. It's what my trade is after all.'

Ainsley beamed up at him. 'If all the villagers and tenants see what a clever man you are, then perhaps they'll understand why you had to leave.'

'Atonement?'

'No, you've nothing to atone for. It is a gift. A symbol of the modern world brought to Strone Bridge by their modern laird.'

Innes laughed. 'I can just about hear my father turning in his grave from here.'

'Good.'

He pulled her closer. 'I saw it this morning at the chapel. The grave I mean, and yes, it was for the first time. I could see you just about chewing your tongue off trying not to ask. Eoin told me about the funeral. It seems I have Mhairi to thank for doing things properly.'

'We have a lot to thank Mhairi for,' Ainsley agreed, enjoying the warmth of his body, the view, the salty tang of the air. 'She's at one with Eoin and everyone else in thinking that you should have come back here earlier, but now you're here, she's of the opinion that you should be given a chance.'

'That's big of her. Mhairi was my father's mistress,' Innes said.

Ainsley jerked her head up to look at him. 'Mhairi! Your father's mistress! Good grief. Are you sure?'

'Eoin told me.' Innes shook his head. 'I still can't believe it. He thought I knew. It seems everyone else does.'

'But—did he leave her anything in his will? You have not mentioned...'

'No. According to Eoin, he'd already made provision. A farm, an annuity. She did not need to stay on at the castle when he died.'

'But she did, so she must have wanted to. How very—surprising. It's funny, when I was talking to her over breakfast yesterday morning, I was thinking that she was an attractive woman and wondering why she had not married. There is something about her. Her mouth, I think. It's very sensual.'

'I believe I've said something similar to you.' Innes pulled her back towards him, tipping up her face. 'Infinitely kissable, that is what your mouth is, and if you don't mind...'

'I don't.'

'Good,' Innes said, and kissed her.

They took the path back up to the castle to-gether. While the track used by the cart wound its serpentine way upwards, the footpath was a sheer climb. Out of breath at the top, Ainsley stood with her chest heaving. 'I don't suppose your engineer-ing skills can come up with a solution for that,' she said.

'I will have my surveyor take a look,' Innes said. 'See if it can be widened, maybe change some of the angles so they're not so sharp. That way we can get bigger vehicles down to collect supplies.'

'And steamer passengers,' Ainsley said. 'Then you can build a tea pavilion up here on the terrace, where the view is best. Although there would be no need to build anything new if you set up a tea-room in that lovely drawing room. Then Mhairi could show the excursionists around the castle for a sixpence. She tells those ghost stories much bet-ter than you do, and she has lots more. There was one about a grey lady in the kitchens that gave me goosebumps.'

They began to walk together up to the castle.

'Mhairi's mother was the village fey wife when I was wee. A witch, though a good one, of course.'

'Better and better. She could make up some potions. You could sell them in the teashop. And some of the local tweed, too,' Ainsley said, handing Innes the keys to the main door, for they were going to inspect the Great Hall together. 'Before you know it, Strone Bridge will be so famous that the steamers will be fighting to berth at this new pier of yours.'

Innes paused in the act of unlocking the door. 'You're not being serious?'

She had forgotten, in her enthusiasm, how he felt about the place. Ainsley's smile faded. 'Don't you think it's a good idea?'

'I think it's a ridiculous idea. Besides the fact that I have no intentions of wasting my fortune having the place made habitable, it's a monstrosity—no one in their right mind would pay to see it.'

'Ridiculous.' She swallowed the lump that had appeared in her throat.

Innes looked immediately contrite. 'Don't take it like that, I didn't mean— It's not the idea. It's the place.'

'Why do you hate it so much? It's your home.'

'No. I could never live here.' He shuddered. 'There are more ghosts here than even Mhairi knows of.'

They were in the courtyard. Ainsley followed his gaze to the tower that stood at the centre. A huge bird of prey circled the parapet. She, too, shuddered, not because she thought it an omen, but at the look on Innes's face. She'd thought she was beginning to understand him, but now she was not so sure. That bleak expression could not merely be attributed to feelings of inadequacy or resentment. There was a reason beyond his quarrel with his father for Innes's absence from this place for fourteen long years. Ghosts. Who would have thought such a confident, practical man as Innes would believe in them, but he very obviously did. Something in his past haunted him. Something here, in this castle.

Above the tower, the sky was empty now. 'Come on,' Ainsley said, slipping her hand into Innes's arm. 'Let's go inside.'

She led him through to the Great Hall, their feet echoing on the stone flags. Innes seemed to have shaken off his black mood, and was now wandering around, sounding panelling, looking up with a worried frown at the high beams. 'I'll get

Robert, my surveyor, to take a look at this while
he's here. He'll be able to tell me if there are any
structural problems.'

He said it hopefully, no doubt thinking that
structural problems would give him the excuse
to pull the place down. The castle seemed sound
enough to her, no smell of damp, no sign of rot,
but she was willing to admit she knew nothing
about it.

Watching him out of the corner of her eye, Ainsley got on with her own measurements. 'I think
we'll have to plan to feed about two hundred, including bairns,' she said. 'Mhairi is overseeing the
work in the kitchens. I reckon we'll need to light
the fires a few days in advance, once the chim-
neys are swept.' She scribbled in her notebook,
which she had reclaimed from Innes, and began
to tick items off from her list. Quickly absorbed
in her task, she was struggling to pull the holland
covers from what she assumed must be the laird's
chair when Innes came to her aid.

'Let me,' he said.

A cloud of dust flew up, making them both
choke. 'Good heavens, it's like a throne.'

Innes laughed. 'Now you can get some idea of

the esteem in which the lairds of Strone Bridge have held themselves.'

Ainsley sat down on the chair. It was so high her feet didn't touch the ground. 'Mhairi would have a fit if she could see me. I'm probably bringing any amount of curses down on myself for daring to occupy the laird's seat.'

'I'm the laird now, and I'd be more than happy for you to occupy my seat.'

'Innes!' He was smiling down at her in a way that made her heart flutter. 'I don't know what you mean by that, but I am sure it is something utterly scurrilous.'

'Scandalous, not scurrilous.' He pulled her to her feet and into his arms. 'Want to find out?'

'Do you even know yourself?'

He laughed. 'No, but I am certain of one thing. It starts with a kiss,' he said, and suited action to words.

The second kiss of the day, and it picked up where the first had left off on the cold pier. Just a kiss at first, his hands on her shoulders, his mouth warm, soft. Then his hands slid down to cup her bottom, pulling her closer, and she twined hers around his neck, reaching up, and his tongue licked into her mouth, and heat flared.

He kissed her. She kissed him back, refusing to let herself think about what she was doing, concentrating her mind on the taste of him, and the smell of him, and the way he felt. The breadth of his shoulders. Her hands smoothing down his coat to the tautness of his buttocks, her fingers curling into him to tug him closer, wanting the shivery thrill of his arousal pressed into her belly.

Hard. Not just there, but all of him, hard muscle, tensed, powerful. She pressed into him, her eyes tight shut, her mouth open to him, her tongue touching his, surrendering to the galloping of her pulses, the flush of heat, the tingle in her breasts. Kissing. Her hands stroking, under the skirts of his coat now, on the leather of his breeches.

His hands were not moving. She wanted them to move. Took a moment to remember the last time, and opened her eyes to whisper to him, 'It's fine. I am— I won't.'

'Tell me,' he said then. 'What am I to do?'

She shook her head. 'Can't,' she mumbled, embarrassed.

He kissed her slowly, deeply. 'Tell me, Ainsley,' he said.

She was losing it, the heat, the shivery feeling, but not the desire. John had never asked what she wanted. Despite all the vague advice Madame Hera doled out about connubial bliss and mutual satisfaction, she had neither the experience nor knowledge of either. 'I don't know,' Ainsley said, sounding petulant, feeling frustrated. *You do it*, was what she wanted to say.

'You do know,' Innes insisted.

He kissed her again. He cupped her face, forcing her to meet his eyes. His own were not mocking, not cruel. Dark blue, slumberous. Colour on his cheeks. Passion, not anger or shame, though it was being held in check. She realised why, with a little shock, remembered how she had been the other night. 'I don't know what to say,' she said.

'Tell me where you feel it when I kiss you,' he said, putting his hand in hers, kissing her. 'Tell me where it makes you want me to touch you.'

'Here,' she said, putting his hand on her breast.

His hand covered the soft swell. Her nipple hardened. She caught her breath as he squeezed her lightly through the layers of her gown and her corsets. 'Like this?' he asked, and she nodded. He kissed her neck, her throat, still stoking, kneading, making her nipple ache for more, then turned his attention to the other breast, and she caught her breath again.

'You like that?' Innes said.

His thumb circled her taut nipple. 'Yes.'

'And that?'

Her other nipple. 'Yes.'

'What else?'

That smile of his. His hands teasing her. She wanted his hands on her skin. His mouth on her nipple. The thought shocked her and excited her and terrified her. Her breasts were so small. John had always said— But she was not going to think about John. And Innes had said— What had Innes said?

He was kissing her neck again, her throat again. And her mouth again. 'Ask me,' he whispered, nibbling on the lobe of her ear. 'Ask me to kiss you. Here,' he said, cupping her breast. 'Ask me to taste you. Tell me what you want, Ainsley. I want to please you. Tell me.'

'I want—I want you to kiss me. Here,' she said, putting her hand over his. 'I want you to— Innes, I want you not to be disappointed.'

'Ainsley, it is not possible. I absolutely assure you that I won't be disappointed,' Innes said, loosening her cloak and turning her around. Kissing the back of her neck, he began to loosen the buttons of her gown, just enough to slide the bodice down her arms. His hands covered her breasts, his body pressed into her back. She could feel his hard, rigid length against the swell of her bottom.

'You see,' he said, nuzzling the nape of her neck. 'You feel what you are doing to me?'

She wriggled, arching her back so that he pressed closer. Innes moaned, and she laughed, a soft, sensual sound deep in her throat, for it was potent, the effect she had on his potency, and it gave her a burst of confidence. 'Touch me,' she said, 'I want you to touch me. Your hands. Your mouth. On me.'

'It will be my pleasure.' He undid the knot of her stays, then turned her round. 'And yours, I hope.'

He dipped his head and kissed the swell of her breasts above her corset. His tongue licked into the valley between them, kissing, his lips soft on her skin. He loosened her stays and freed her breasts, cupping them, one in each hand. Her nipples were dark pink, tight. Innes's eyes were dark with excitement. 'I told you,' he said with a wicked smile. 'I told you.'

He dipped his head and took her nipple in his mouth and sucked. She jerked, the drag of sensation connecting directly with the growing tightness between her legs. He sucked again, slowly, and it was like the tightening of a cord. He kissed her. He traced the shape of her breast with his tongue and kissed his way over to the other one. Sucking. Dragging. She moaned. Sucking. Tension. She said his name in a voice she hardly recognised.

'What?' he asked, sounding just as ragged. 'Tell me what you want.'

'I can't.'

More sucking. Nipping. She clutched at his shoulders, for her knees had begun to shake. 'Tell me,' Innes insisted.

She felt as if her insides were coiling. She was so hot, and the heat was concentrated between her legs. There had been echoes of this before. She had forgotten that, but it had been further away, not like this, not so close. 'I don't know,' she said, frustration making her voice tense, her fingers digging deep into his shoulders. 'Innes, I really don't know.'

She thought he would stop. Or he would tell her what it was. That he would give her the words. That he would simply act. But he did none of those things. He smiled at her, his mouth curling in a way that made her insides tighten even more. 'Oh, I think you do,' he said.

His hand slid down, between her legs, and curled into her, through her gown. Instinctively she tilted up. 'Yes,' she said. 'Yes, I do.'

He caressed her, the flat of his palm against her skirts, her skirts and petticoats flattened, rubbing into the heat between her legs, and she realised that was what she wanted. 'More,' she said, helping him, arching her spine. 'More. No, less—no skirts.'

She pulled up her gown, her petticoats, shamelessly, not caring now, and put his hand underneath. Innes groaned. She pulled his face to hers and kissed him desperately. He groaned again. 'Innes,' she said, 'Innes I want— I think I want— Innes, for goodness' sake.'

He cupped her again, between her legs, only this time there was only the thin linen of her pantaloons between her and his hand. She was throbbing. There was a hard knot of her throbbing against his hand. And then he began to stroke her and the knot tightened, and throbbed, contracted and she thought she wouldn't be able to bear it, and for a few seconds she felt as if she were hovering, quivering, and then it broke, pulsing, the most delightful pulsing, making her cry out in pleasure, over and over, until it slowed, stopped, and she clung to him, her hair falling down her shoulders, panting, utterly abandoned, and for the first time in her life, utterly spent.

'I didn't know,' she said simply to Innes when she finally managed to let go her grip on him, surprised at her utter lack of embarrassment.

'Then I'm honoured.'

'Palpitations. That is how one woman described it to Madame Hera in a letter I read yesterday. "He does not give me the palpitations I can give myself."' Ainsley covered her mouth, her eyes wide. 'Good grief, does that mean that she...?'

'I reckon it does.'

She laughed. 'It is a whole new world. I thought the woman was talking about some sort of nervous condition. It's as well I've not replied yet.'

'I look forward to reading your reply.'

He was looking distinctly uncomfortable as he tried to arrange his coat around the very obvious swelling in his trousers. Catching Ainsley's eye, he blushed faintly. 'It's at times like this I can see the merit of a kilt.'

Were there rules that applied to this sort of situation? 'Should I do something to—to relieve you?' she blurted out, then flushed bright red. She sounded as if she was offering to bathe his wounds and not—not… She made a helpless gesture. 'I don't know the—the form.'

Innes burst out laughing. 'This is not a sport! Oh, don't go all prickly, I didn't mean— Ainsley, I would love you to *relieve* me, but there is no need. Well, there is, but I will— It will go away if we talk of something else.' He stroked her tangle of hair back from her face, his smile gentling. 'Your pleasure was very much mine, I assure you.'

Was he merely being nice? Polite? She eyed him dubiously. She had always suspected there was something missing even in the early days of her marriage before John began to find her body so repellent, but she had always been under the apprehension that the main event, so to speak, was a man's pleasure. Not that John had taken much pleasure latterly. A chore. Then a failure. Though he had not seemed to have any such problems alone. She shuddered, still mortified by that discovery.

'Ainsley, what is it?'

She was about to shake her head, but then she paused. 'Palpitations. The woman who wrote to Madame Hera, she gives them to herself because her husband does not—cannot. There is something wrong with her husband, then, is there not?'

'Ignorance, or perhaps he's just selfish. Is this another of Madame's problems?'

'It made me wonder,' Ainsley said, ignoring this question. 'Would a man—a husband— If he cannot, with his wife, I mean, but he can—you know, do that...' She swallowed. She did know the words for this, they had been thrown in her face. 'Bring pleasure to himself. If he can do that for himself, but he can't with his wife, then there is something wrong with his wife, isn't there?'

Innes looked at her strangely. 'I thought only women wrote to you?'

Ainsley managed a noncommittal shrug.

'Do you mean can't or won't?'

Were they the same thing? She forced herself to think back. No. John had tried, and it had shamed him. 'Can't,' Ainsley said sadly.

He touched her cheek gently. 'Poor wife. And poor husband. Though I'd say the problem was most definitely his.'

Chapter Seven

August 1840, three weeks later

Felicity threw herself down on the bed, careless of the creases it would put in the emerald-green gown she wore for the Rescinding ceremony. 'So tell me, since this looks like the only opportunity I'll have to get you to myself, how are you enjoying married life?'

Ainsley, still in the woollen wrapper she had donned after her bath, was perched on a stool in front of the dressing table. Her hair ought to be curled, but it would take for ever, and in the breeze that would no doubt be blowing outside, it would probably be straight again by the time they reached the church. 'We're not really married. I like it a lot better than my real marriage was.'

'I'm sorry I couldn't get here until yesterday.

I've been so busy. I've barely had a chance to talk to your Mr Drummond.'

'I've barely had a chance myself lately, there's been so much to do to get this ceremony organised, and when Innes has not been closeted with Eoin talking agriculture, he's been with his surveyor, Robert Alexander, talking engineering. They're finalising the plans for a new pier and road. Mr Alexander has made a model of the pier and the road out of paper and paste. It is quite realistic. Innes will unveil it today, after the Rescinding.' Ainsley picked up her brush but made no attempt to apply it. 'So I suppose it's no surprise that we've been like ships that pass in the night.'

'I'd have thought you'd be happy about that, not having to live in his pocket.'

'I am. I don't want to. You're right.' Ainsley put the brush down and picked up a comb.

'You don't sound very convincing. Please don't tell me you're falling in love with the man.'

'That is one mistake I won't make twice,' Ainsley said scornfully, 'and even if I did—which I assure you I won't—Innes has made it very clear that he will not.'

Felicity raised her brows. 'Has he, now? Why not?'

'He likes his independence too much.'

'Marriage makes no difference to independence for a man, they carry on just as they please, regardless of the little woman waiting at home. It is only a wife who is shackled by matrimony.'

'You sound so bitter, Felicity.'

'Now, that is definitely a case of the pot calling the kettle black.'

Ainsley nodded. 'Yes, but I have reason to be bitter. My marriage—you know what it was like.'

'I know what it did to you, even though you refused to confide the particulars.' Felicity's smile was twisted. 'And as you must have guessed, I know enough, from being the other woman, not to want to be the wife. But that is over now.'

'You mean your—your…'

'*Affaire*, why not call it what it was.'

'Why did you not say?'

'Because I'm ashamed, and because it has taken up quite enough of my life for me to wish to grant it any more,' Felicity said bracingly. 'I read Madame Hera's latest batch of correspondence last night, by the light of a candle that threatened to blow out in the gale that was howling through my bedchamber.'

Ainsley and Mhairi had been forced to put all their visitors up in the west wing of the castle, which had latterly been the old laird's quarters. 'I'm so sorry,' she said. 'Were you freezing?'

'I certainly don't fancy being here in the winter. Though Madame's correspondence heated me up,' Felicity said with a saucy smile. 'I assume that you and Mr Drummond have not been ships that passed each other every night.'

Ainsley flushed. 'Well, I know now that palpitations are not necessarily the prelude to a fainting attack,' she said. 'The rest you can deduce from Madame Hera's letters.'

'Does he know that you're writing them?'

'Yes. And before you ask, you were right. I owe you five pounds. He thought it was fun.' Ainsley's laughter faded. 'He made me realise that some of my advice has been— Well, frankly, not the best, Felicity. I don't mean because I've been forced to modify my language to avoid offence—'

'I did notice a tendency to use rather less euphemisms and rather more—shall we say colloquial terms, in those personal replies,' Felicity interjected. 'I take it those were Mr Drummond's phrases?'

'Do you think they are too much?'

'I think they make it impossible for the recipients to misunderstand. We shall see. I have found in this business that while people rarely praise, they are very quick to let you know when they're not happy. But I interrupted you. You were saying, about your advice...'

Ainsley finished combing her hair and began to pin it up in what she hoped would be a wind-resistant knot. 'Looking back over my replies since Madame Hera came into being, I realised my advice has often been—defensive? No, sometimes rather combative. I assumed, you see, that the women who write are in need of— That they need to stand up for themselves. Madame Hera is very belligerent. She sees marriage as a battlefield.'

'In many cases she's right.'

'Yes.' Ainsley turned away from the mirror to face her friend, her hair half-pinned. 'Madame Hera was born of war. She ought to have been called Madame Mars, or whatever the female equivalent is.'

'Athena. No, she is Greek.' Felicity shook her head impatiently. 'It doesn't matter. Go on.'

'I've been thinking about John a lot these past few weeks. I blamed him for everything. I hated him, in the end, for what he did to me, for the constant undermining and the—the other things. I was furious about the debts, and about the mess he left me in. Much of it was his fault, of course. He was weak and he was a spendthrift and he was completely gullible when it came to moneymaking schemes, but I wonder how different things would have been if, instead of blaming him and shutting him out, and setting off on my own vengeful path, I had shown him a little understanding.'

'None at all!' Felicity said scornfully. 'The man was a useless profligate and you are better off by far without him.'

'Perhaps he would have been better off without me.'

'What do you mean?'

'When things started to go wrong, I didn't try very hard to make them right. Oh, I challenged him about the money—but not really with the conviction I thought I had at the time. I think— this is awful—but I think I *wanted* him to be in the wrong, more than I wanted to make things right between us.'

'Ainsley, he *was* in the wrong.'

'Yes, but so, too, was I. I would do things differently if I got the chance again.'

'But you are getting the chance again. Don't tell me it doesn't count because you're not really married, Ainsley, you know what I mean. I hope you're not letting Drummond walk all over you?'

'Not exactly. I don't think he deliberately excludes me, but he's not in the habit of including anyone in his life. I told you, he is very attached to his independence.'

'Blasted men,' Felicity said feelingly. Looking down at the little gold watch she always wore on a fob on her gown, she clapped her hand over her mouth in dismay. 'Ainsley, we've to be at the chapel for the start of proceedings in an hour and you haven't even done your hair. Turn round. Let me.' Jumping to her feet, she gathered up a handful of pins. 'You could come back to Edinburgh with me after this, you know.'

'Thank you, but no.' Ainsley met her friend's eyes in the mirror and smiled. 'It's good for me, being here at the moment. It's helped me think.'

'Don't think too hard, else you'll be turning that John McBrayne into a saint, and that he was not,' Felicity said, pinning frantically.

'No, but I had turned him into a devil, and he wasn't that, either.'

'Hmm.' Felicity carried on pinning. 'I'm sorry I can't stay longer. You know how it is, being a female in a man's world. If I'm not back, they'll replace me.'

'It's fine. I know how important your job is to you. And to me. Madame Hera depends on you.'

'Madame Hera is becoming so popular that she doesn't need my support. There.' Felicity threw down the remainder of the pins. 'Let's get you into your gown.' She pulled the dress from its hanger and gave it a shake.

'I'm getting nervous,' Ainsley said as she stepped into it. 'I haven't thought about it until now. I've been too busy planning it, but it's a big thing, Felicity. It's really important for Innes that it goes well. I thought about asking Mhairi for a good luck spell, but asking her is probably bad luck. You've no idea how superstitious she can be.'

'The housekeeper?' Felicity was busy hooking the buttons on Ainsley's gown. 'Is she the witch?'

'Her mother was.'

'And she was the old laird's mistress, too, you tell me. You should ask her for a potion. You know, just to make sure that there are no consequences from the palpitations your husband is giving you.'

Ainsley's face fell. 'I don't think that will be necessary.'

'Oh, Ainsley, I'm so sorry. I didn't think.'

'It doesn't matter.' Ainsley managed to smile. 'Really. Are you done? May I look?' Ainsley turned towards the mirror and shook out her skirts.

'I do hope your Mr Drummond is making sure he takes appropriate measures.' Felicity gave her a grave look. 'You cannot take the risk.'

'There is no risk, and even if there were, I am very sure that the last thing Innes would risk is such a complication.' Seeing that her friend was about to question her further, Ainsley picked up her shawl. 'We should go.'

'Wait. I brought you something.' Felicity handed her a velvet-covered box. 'A belated wedding present. It's not much, but it's pretty.'

It was a gold pendant set with a tiny cluster of diamonds around an amethyst. Ainsley hugged her tightly. 'It's lovely. Thank you.' She hugged Felicity again, then handed her the necklace to fasten. She stared down at her left hand, with the simple gold band Innes had given her more than

two months ago. 'Do you think I'll pass muster.
As the laird's wife, I mean?' she asked anxiously.
'I don't want to let Innes down.'

'That is exactly the kind of talk I don't want to
hear. You will do your best, and that's all you can
do. The rest is up to him. He's lucky to have you,
Ainsley. Am I permitted to wish you good luck,
or is that bad luck?'

'I don't know, probably.'

'Then I will say what the actors say. Break a leg.
But make sure that you do not break your heart.'
Felicity cast a quick glance at the mirror. 'My hair.
As usual. Give me just a minute, for that rather
gorgeous man who brought me over in his rather
rustic fishing boat yesterday is to be one of your
escorts, and I'd like to look a little less ravaged
than I did the last time he saw me.'

'You mean Eoin?'

'That's the one. I am to be one of your Mr
Drummond's escorts in the walk to the chapel.
He asked me last night.' Felicity grimaced. 'Two
virgins, it's supposed to be. I hope my lack of
maidenhead will not bring you bad luck.'

Ainsley choked. 'I think what matters is that
you are unmarried. Shall we go?'

'Are you ready?'

Ainsley kissed her cheek. 'As I'll ever be,' she said.

Innes hadn't thought about the ceremony until he was walking to the church between his escorts, with what felt like the entire population of Strone Bridge behind him. He was putting on a show, that was all. It was just a daft tradition; it meant something to the people who would be attending, but nothing to him. Except he felt nervous, and it did matter, and realising that made him feel slightly sick, because that meant Strone Bridge had come to matter, and that complicated everything.

It was not raining, which Eoin had assured him was a good sign. From somewhere behind him came the skirl of the bagpipes. On one side of him Felicity, Ainsley's eccentric friend, picked her way along the path, sliding him what he could only describe as assessing glances every now and then. He wondered what Ainsley had told her. He doubted very much that this very self-assured and rather sultrily attractive woman fulfilled the criteria expected of his escort. Of Mhairi's niece Flora's qualifications, he had no doubt at all.

They arrived at the door of the church, and the crowd behind him filtered in to become the congregation. Begging a moment of privacy, Innes made his way alone to the Drummond Celtic cross, not to commune with the dead man so recently interred there, but the one whose corpse lay elsewhere. In a few moments, he was going to have to stand at that altar, in front of those people, and be blessed as the new laird. It should have been Malcolm standing there. If things had gone as they had been planned, as his brother had so desperately wanted them to, Malcolm would have been standing at that altar fourteen years ago beside Blanche, taking part in another ritual.

Blanche. He never allowed her name into his head. Until he'd come back to Strone Bridge, he rarely even allowed himself to think of Malcolm. Now, standing in front of the cross where Malcolm should have been buried, Innes felt overwhelmed with grief and regrets. If he could turn back time, make it all as it should be—Malcolm leading the Rescinding, Blanche at his side, and perhaps three or four bairns, too. Strone Bridge would be flourishing. The congregation would be celebrating.

'And you,' he hissed at the cross, 'you would

have gone to your grave a damn sight happier, that's for sure. You never thought you'd see this day, any more than I did.'

Innes leaned his forehead on the cold stone and closed his eyes. If Malcolm could see what had happened to his precious lands, he'd be appalled. He could not bring his brother back, but he could do his damnedest to restore the lands to what they had been. 'No, I can do better,' Innes said to the stone. 'I will make them flourish, better than they have ever, and what's more, I'll do it my way.'

For better or for worse, he thought to himself, turning his back on the cross. The same words he'd said in front of another altar not so very long ago, with Ainsley by his side. For better or for worse, it looked as if he'd made up his mind to stay here, for the time being. He'd rather have Ainsley by his side than any other woman. 'For the time being, any road,' he muttered, squaring his shoulders and making his way towards the chapel.

She was waiting at the porch, with Eoin and Robert by her side. She looked so nervous as she made her way towards him, Innes was worried for a moment that she might actually faint. Her gown was of pale silk, embroidered with pink and blue flowers. The long puffed sleeves gave it a demure look, at odds with the ruffled neckline. She wore a pretty pendant he had not seen before.

Her hand, when he took it, was icy cold. Muttering an apology, Innes squeezed it reassuringly. Was she thinking as he was, how like a wedding this whole thing was turning out to be? Was she thinking back to the other time, when she had stood beside another man, in another church? It shouldn't bother him. He hadn't thought about it before, and wished he had not now. It shouldn't bother him, any more than the idea, which had only just occurred to him, that she would leave here soon. He might have committed to the place, but it had always been a temporary location for her. There would come a time when he'd be here alone. When things were clearer. They were very far from clear now. No need to think of that just yet.

Ainsley winced, and Innes immediately loosened his grip. 'Ready?' he asked. She nodded. She put her arm in his and prepared to walk down the aisle with him, and Innes closed his mind to everything save playing his part.

Standing in the church porch, offering her cheek to be kissed by yet another well-wisher, Ainsley felt as if her smile was frozen to her face. The Drummond ring that Innes had placed on the middle finger of her right hand felt strange. It was apparently worn by every laird's wife. A rose-tinted diamond coincidentally almost the same colour as the pendant Felicity had given her, surrounded by a cluster of smaller stones, it was obviously an heirloom. She felt quite ambivalent about it, for there was bound to be some sort of curse attached to anyone who wore it under false pretences. She would ask Innes. No, she decided almost immediately, she would rather not know.

The last of the men kissed her cheek. The church door closed and the minister shook Innes's hand before heading along the path to join the rest of the guests at the castle. 'They can wait for us a bit,' Innes said when she made to follow him. 'I haven't even had the chance to tell you that you look lovely.'

'Don't be daft. There's no one watching.'

'I know. Why do you think I kept you here?' he asked, smiling down at her. 'I believe the laird has the right to kiss his lady.'

'You already have, at the end of the blessing.'

He laughed, that low, growling laugh that did

things to her insides. 'That wasn't what I had in mind,' he said, and pulled her into his arms.

His kiss was gentle, reassuring. He held her tightly, as if he, too, needed reassurance. Her poke bonnet bumped against his forehead, and they broke apart. 'I didn't think it would matter,' Innes said, running a hand through his carefully combed hair.

'Do you feel like a real laird now?'

She meant it lightly, but Innes took the question seriously. 'I feel as though I've made a promise to the place,' he said. 'I think— I don't know how I will manage it, but I owe it to Strone Bridge to restore it. Somehow.' He pulled her back into his arms. 'I know I was sceptical about the Rescinding, but I think it was a good idea, and it was your idea. So thank you.'

She was touched as well as gratified. Unwilling to show it, she looked down at the ring. 'Was this your mother's?'

'And my grandmother's and so on. Do you like it? Don't tell me you're worried that there's some sort of curse attached to it.'

She laughed. 'I don't appreciate having my mind read. I was worried that it would be bad luck to wear it, since I'm not really the laird's lady.'

'There's no need to worry, I promise you. Generations of Drummond men have married for the good of Strone Bridge before all else, and that's exactly what I've done,' Innes said. 'In our own way, we're carrying on a tradition. Drummonds don't marry for love.' His expression darkened. 'It's when they try to, that's when they become cursed.'

She wanted to ask him what he meant, but she was afraid, looking at his face. He could only be thinking of himself. It was so obvious; she couldn't believe she hadn't thought of it before. That was why he was so insistent he'd never fall in love. Because he already had, and it had come to nothing.

She felt slightly sick. She oughtn't to. The pair of them were even better matched than she had realised, both of them burned by that most revered of emotions. She should be relieved to finally understand. Actually, there was no cause for her to feel anything at all. Innes's heart was no concern of hers.

'We should go,' Innes said, dragging his mind back from whatever dark place he had gone to. 'I want to get the formal Rescinding out of the way before too much whisky had been taken. What is it? You look as if you've seen a ghost.'

Ainsley managed to smile. 'Just my husband, in his full Highland regalia, looking every bit the part of the laird. I have not told you how very handsome you look.'

He tucked her hand in his, smiling down at her wickedly, his black mood seemingly vanished. 'Do I live up to your expectations of a wild Highlander?'

Her own mood lightened. 'I don't know.' Ainsley gave him a teasing smile. 'It's a shame we have a party to attend, else I would say I was looking forward to finding out.'

A fire had been burning constantly in the huge hearth of the Great Hall for the past few days. The mantel was of carved oak set on two huge marble pillars, and the hearth itself was big enough to hold a massive log cut from a very old tree in one whole piece. The Great Hall was a long, narrow room done in the Elizabethan style, though it had been created less than a hundred years before. The walls were panelled to head height, then timbered and rendered, giving the impression of great age, as did the vaulted oak ceiling. Ainsley stood at the far end of the room, where a balconied recess had been formed with yet more oak, this time in the form of three arches rather like a rood screen.

The hall was full of people, very few of whom she recognised. Innes had not wanted anyone from his old life here. When Ainsley had enquired about inviting other local gentry, having heard the name Caldwell mentioned as the owners of the next estate, she thought he had flinched, though she could not be sure. 'We've enough to do, to win the hearts and minds of our own,' he'd said quickly. 'Let's keep it a Strone Bridge celebration.' Everyone present, save herself, Felicity and Robert Alexander had been born here, or had married someone who had been born here. Which for now included her, though she did not really count.

Innes was standing a few feet away, holding one of those intense conversations with his surveyor that seemed to require Robert Alexander to flap his arms about a lot. The model of the pier and the new road was to be revealed after the Rescinding. Mr Alexander was nervous. She could see that Innes was reassuring him.

The laird. Her husband, in his Highland dress, which he claimed to have worn just for her, though she knew he was only teasing. He had opted for the short jacket, and not the long, cloak-like plaid, of a dark wool that was fitted tight across his shoulders, the front cut in a curve, finishing at his neat waist. Under it, he wore a waistcoat and a white shirt. And below it, the kilt, a long length of wool folded into narrow pleats and held in place by a thick leather belt with a large silver buckle. When he turned, as he did now, granting her a delightful view of his rear, the pleats swung out. As she suspected, he had very shapely legs, not at all scrawny, but muscled. His long, knit hose covered what Mhairi called a fine calf, and Ainsley had to agree. There was a small jewelled dagger tucked into one of his hose, and another, longer dagger attached to his belt. The kilt stopped at his knee. He could not possibly be wearing undergarments.

He caught her looking at him and came to join her. 'I would very much like to ask you what you're thinking,' he said softly into her ear, 'but if you told me, I reckon I'd have to carry you off and have my wicked Highland way with you, and we've a lot of ceremony to get through, unfortunately.'

'And a party to attend afterwards.'

'Actually, Eoin was just telling me that it's customary for the laird and his lady to celebrate their new life alone.'

'I read nothing of that in the book.'

'It's known as the—the Bonding,' Innes said.

She bit her lip, trying not to laugh. 'You made that up.'

'It's one of the new traditions I'm thinking of establishing.' Innes smiled one of his sinful smiles that made her feel as if she were blushing inside. 'What do you say?'

'I would certainly not wish to break with tradition on a night like this. And I would not wish all that effort you've made with your Highland dress to go to waste.'

His eyes darkened. She felt the flush inside her spreading. 'If it were not for the Rescinding, I would carry you off right now.'

'I have gone to an enormous effort to get this Rescinding organised, Laird. You are not going to spoil it for me.'

'No. I would not dream of it. I'm truly grateful, Ainsley.' He kissed her cheek. 'But just as soon as it's over, my lady...'

'I know. A Bonding! Whatever that entails.'

'Haven't you imagined it? I know I have. Lots of times.'

'Innes! Let us concentrate on one ceremony before we start discussing another.'

He laughed. 'Very well. I see your Miss Blair conferring with Eoin. Again. Is she spoken for?' Innes asked.

'She's wedded to her career,' Ainsley replied.

'Do you know, you have a way of pursing up your mouth just at one corner when you fib, as if you're trying to swallow whatever it is you're determined not to say.'

'I was not fibbing.'

'You weren't telling the truth, either.' Innes smiled down at her. 'I suspect your Felicity is a woman of many secrets.' Innes put his arm around her waist, pulling her into his side. 'I'm not really interested in Miss Blair's private life, nor indeed Eoin's. I'm more interested in our own. But first, it's time for the Rescinding. Are you ready?'

'What if I forget something?' Ainsley asked, suddenly panicked.

'You've made the whole thing go like a dream so far. Now all you have to do is to remember all the promises I make, lest I forget any. And I must forgive and forget.' Innes rolled his eyes. 'I cannot believe my father did this and meant it.'

The chair, like most of the Great Hall, was carved in oak and had been polished to a soft gleam. The canopy that covered it was of the same faded green velvet as the cushion. After handing Ainsley into the much simpler chair by his side, Innes sat down. He felt part foolish, part—good grief, surely not proud? No, but it was something close. The ghosts of his ancestors had got into his blood. Or having all those eyes on him had gone to his head. Or maybe it was this chair, and the hall, which was only ever used for formal occasions. His father's birthday had always been celebrated here. The annual party for the tenants and cotters. His and Malcolm's coming of age.

No. This was a time to look forward, not back. Innes jumped up. The room fell silent. He picked up the sword that lay at his feet, the wicked blade glittering. The sheath lay beside it. Carefully, he placed the sword inside the sheath, a signal of peace, and handed it to Eoin, who was once again playing the part of the nearest living blood relative. All of this was prescribed in the book that Ainsley had shown him. *The Customs and Ways of the Family Drummond of Strone Bridge*, it pompously declared itself in faded gold script. Mhairi had been insulted when he'd laughed. Ainsley had apologised on his behalf. Later, she'd teased him, calling it the *Drummond Self-Help Manual*. Now he was simply glad Ainsley had read it so carefully for him.

'Friends,' Innes said, 'I bid you welcome. Before we begin the ceremony, it is traditional to toast the departed.' He lifted the glass of whisky that lay ready, nodding to Ainsley to do the same, and waiting to make sure everyone watching had a glass. *'Slàinte!'* he said. 'To the old laird, my father. *Cha bhithidh a leithid ami riamh.* We'll never see his like again.' He drank, surprised to discover that the toast had not stuck in his craw quite as much as he'd thought it would. Perhaps it was because it was true, he thought to himself wryly. He was making sure of it.

Innes put his glass down. 'The laird has met his maker. With him must be buried all grudges, all debts, all quarrels. A forgiving and forgetting. A Rescinding. A new beginning. And I promise you,' he said, departing from his script, 'that it is not the case of sweeping the dirt out of one door and blowing it into the other. That is one change.

The first, I hope of many. This Rescinding is an old tradition, but today it will be done in quite a new way. No recriminations. No half measures. No payback. That is my vow to you. Let us begin.'

He sat down heavily. Sweat trickled down his back. He never made speeches. The words, his words, had not been planned, but they were *his*, and he'd meant them. Scanning the room anxiously, he waited for the reaction. They were an inscrutable lot, the people of Strone Bridge. The lightest of touches on his hand, which was resting by the side of his chair, made him look over at Ainsley. 'Perfect,' she mouthed, and smiled at him. When she made to take her hand away, he captured it, twining his fingers in hers. He felt good.

Ainsley waited anxiously. Innes had been nervous making his speech. His palm was damp. He'd been treating the Rescinding almost as a joke, at the very least a mere formality, but when he spoke it was clear that he meant every word he said. Such a confident man, and such a successful one, she had assumed speech-making came easily to him. It was oddly reassuring to discover it did not. She couldn't decide whether she wanted there to be lots of petitioners or few, but she was vastly relieved when the first came forward, for none at all would have been a disaster.

The man was a tenant, and by the looks of him, one of long standing. 'Mr Stewart,' Innes said, 'of Auchenlochan farm. What is it you wish from me?'

The old man, who had been gazing anxiously down at his booted feet, straightened and looked Innes firmly in the eye. 'I petition the laird to forgive two wrongs,' he said. 'For my son, John Angus Stewart, who left two quarters rent unpaid on Auchenlochan Beag farm when he sailed for Canada. And for myself, for failing to inform the laird that the rent was unpaid.' Mr Stewart looked over his shoulder at the rest of the room, before turning back to Innes. 'The laird did raise the rents far beyond the value of the farms, it is true, and many of us here felt the injustice of that, but…' He waved his hand, to silence the rumbles of agreement emanating from behind him. 'But it was his right, and those of us who took advantage of his failing to collect were wrong, and they should be saying so now,' he finished pointedly.

Innes got to his feet, and said the words as specified in the Drummond manual. 'Angus Stewart of Auchenlochan, and John Angus Stewart, who was of Auchenlochan Beag, your petitions are granted, the debt is Rescinded.'

Mr Stewart nodded, his lips pursed. Before he had reached his wife, another man had come forward to proclaim another unpaid rent, and after him another, and another. Some went reluctantly, some resignedly, some went in response to Crofter Stewart's beady-eyed stare, but they all went. The debts Innes was waiving amounted to a large sum of money. Ainsley couldn't understand the old laird—the man was something of a conundrum—putting rents sky-high on one hand, then failing to collect them on the other. Since Mhairi assured her the laird's mind had not wandered, she could only assume that it must have been severely warped. *Twisted.* That was a better word.

As Innes continued to forgive and forget, the Rescinding began to take on a lighter note. A woman admitted to burying a dog along with her husband in the graveyard of the Strone Bridge chapel. 'Though I know it is forbidden, but he always preferred that beast's company to mine, and the pair of them were that crabbit, I thought they would be happy together,' she declared, arms akimbo. Laughter greeted this confession, and

Innes earned himself a fat kiss when he promised the dog and the master's mortal remains would not be torn asunder.

Whisky flowed, and wine, too, along with the strong local heather ale. Innes was preparing to end the ceremony when a man came forward whom Ainsley recognised as Mhairi's taciturn brother, the father of Flora, the pretty lass who had been one half of Innes's escort.

'Donald McIntosh of High Strone farm.' Expecting another case of rent arrears, Ainsley's mind was on the banquet, which would be needed to sop up some of the drink that had been taken. She was trying to catch Mhairi's eye, and was surprised to see the housekeeper stiffen, her gaze fixed on her brother.

'Your father did wrong by my sister for many years,' Donald McIntosh said.

'Dodds!' Mhairi protested, but her brother ignored her.

'The laird took my sister's innocence and spoilt her for any other man. He shamed my sister. He shamed my family.'

'Dodds!' Mhairi grabbed her brother by the arm, her face set. 'I loved the man, will you not understand that? He did not take anything from me.'

'Love! That cold-hearted, thrawn old bastard didn't love you. You were fit to warm his bed, but not fit to bear his name. You were his hoor, Mhairi.'

Hoor? Shocked, Ainsley realised he meant *whore*.

Mhairi paled, taking a staggering step back. 'It's true, he didn't love me, but I loved him. I don't care if that makes me his hoor, and I don't know what you think you're doing, standing here in front of the man's son. This is a celebration.'

'It's a Rescinding.' Donald McIntosh turned back towards Innes. 'I beg forgiveness for the curse I put upon your family.'

Along with almost everyone else in the room, Ainsley gasped. Almost everyone else. Felicity, she noticed, was looking fascinated rather than shocked. What Innes thought, she could not tell. 'What particular curse?' he asked.

'That the bloodline would fail.' Donald spoke not to Innes, but to his sister. 'I had the spell from our mother, though she made me swear not to use it.'

'No. *Màthair* would never have told *you* her magic, Dodds McIntosh. No fey wife worth her salt would have trusted a mere man.'

'You're wrong, Mhairi. Like me, she felt the shame that man brought on our family.'

Mhairi's mouth fell open. 'And now she is dead it cannot be retracted. What have you done?'

Donald stiffened. 'I am entitled to be forgiven.'

'And forgiven you shall be,' Innes said, breaking the tense silence. 'The potency of the Drummond men is legendary. I refuse to believe that any curse could interfere with it.'

The mood eased. Laughter once more echoed around the hall, and another supplicant shuffled forward. Stricken, Ainsley barely heard his petition. Until she came to Strone Bridge, she had not considered herself superstitious, but Mhairi's tireless efforts to appease the wee people and to keep the changelings at bay seemed to have infected her. By some terrible quirk of fate, Dodds McIntosh's curse had come true. Ainsley felt doubly cursed.

Faintly, she was aware of Innes bringing proceedings to a close. Mechanically, she got to her feet while he said the final words. It didn't matter, she told herself. It would matter if she and Innes were truly married, but they were not. Innes did not want a child. He'd told her so on that very first day, hadn't he? She tried to remember his precise words. No, he'd said he didn't want a wife. *One must necessarily precede the other*, that was what he had said. But she was his wife. And she could not— But she wasn't really his wife. She could not let him down in this most basic of things, because he did not require it of her. She clung to this, and told herself it was a comfort.

'I declare the Rescinding complete, the door closed on the old and open on the new,' Innes was saying. 'It's time to celebrate. Mr Alexander here will fill you all in on the details of our plans for a new pier and a new road, too. There is food and drink aplenty to be had, but first, and most important, one last toast.' Innes lifted his glass and turned towards Ainsley. 'To my lady wife, who made this day possible. I thank you. I could not have done this without you.'

He kissed her full on the lips; the guests roared their approval and Ainsley's heart swelled with pride. She had done this. She had proved something by doing this. For the moment, at least, nothing else mattered.

Chapter Eight

It was dark, but the party was only just hotting up, thanks to the fiddlers. A bundle of bairns slept snuggled together like a litter of puppies, some of them still clutching their sugar candy. In the recess at the far end of the room, in front of Robert Alexander's model of the pier, Mhairi was holding court with a group of local wives. Miss Blair was dancing a wild reel with Eoin. This, Innes decided, was as good a time as any for them to make their getaway unobserved.

The night air was cool. He wrapped a soft shawl around Ainsley's shoulders and led her down to her favourite spot, overlooking the Kyles. Above them, the stars formed a carpet of twinkling lights in the unusually clear sky. 'It went well, didn't it?' she asked. 'Save for that curse Mhairi's brother made.'

'Stupid man. If he really was so ashamed, he should have done something about it when my father was alive.'

'From what you've told me about your father, Mr McIntosh would then have found himself homeless.'

Innes considered this for a few moments. 'No. More likely my father despised Dodds McIntosh for not challenging him. His sense of honour was twisted, but he did have one.'

'Perhaps he did love Mhairi, in his own way.'

'My father never loved anyone, save himself.'

'Not even your brother?'

Ainsley spoke so tentatively, Innes could not but realise she knew perfectly well how sensitive was the subject. He hesitated on the brink of a dismissive shrug, but she had done so much for him today, he felt he wanted to give her something back. 'You're thinking that my father's wilful neglect of Strone Bridge is evidence of his grief for my brother, is that it?'

'Yes.'

'I'm not so sure. My brother loved this place. If my father really cared, why would he destroy the thing Malcolm loved the most? Besides, Eoin said it was a gradual thing, the neglect.'

'A slow realisation of what he'd lost?'

Innes shook his head. 'A slow realisation that I was not coming back, more like. He destroyed it so that I would be left with nothing.'

'And you are determined to prove him wrong?'

'I'd prefer to say that I'm determined to put things right.'

'How will you do that?'

'I have no idea, and at the moment I have better things to think about.'

He kissed her in the moonlight, underneath the stars, to the accompaniment of the scrape of fiddles and the stomping of feet in the distance. She was not really his wife, but she understood him in a way that no one else did. He kissed her, telling her with his lips and his tongue and his hands not only of his desire, but that he wanted her here, like this.

'Are you sure someone won't come chasing after us to come back to the party?' Ainsley whispered.

'If they do, I'll tell them they're in danger of incurring a year of bad luck for interfering with the ancient and revered tradition of the Bonding,' Innes replied.

He felt the soft tremor of her laughter. 'Will

you run up a special flag to declare it over, in the morning?'

'I haven't thought that far ahead. You know that you can change your mind if you don't want to do this, don't you? You must be tired.'

'I'm not the least bit tired, and I don't want to change my mind,' she answered. 'I think we've waited long enough.'

He kissed her again. She tasted so sweet. Her skin was luminous in the moonlight, her eyes dark. He kissed her, and she wrapped herself around him and kissed him back, and their kisses moved from sweet to urgent. Panting, Innes tore his mouth from hers. 'I meant it,' he said. 'I am not expecting you to— We don't have to...'

'But you want to?' she asked, with that smile of hers that seemed to connect straight to his groin.

'I don't think there can be any mistaking that.'

And she laughed, that other sound that connected up to his groin. 'Good,' she said, 'because I want you, too.'

It was the way she said it, with confidence, unprompted, that delighted him most. He grabbed her hand, not trusting himself to kiss her again, and began to walk, as quickly as he could, towards the Home Farm. Ten minutes. It felt like an hour.

'Does this Bonding take place in the laird's bed or his lady's?' Ainsley asked as Innes opened the front door.

He kicked it shut, locking it securely, before he swept her up into his arms. 'Right now, I'm not even sure we'll make it to the bed.'

They did at least make it to her bedchamber. A fire burned in the cast-iron grate. Mhairi must have sent someone down from the castle to tend it. The curtains were drawn. A lamp stood on the hearth, another one on the nightstand, lending the room a pleasant glow. Ainsley stood, clasping her hands and wondering what she ought to do now. The excitement that had bubbled inside her dissipated as she eyed the bed, and memories of that other first night tried to poke their way into this one. She shivered, though it was not at all cold.

'You can still change your mind,' Innes said gently.

He meant it, too. A few days ago, Ainsley would have assumed that what he meant was that *he* had changed *his* mind. Even now, despite the fact that she knew how much he wanted her, she had to work to believe it. 'No,' she said. 'I don't want to change my mind. I don't.' She looked at the lamps, wondering.

'Do you want me to put them out?'

Like the last time. Like all of the last times. She shook her head. She would not have it like any other time.

'Do you want me to leave you to undress?' Innes asked.

'I want...' She studied him, focusing on him, drinking him in so that he was the only one there in the room with her. 'I want you inside me,' she said, meaning in her head, not meaning it how it sounded, though when she saw the results, the leap of desire in his eyes, the way he looked at her, with such passion, she meant that, too. 'I want *you,*' she said, closing the space between them, 'and I want you to show me just how much you want me. That's what I want.'

Innes pulled her tight up against him, lifting her off her feet. 'I think I can manage that,' he said, and kissed her, and she realised that he already had.

He picked her up, but instead of laying her down on the bed, he pulled the quilt onto the floor and laid her down by the fire. Quickly divest-

ing himself of his jacket, his waistcoat, his boots
and stockings, he stood over her wearing just his
plaid and his shirt. The firelight flickered over the
naked flesh of his legs. She caught a glimpse of
muscled thighs as he knelt down beside her, pulling her into his arms again to kiss her. There was
heat inside her. There was heat on her skin from
the fire. There were little trails of heat where he
touched her. Her face. Her neck. His mouth on
her throat. Kissing his way along the curve of her
décolletage, his tongue licking the swell of her
breasts, his hands splayed on her back, feathering over the exposed skin of her nape, the knot at
the top of her spine, then down to pick open the
buttons of her gown.

He kissed the tender spot behind her ears. He
slid her gown over her arms, kissing her shoulders, the crook of her elbow, her wrists, tilting her
gently back to work her gown down, over her legs.
When he took off her shoes, he kissed her ankles
through the silk of her stockings. And her calves.
The backs of her knees. His mouth, thin silk, her
skin. She watched him, her eyes wide open, not
wanting to miss a moment, enthralled, astonished
that simply watching could be so stimulating. His
cheeks were flushed. His blue-black hair, grown

longer since he came to Strone Bridge, was ruffled. She ran her fingers through it. Soft as silk. She pulled him down towards her, wanting the weight of him on her, and claimed his mouth. Hot, his mouth was. 'Sinful,' she murmured, lips against lips. 'I want to be sinful.'

Innes laughed, rolling to his knees again, pulling her with him to work at the ties of her stays. His eyes were dark in this light, midnight blue, his pupils dilated. His shirt was open at the neck. The firelight danced over it, showing her shadows of muscle, making her ache to touch him. While he worked on her corsets, cursing under his breath at the time it was taking, she tugged at the shirt, pulling it free from the leather belt, sighing as her palms found his flesh, sighing again when he flexed and his muscles tensed. Flesh. Heated flesh. She pressed her mouth to his throat and licked his skin, feeling the vibration of his response. Then his triumphant growl as he finally cast her corsets aside and tore at her shift, leaving her in just her pantaloons and her stockings, the bright pink of her garters, which perfectly matched the flowers on her gown.

A fleeting urge to cover up her breasts faded as Innes devoured her with his eyes and then feasted on her with his mouth. Sucking. Nipping. Stroking. Setting up paths of heat, making her blood pulse and the muscles inside her contract. She fell back onto the quilt, tensing, heating, watching him kiss her, touch her, watching his hands on her skin, tanned, rough hands, covering her breasts, flattened over her belly, then pulling at the drawstring of her last undergarment. She looked so pale in the firelight. Her skin milky. The curls between her thighs seemed tinged with autumn colours.

Innes smiled at her. She smiled back. Sinful. Sure. He pulled his shirt over his head, and she watched, clenching inside, the revelation of flesh and muscle, the smattering of dark hair on his chest, the thinner line from his navel to the belt of his kilt. The plaid tickled her thighs and her belly as he knelt over to kiss her. She could feel the tip of his shaft nudging between her legs. She tilted towards him, her fingers gripping into the muscles of his shoulders, and it touched her, the tensest part of her. 'Yes,' she said, not meaning to, not quite sure what she meant.

He sat up, still straddling her, and reached under his kilt, which was spread over the two of them.

She could not see what he did, but she could see the intent in his eyes. Stroking, up and down, slick sliding, unmistakably not his hand, sliding. He was watching her. 'Yes,' she said, quite deliberately, 'again.'

Stroking. Sliding. She must be wet. She was tight. She was getting tighter. Stroking and sliding. And then more stroking. And more sliding. And she came. Suddenly. What she now knew was a climax, though it felt like an explosion. He lifted her, his hands under her, cupping the bare flesh of her bottom as she cried out, and the pulsing took her over, and he pushed his way inside her, thick, hard, pushing her apart, finding his way higher as her muscles pulsed around him, pulling him in, tighter, and higher and tighter.

He paused, his face tense, his breathing heavy. 'Ainsley?'

'Yes. Oh, yes.' She dug her fingers into his shoulder, remembering just in time Felicity's caution. 'But, Innes, be careful.'

'Of course. I promise. Always.' It pained her that he believed there was a need, then he tilted her farther, his hands cupping her bottom, and she forgot about it. She wrapped her legs around him, anxious, feeling anxious, not nervous, but like a runner, wanting to run, wanting to be off, wanting.

And then she was. Not running but better. He thrust inside her, and she met him, held him, thrust back. He thrust again, and she met him again. Not a race. But like a race. Inside her, tensing again, pooling, holding him tight. His chest was slick with sweat. The firelight danced over the planes of his chest. His eyes, midnight-dark eyes, were on her, watching her. She did not look away. She looked down at their bodies. At the dark, hard peaks of her nipples, at the shudder of her breasts as he thrust, and the entity that they were beneath his kilt, joined, flesh melding into flesh, heat and sweat. And then it happened, different but the same, a climax pulsing, and she heard him cry out, and pull away from her, chest heaving, as his climax took him, too.

Afterwards, she wanted to laugh with the sheer delight of it. Fun and pleasure, Felicity had said, and she had been right. 'Astonishing,' she said to Innes, and he laughed. 'I had no idea,' she said, and he laughed again, only it was a different kind of laugh. There was pride in it, and something proprietary. She would have minded that, under any other circumstances. Tonight, on what Madame Hera would no doubt call a voyage of discovery, Ainsley found that there was something rather exciting about a man in a kilt who looked as if he would like to mark every bit of her body as his own. She wanted to do the same to him herself.

She kissed him, tangling her tongue with his, pressing her breasts into the still-damp skin of his chest, relishing the *frisson* that the contact made, the roughness of his hair on the sensitive skin of her nipples. She straddled him in the firelight, as he had straddled her, and felt the stirrings of his member against her. Deciding that this time she wanted to see for herself, she undid the ornate buckle of his belt. The kilt fell open. She watched, fascinated, as he thickened and hardened before her eyes. She wanted to touch him, but this was quite new territory for her. Even the wanting was new.

Innes was leaning up on his elbows. She could see the ripple of his belly muscles as he breathed. His eyes on her. Waiting for her. 'Tell me what you want,' she said, an echo of what he had said, wanting to know, sure that what he wanted so too would she.

'Touch me.' She reached for him, running a tentative finger down the sleek length of him. He shuddered. She did it again. A finger, from the thick base of him, to the tip.

Innes's chest rose and fell. 'More,' he said.

She could guess what he wanted now, but she would not. 'Tell me,' she said.

He knew she was playing. She could see he liked it. 'Stroke me,' he said.

She did, feathering her fingers up and down the length of him. 'Like that?'

'No. You know what I want.'

She leaned forward again, brushing her breasts against his chest. Her nipples ached. 'Then tell me, Innes,' she said, nipping his earlobe. 'Tell me exactly what you want.'

'Put your hands around me, Ainsley.'

She was shocked, not by what he asked, but by the effect it had on her. She sat up, sliding against him so that the soft folds of her sex touched his body, enjoying the separate *frisson* of pleasure this sent through her. Then she did what he asked. She wrapped her hand around his girth, and stroked. 'Like that?'

He groaned.

She did it again. 'Like that, Innes?'

'Yes. Oh, Ainsley, yes.'

'Not like this,' she said, squeezing him lightly. He swore.

'Or like this?' She slid herself against him. Her skin on his, her hand, her sex. Different textures. Same heat. She stroked. 'Do you mean like this, Innes?' she persisted.

'You are a witch.'

'A white witch, or a black witch?' she asked, her fingers tightening and releasing, tightening and releasing.

He put his hands around her waist and lifted her, pulling her swiftly back down on top of him, entering her in one long, hard thrust. 'A very, very bad witch,' he said, pulling her down towards him and kissing her hard.

His kisses matched his thrusts. She matched his kisses first, and then dragged her mouth away to push back, to force him to match his thrusts to hers as she rode him, harder, faster and harder again, until they were both shouting, crying out. Hearing him, the change of note, feeling him, the thickening, feeling herself topple over the edge, she heaved herself free of him just in time to lie panting by his side on the quilt, by the fireside, utterly abandoned, utterly wanton, utterly satisfied.

'So did you enjoy your wild Highlander?' Innes asked her a few moments later.

'I did not know it was expected that a lady should compliment a laird on his performance.'

'Contrary to what you seem to think, we men like to know that we've pleased.'

Ainsley chuckled. 'You definitely pleased, as you very well know.'

'I'm glad you think so,' Innes said with a teasing smile, 'for I most certainly agree. In fact, it was so delightful I think we might even try it again in a wee while.'

'I'm extremely sorry to intrude, but I could wait no longer, and your housekeeper told me she would not be the one to interrupt you, so— so here I am.'

Innes, clad only in his hastily donned plaid, sketched Felicity a bow. 'I'll leave you to it.'

Felicity handed the breakfast tray to Ainsley, flushing. 'Never fear, I will not keep her long. I came only to bid you good morning and good-bye.' As the door closed behind him, she turned towards Ainsley. 'Not quite true, of course. I came to make sure you made it through the night un-scathed. Did you?'

Ainsley, who had scrambled into the nightgown she had not worn last night, now pushed back the covers, blushing wildly, picking up her woollen wrapper from where it had fallen on the floor. 'You can see I did.'

Felicity put her hands on her hips. 'Well? Come on, I guessed after what you told me yesterday that it was your first time together.'

'You were right. *Again*. It was both fun and pleasurable. And that's all you're getting,' Ainsley said, sticking her nose in the air and trying to look smug. 'Is that coffee? Would you like some?'

'Yes, it is and no, I won't, thank you. That scary housekeeper of yours produced breakfast for everyone who was left up at the Great Hall hours ago. Eoin said it's true, her mother really was a witch.'

'Do you mean you were there all night?'

'Lots of people stayed. There's not been a ceilidh at the castle for years. Did you know that the old laird stopped holding the Hogmanay celebrations when—'

'The old laird! You've gone native, Felicity Blair. Was it Eoin who told you this, by chance?'

Felicity, to Ainsley's amazement, blushed. 'People used to look forward to the Hogmanay party for months,' she said. 'They're already wondering, after yesterday, whether Innes will be holding one.'

'And I'm wondering why you're avoiding answering my question.'

'Because I'm going back to Edinburgh today, and my life is complicated enough without adding a farmer who lives in the middle of nowhere into the mix,' Felicity said tartly. 'Sorry, Ains. Sorry.'

'What's wrong, Fliss?'

Her friend shook her head, blinking rapidly. 'Nothing. I am tired from all that dancing and too much whisky, probably, and I have to go and pack, for the steamer leaves Rothesay this afternoon and I can't afford to miss it.'

'But...'

'No. I'm fine.' Felicity spoke brusquely. 'Much more important, I can see that you are fine, so I can leave you without worrying too much. I've some more letters for Madame Hera. They're on the dressing table in my room at the castle. And I've got the ones you've written to take with me. I think that Madame Hera's latest venture is going to prove very popular. You are going to carry on with her, aren't you?'

'Of course I am,' Ainsley said. 'Why wouldn't

I? This— You know I'm only here temporarily. I'll be back in Edinburgh soon enough.'

'Or sooner, if you are unhappy. You promised, you remember?'

'Yes, but...' Ainsley stopped, on the verge of saying that she could not imagine being unhappy. She'd thought that before. 'I remember,' she said.

Felicity hugged her. 'I'd better go. Just be careful, Ainsley, your Mr Drummond is a charmer. Don't let him charm you too much. Take care of yourself, dearest. I'll write.'

A kiss on the cheek, a flutter of her hands, the fainter sound of her bidding farewell to Innes and she was gone.

'It's bad luck to frown on the morning after the Bonding,' Innes said, closing the bedroom door behind him. 'What has Miss Blair said to upset you?'

'Nothing.' Ainsley poured the coffee. 'I don't know where we're going to sit for breakfast. There are no chairs.'

'We'll take it in bed.' Innes placed the tray in the centre of the mattress, patting the place beside him.

'I wonder what possessed Mhairi to send up a tray? She never has before.'

'Second sight,' Innes said flippantly, handing her an oatcake. 'She knew today was a holiday.'

'I suppose that's part of the tradition, is it?'

Innes grinned. 'It is now.'

Ainsley looked down at the oatcake, which was spread with a generous layer of crowdie, just exactly as she liked it. She wondered if Innes would return to his own room tonight. She took a sip of coffee. It had always been John who decided whether or not to visit her. She had never once been in his bed. He had never once slept in hers. She took another sip of coffee. Not even in the earliest days of her marriage had John made love to her twice in one night. He'd never asked her what she wanted. Never seemed to imagine that she could want something more. It had never been fun, and there had been very little pleasure. This was different in every way.

'What are you smiling at?'

Ainsley's smile widened. 'You'd think, after last night, that we'd want to spend the day in bed. Sleeping,' she clarified hastily.

Innes refilled their coffee cups, and cut into a slice of ham. 'Tempting as it sounds, I have other plans.'

'You've tired of my charms already,' Ainsley said, through a mouthful of oatcake.

'I said I didn't want to spend the day in bed, I did not say that I didn't want to experience more of your charms.'

'The palace of pleasures. There's more, then?'

'Keep looking at me like that and I'll show you more right now.'

'No, thank you, I'm much more interested in my breakfast,' Ainsley said primly.

Innes leaned across the tray to lick a smear of crowdie from the corner of her mouth. 'Fibber,' he said.

She touched the tip of her tongue to his, then pushed him away. 'You are not irresistible, Innes Drummond.'

'No, I'm not.' He pulled the oatcake from her hand and put it back down on the tray. 'But you are,' he said.

Ainsley leaned back, tilting her face to the sky. It was a guileless blue today, with not even a trace of puffy cloud as yet, and the sun was high enough to have some real warmth in it. The boat scudded along, bumping over the white-crested waves. The breeze was just sufficient to fill the red sail, to flick spray on to her face, but not enough to chill her. 'It's perfect,' she said.

Innes took her hand and placed it on the tiller on top of his. 'You're supposed to be helping,' he said.

'I am.' She smiled at him lazily. 'By not interfering. Besides, I want to look at the view, it's so lovely.'

They had sailed south down the Kyles of Bute towards the Isle of Arran, whose craggy peaks were such a contrast to the gentle, greener Isle of Bute, before veering east, round the very tip of the peninsula on which Strone Bridge was built, to follow the coastline north. 'It's only about fifteen miles overland from the castle,' Innes told her, 'but there's just the drover's roads and sheep tracks to follow.'

'This is much nicer.' Innes was wearing a thick fisherman's jumper in navy blue that made his eyes seem the colour of the sea. With his tweed trews and heavy boots, his hair wildly tumbled and his jaw blue-black, for he had not shaved that morning, he looked very different from the man she had met all those weeks, months ago, at the lawyer's office in Edinburgh. 'Your London friends would not recognise you,' she said. 'You look like a native.'

'A wild Highlander.'

She smoothed her palm over the roughness of his stubble. 'Is this for me, then? Is this the day you drag me off to your lair and have your wicked way with me?'

'Wasn't last night enough?'

'Didn't you say this morning that there was more?'

Innes caught her hand and kissed it. His lips cold on her palm, then his mouth warm on each of her fingers. 'Are you going to prove insatiable?'

'Will that be a problem?'

Innes gave a shout of laughter. 'It's every man's dream. There's plenty more,' he said, releasing her and hauling at the tiller to straighten the dinghy, 'but unless you want us to end up on the rocks, maybe not just yet.'

Ainsley shuffled over on the narrow bench. 'Where are we going?'

'Wait and see. This is Ardlamont Bay. We are headed to the next one round. You can see now that we've not really come that far. If you look straight across, you'll get a glimpse of the castle's turrets.'

The breeze began to die down as they headed into St Ostell Bay. Directly across, the Isle of Arran lay like a sleeping lion, a bank of low, pinkish cloud that looked more like mist sitting behind it and giving it a mysterious air. In front of them stretched a crescent of beach, the sand turning from golden at the water's edge to silver where high dunes covered in rough grass formed the border. Behind, a dark forest made the bay feel completely secluded.

The waters were very shallow. Innes pulled off his boots and stockings and rolled his trews up before jumping in and hauling the boat by the prow. Seeing that the water lapped only as high as his knees, Ainsley, who was wearing a skirt made from the local tweed, pulled off her stockings and shoes and followed suit. The little boat rocked precariously as she jumped over the side, and she gasped with the cold, stumbling as her feet sank into the soft sand.

The tide was on the ebb. Leaving the boat at the water's edge, they made their way up the beach, Innes carrying the basket that he'd had Mhairi pack. There was not a trace of a breeze. The sun blazed down on them, giving the illusion of summer. The air was heady with salt and the scent of the pine trees. Shaking out her dripping skirts, Ainsley stopped to breathe it in, gazing around her with wonder. 'It's just beautiful.'

'I'm glad you like it.'

They deposited the hamper and their shoes in the shelter of a high dune before picking their way along the stretch of the sands. 'I like your Highland outfit,' Innes said. 'I'm not the only one who would be unrecognisable to their friends.'

Ainsley's skirt was cut short, the hem finishing at her calf, in the local style, which gave her considerably more freedom of movement. She wore only a thin petticoat beneath, not the layers that were required to give fullness to her usual gowns, and a simple blouse on top, with a plaid. 'It took me hours of practice to get this right,' she said. 'You see how it is folded to form these pockets? The local women have their knitting tucked into them. They can knit without even looking, have you noticed?'

'Are you planning on making me a jersey?'

'Good grief, no. I'll wager Mhairi knitted that one.'

'She did.' Innes caught her as she stumbled, and tucked her hand into his. They headed down to the shoreline where the sand was harder packed and easier to walk on, but he did not release her. The wavelets were icy on her toes. In the shallows, flounders rippled under the sand. Spoots, the long, thin razor clams, blew up giveaway bubbles. At the western tip of the beach, a river burbled into the sea. 'The Allt Osda,' Innes said. 'There's often otters here. I don't see any today.'

It was only then that she realised he must have come here as a boy. He talked about his childhood so rarely, it was easy to forget that he must have a host of memories attached to all these beautiful places, must have sailed around that coastline countless times. It was obvious, when she thought about it. The way he handled the boat. The fact that he'd navigated almost without looking. As they followed the river upstream on banks where the sand became dotted with shale, Ainsley puzzled over this. She still had no idea what haunted him, but she was certain something did.

The river narrowed before twisting onto higher ground. They crossed it, Innes holding her close as her feet slid on the weed-covered rocks, his own grip sure. It was odd, knowing him so well in some ways yet knowing so little of his past. Strange, for they had shared so much last night, yet she had no idea whatsoever right now of what he might be thinking, no idea of the memories he associated with this place, save they could not be bad. No, definitely not bad. He was distant but not defensive, simply lost in his thoughts.

It was a different ache, she felt. Not the sharp pang of feeling excluded, but something akin to nostalgia. Like pressing her nose against a toyshop as a child and seeing all the things she could not have. Silly. Fanciful. Wrong. It was not as if Innes had any more idea of what she was thinking after all. Nor cared. She caught herself short on that thought. Last night had been a revelation, but it was fun and pleasure, nothing more. Surprising as it was, this discovery that she could be so un-inhibited, that the body she had been so ashamed of could be the source of such delight, she would do well not to read anything more into it. She and Innes were, as luck would have it, extremely well matched physically. No, it was not luck. That connection had been evident right from the start. And that was all it was. She'd better remember that.

Innes left her to unpack the basket while he went into the forest in search of wood. The sun was so warm, and the dune in which they sat so sheltered, that Ainsley could see no need for a fire, but when she said so, he told her she would be glad of it when she had had her swim.

'You were teasing me,' she said later, watching him as he made a small pit in the sand and lined it with stones. 'The water is freezing.'

Innes began to kindle the sticks. 'That's why we need the fire.'

'I can't swim.'

'Do you want to learn?'

Ainsley looked at the sea. Turquoise-blue, and, she had to admit, extremely alluring, with the sun sparkling on the shallows, the little wavelets making a shushing noise. Then she remembered the shock of cold on her feet when they had first landed. 'No,' she said decisively. 'Perhaps another day, when it's warmer.'

Innes, feeding bigger sticks to the small flame, shook his head. 'It's nearly September, the end of the summer—it doesn't get much warmer, nor much colder, either.' He settled a larger piece of wood on the fire, before joining her on the blanket. 'We used to…'

The fire sparked. Innes put his arms around his knees, staring out at the sea. She waited for him to change the subject, as he always did when he stumbled on a memory, but he surprised her. 'Malcolm and I,' he said. 'We used to come here the first day of the New Year to swim. It was our own personal ritual, after the Hogmanay celebrations.'

'A cleansing?' Ainsley joked. 'Another form of a fresh start?'

'Aye, the Drummonds are fond of those, aren't they?' Innes said ruefully. 'Funnily enough, that's how my brother always put it. He was an awful one for dressing things up, but the truth is, a dip in water that cold is the best cure for a whisky head that I know.'

'Did you and your brother often have whisky heads, then?'

'Only on special occasions, and in truth, it was mostly me. My father believed that the laird should be able to drink everyone under the table. When he gave Malcolm his first dram, he made him drink the whole lot in one swallow. Malcolm was sick. He never could hold his drink, but he became very good at pouring it down his sleeve or over his shoulder, or on one occasion into a suit of armour.' Innes picked up a handful of soft sand, and watched as the grains trickled through his fingers. 'Since I was not obliged to prove my-self, I could drink until I was stotious.'

'Like I was, on the sherry?' Ainsley said, blushing faintly.

'You were endearing. I fear that I was simply obnoxious, which is why I take good care not to drink too much these days.' Innes wiped the last few grains of sand from his palm and pulled his jumper over his head. 'Right, it's now or never.'

'You're not really going to swim?'

'I am.' Innes pulled off his shirt and got to his feet. 'I take it you'll not be coming with me?'

'I think this is one ritual you had better perform on your own,' Ainsley said.

Innes paused in the act of unbuckling his belt. 'I think I've told you before that you see a deal too much,' he said. Before she could answer, he grinned and began to unfasten his trews. 'Now, if you don't turn your back, you're going to see a great deal more.'

Ainsley looked up, deliberately running the tip of her tongue over her lower lip. 'I think the view from here is going to prove even more attractive than the one out there,' she said, waving vaguely in the direction of Arran without taking her eyes from Innes.

'If you keep looking at me like that, the view will be considerably more defined than it is right now.'

She got to her feet, unable to resist flattening her palms over the hard breadth of his shoulders, down over his chest, grazing the hard nubs of his nipples. Innes's eyes were beginning to glaze. Her own breathing was becoming rapid. He did not move. She slid her hands lower, to cup him through his trews. She trailed her fingers up his satisfyingly hard shaft. 'I do believe you are my idea of perfect Highland scenery.'

Innes pulled her to him roughly. 'Did I tell you that you're a witch?'

She wanted him. He was more than ready. His mouth was inches away from hers. All she had to do was tilt her head. Ainsley laughed, that soft, guttural sound she knew he found arousing. 'I think I'll be perfectly satisfied just taking in the view,' she said, freeing herself.

She turned away, but Innes caught her and hauled her back. His smile looked like hers felt. Teasing. Aroused. 'I'll be cold when I come out of the water.'

'And wet,' she said.

'And wet,' he said softly.

His hand covered her breast. Even through her corset, she felt her nipple harden in response. She shuddered. 'I'll keep the fire going.'

Innes nipped her ear lobe. 'I hope so, though I suspect that I'll need a little help with my blood flow.'

Her own blood was positively pulsing. 'What did you have in mind?' Ainsley whispered.

'I am sure you'll think of something.' His lips found hers in the briefest of kisses. 'Unless you've changed your mind and decided to swim with me?'

It was tempting, but she forced herself to wriggle free. 'The best things come to those who wait, isn't that what they say?'

'I just hope it's worth it,' Innes said, laughing, pulling off the rest of his clothes.

He stood before her quite naked, and completely aroused. Ainsley watched him making his way down the beach, long legs, tight, muscled buttocks, and thought she had never seen such a wickedly tempting sight in her life. 'Innes,' she called, waiting for him to turn around. 'It already is.'

Innes began to run down the beach, forcing himself to continue as he hit the shallows, knowing that if he stopped, if he turned around, he would immediately turn back. The water was freezing. He'd forgotten. With the tide out, the shallows went on for ever. He'd forgotten that, too. It had been a joke between them, he and Malcolm, that you would reach Arran before it was deep enough to swim.

It was over his knees now, and up to his thighs. He slowed, took to wading, his feet sinking into the soft sand, the flounder scooting out from under him the merest ripple of sand. When a wave hit his groin, he gasped and looked ruefully down. It wasn't just a whisky head the water cured. He dipped his hands into the water, and splashed water over his arms, his shoulders, then caught himself as he dipped his head down to throw more over his face. Malcolm, who always dived straight under, used to laugh at him when he did this. Innes stood up, closing his eyes and lifting his face up to the sun. It didn't hurt here. It didn't hurt to think of him. The memories here were all good. Looking over his shoulder, he saw that Ainsley had followed him down the beach and was standing in the shadows, clutching the blanket. He gave her a mocking salute and dived in.

* * *

When he emerged, fifteen minutes later, she was still there, holding the blanket open. Innes was shivering, and embarrassed at the effect the icy water had had on him. Instinctively, his hand moved to cover himself, but she was watching him, and her watching him was far better for his condition than the cold skin of his own hand. He waded out slowly, pushing his hair out of his eyes, relishing the rays of the sun on his back, his skin tingling from the salt. He liked to look at women naked, and he liked them to look at him, but it had always been in the privacy of a bedchamber, and it had never been like this. Ainsley found the idea of him as some sort of savage Highlander arousing, and he found that he liked playing the part. He'd never done that before.

By the time he reached her, the effect of the cold was definitely wearing off. Ainsley handed him the blanket, which he wrapped around his shoulders. 'Well?' he asked.

'The scenery was most elevating,' she said, then blushed. 'I did not mean…'

Innes laughed. 'Not quite, but it will be.'

'I don't know how it is, but when I am with you I say the most shocking things.'

'Delightful is what I'd call them. Why is it, do you think?'

'I will not pander to your ego by telling you.'

They had reached the dune. Innes put some wood on the fire. 'That's a shame, because I rather like the idea of you pandering to me.'

'What particular kind of pandering do you have in mind?'

'You could heat me up.'

'It's only fair, I suppose, since you got so cold at my request.'

'I did.' He made a point of shivering, and tried to look soulful. 'You could rub me down with the blanket.'

She eyed him speculatively. 'I could certainly rub you down,' she said, pulling the blanket from his shoulders and shaking it out onto the sand, 'but I don't think we need the blanket. Lie down.'

He did as she asked, his body already stirring in anticipation. Ainsley slipped off her undergarments, then sat on top of him. She was warm and wet. His shaft thickened, eager to be inside her, but she slid away from him, spreading her skirts around them, just as he had spread his kilt over the pair of them last night. Then she touched him, her hands forming a cocoon around him, and slowly, gently, delightfully, began to stroke.

He bucked under her. She gripped him with her thighs. He closed his eyes, praying for control. It was agonising, her touch feathery, the slightest of friction, not enough but almost too much. He dug his hands into the sand. He dug his heels in, but it was unbearable. With a guttural cry and a surge of desire he would have thought impossible after the night's exertions, Innes rolled her over onto her back, imprisoning her wrists above her head. 'Please,' he said, in a voice he barely recognised, 'say that you are ready, because I don't want to wait.'

'Then don't,' she said.

He kissed her, plunging his tongue into her mouth and entering her at the same time in one long, deep thrust. She met him, pushing up underneath him, clenching hard around him. He thrust again. Her mouth was hot on his, her kisses wild. She struggled to release her arms. When he held her, she dug her heels into his behind. He thrust again, and she met him with equal force, and he felt her tense, the sudden stillness before the crash that made him contract and sent the blood rushing, and he thrust again, hard, and again, deeper, with her crying out and holding him and digging her heels in and urging him on, to pound deep, deep inside her, so that when she came, pulsing around him, it took every ounce of his resolution to pull away, spilling onto the sand, then falling down onto the blanket, gasping, slick with sweat, panting, pulling her on top of him, the frantic beat of her heart clashing with his.

Chapter Nine

Dear Madame Hera,

I have been married for eighteen months. I love my husband very much, and relations between us have always been most satisfactory, him being a perfect gentleman, if you understand my meaning. Indeed, I had no cause at all to complain, until that fateful tea party with my three closest friends several weeks ago. It was my birthday, and I must confess that along with tea, we did partake of some strong drink. Conversation turned to intimate matters. I was shocked to discover that my husband's method of ministering to my needs was considered by my friends to be downright old-fashioned. Imagine my astonishment when they revealed the variety of other ways—well, I will draw a veil over that.

But the problem was that I could not. Draw a veil, that is. For my curiosity was aroused. Alas! Would that I had been content with what I had. When my husband came to my arms as usual on the following Saturday night, I tried to instruct him in one of these variations. It is true, I did fortify myself with a glass or two of his special port beforehand, but I rather think it was my inadequate instructions that were to blame. With hindsight, it is clear that his failure was not a cause for merriment, and that perhaps it was a mistake, after he had expended so much energy, to expect him to renew his efforts in the traditional way.

Now no amount of reassurance will convince my husband to repeat the attempt, despite the fact that I have obtained more complete instructions from my friends. Worse still, my husband assumes my desire to introduce an element of diversity into the bedchamber is actually implied criticism of his previous efforts, and has accused me of having simulated satisfaction in the past. As a result, my Saturday evenings are utterly bereft of marital comfort. What should I do?

Mrs J-A

September, 1840

Ainsley finished reading the letter aloud and looked enquiringly at Innes, seated at his desk and frowning as usual over the account books. 'There, I told you I'd find something to distract you. What do you think she means when she said that her husband is a "perfect gentleman"? I'm assuming it is not that he gets to his feet when she enters a room.'

Innes pushed his papers away and came to join her on the large, overstuffed sofa that sat in front of the hearth. 'She means that he ensures she is satisfied before he allows himself to complete his own pleasure.'

'Oh.' Ainsley grimaced, scanning the letter again. 'I had no idea. I hate to think how many times Madame Hera has quite missed the point of some of her letters.'

'What proportion of her correspondence do these sorts of problems form?'

'That's a good point.' Ainsley brightened. 'It is only since Felicity launched our personal answering service that they have grown. What do you think Madame Hera should advise Mrs J-A? Her poor husband is most likely imagining himself wholly inadequate. She will have to do something to reassure him.'

'Not so long ago, Madame Hera would have been pretty certain that the problem lay with that poor husband.'

'Not so long ago, Madame Hera wouldn't have had an inkling as to what Mrs J-A meant by variety,' Ainsley said drily, 'and she would most certainly never have believed that it was acceptable for a woman to make actual requests. Though perhaps it is not, in general, acceptable at all. I have no idea how other men feel about it. Are you an exception?'

She looked expectantly at Innes, who laughed. 'I have no idea, but I doubt it.'

'I do feel it's a shame that so many women know so little about the variations, as Mrs J-A calls them.'

'Because variety really is the spice of life?'

He was teasing her. She felt the now-familiar tingle make itself known, but refused to be drawn. 'Because it seems wrong that only men do,' Ainsley said.

'Not *only* men, else…'

'You know what I mean, Innes. Lots of women think it is wrong to enjoy what is perfectly natural, and downright sinful to want to enjoy it any way other than what this woman calls traditional.'

'So we are conspiring to keep our wives ignorant, is that what you're saying? Because I'd like to point out to you that you're my wife, and I've been doing my very best, to the point of exhaustion, to enlighten you. In fact, if you would care to set that letter aside, I'd be happy to oblige you right now with a—what was it—variation?'

'Really?' Ainsley bit her lip, trying not to respond to that wicked smile of his. 'I thought you were exhausted?'

He pulled her stocking-clad foot onto his lap and began to caress her leg from ankle to knee. 'I'm also dedicated to providing Madame Hera with the raw material she needs to write the fullest of replies.'

'You have provided Madame Hera with enough material to fill a book.'

'Well, why don't you?'

She was somehow lying back on the sofa with both of her feet on his lap. Innes had found his way to the top of her stockings and the absurdly sensitive skin there. Stroking. How did he know that she liked that? 'Why don't I what?' Ainsley asked, distracted.

'Write a book.'

His fingers traced a smooth line from her knee to her thigh, stroking her through the linen of her pantaloons. Down, then up. Down. Then up. Then higher. Finding the opening in her undergarments. Her flesh. More stroking. 'What kind of book?'

Sliding inside her. Stroking. 'An instruction book.' Sliding. 'A guide to health and matrimonial well-being, or something along those lines,' Innes said. 'Didn't you mention to me once that you thought it would be a good idea? Madame could offer copies to her private correspondents. I'm sure your Miss Blair would be more than happy to advertise something of that sort discreetly in her magazine.'

'I'd quite forgotten that conversation. Do you really think such a book would sell?'

'You're the expert, what do you think?'

She seemed to have stopped thinking. He was still stroking her. And thrusting now, with his fingers. And she was already tensing around him. Was it faster, her response, because of the experience of these past few weeks? Or was she making up for years of deprivation? Perhaps she was a wanton? Could one be a wanton and not realise it? The stroking stopped. Innes slid onto the floor. She opened her eyes. 'What are you doing?'

'Making sure your instruction manual covers every eventuality,' he said, disappearing under her skirts.

When he licked her she cried out in surprise. Then his mouth possessed her in the most devastating way, and she moaned. Heat twisted inside her, and she began to tense, already teetering on the edge, as he licked and thrust and stroked. She gathered handfuls of her skirts between her fingers, clutching at her gown in an effort to hold on, but it was impossible. Such delight, such unbearable delight as he teased from her, that she tumbled over into her climax, shuddering, and shuddering again as he licked her into another wave, and another, until she cried out for him to stop because she really thought that the next wave would send her into oblivion.

'What is it in those account books that is causing you to sigh so much?' Several hours later, Ainsley was pouring their after-dinner coffee. The maid who helped out in the house had left, along with Mhairi, once dinner had been served, for the housekeeper preferred to sleep where she had always slept, in her quarters at the castle.

Innes stretched his feet out towards the fire and shook his head wearily. 'It doesn't matter.'

'It obviously does, else you would not have been sighing.'

'When it comes to sighing, I seem to recall there was someone else in this room doing their fair share earlier this evening. You didn't say whether you approved of that particular variation, now I come to think of it.'

'I thought it was obvious.'

'A man likes to know he's appreciated.'

'You are.'

'I'm looking forward to reading that particular chapter of your guidebook. I reckon it will tax even Madame Hera's newfound vocabulary to describe it.'

'So you were serious when you suggested that I write it?' Her smile was perfunctory.

Innes frowned. 'Why not? It makes perfect sense.'

'And it will give me something to do.'

Innes put his coffee cup down. 'Have you something on your mind?'

'It's been more than three weeks since the Rescinding. I don't have anything to do, yet every time I ask you how things are going with the lands, you find something else to distract me. I'm wondering if tonight's *variation*, as you call it, was simply a better tactic than telling me it was late, and that you were tired.'

'What's that supposed to mean?'

'Nothing.' She set down her cup. 'They are your lands,' she said, getting to her feet. 'You are the one who has set himself the task of making Strone Bridge better than it ever has been. You did not consult me before you made that decision. Why should I possibly imagine that you would think my opinion worthwhile now, when you obviously have no idea how to go about it?'

'Where on earth did that come from?'

'From being ignored! I have tried. I have tried several times now to remind you of the terms on which I agreed to come here, and you've ignored me.'

'But you have helped. The Home Farm. The Rescinding...'

'And I've entertained you, too, when you've found the real problems of this place overwhelming.'

'You're joking.'

He looked at her aghast, but she was too angry to care, and had bottled up her feelings for too long to hold them in. 'I don't know why I'm still here,' Ainsley said. 'I'm not serving any purpose, and I'm a long way from earning back that money you lent me.'

'Gave you.'

'It was supposed to be a fee. A professional fee. Unless you're thinking that it was the other sort of profession after all.'

'Ainsley, that's enough.' Innes caught her arm as she tried to brush past him. 'What has got into you? You can't honestly believe that I deliberately—what was it you said?—distract you by making love to you?'

Ainsley stared at him stonily.

'What?'

She shook her head. 'It doesn't matter.'

'Which means that it does,' Innes said wryly. 'You should put that in your book, you know, if you're including a section for husbands. Whenever your wife says it doesn't matter, you can be sure it's of dire importance.'

'I could write the same advice for wives.'

'I suppose I asked for that.' Innes held out his hand. 'Don't go, Ainsley.'

She hesitated, but she did not really want to run away, so she allowed him to pull her down on to the arm of his chair. 'I don't think it's deliberate,' she said, 'but when you don't want to talk about something, you—you distract yourself. With me, I mean.' She made a wry face. 'I am not complaining. I did not even notice it until tonight.'

'And you immediately decided that I was pulling the wool over your eyes. You should know me better.'

She flinched at the roughness in his voice. 'I do. That was not deliberate, either.'

Innes rested his head against the back of the chair, closing his eyes with a heavy sigh. 'You do know me, better than I know myself, it seems.'

He looked unutterably weary. Ainsley slid off the chair to stand behind him, put her hand on his temples. 'Do you have a headache?'

'I do, but I'm not going to risk another excuse,' he said with a shadow of a smile.

'Why won't you talk to me, Innes?'

'Because despite my resolve to be the saviour of Strone Bridge, I can't see how it's to be done. There's nothing to discuss, Ainsley, and I'm gutted. That's why I've not wanted to talk to you.'

She pushed him gently forward and began to

knead the knots in his shoulders. 'If the situation truly is irredeemable, you should turn your mind to something else more constructive, such as that pier of yours.'

'Now that Robert has started work on the foundations and we have most of the supplies in hand, that pier of mine needs little of my time.' Innes sighed. 'That's nice.'

Ainsley said nothing but continued to ease the tension in his shoulders, her fingers working deep into his muscles.

'It's different,' Innes said after a little while. 'The pier, the new road. I know what I'm doing with those. When things go wrong—as they no doubt will—I know how to put them right. You can't just pluck new tenant farmers out of thin air. You can't put heart back into the soil overnight. You can't make a soil fit only for oats and barley yield wheat or hops, and even if you could, you can't do anything about the rain or the cold. There's so much wrong, and every solution I think of causes another problem somewhere else. There isn't a solution, Ainsley. If the lands here were ever profitable, then it was a long time ago, and I will not clear the land just to turn a profit. I go round in circles with it all.'

'If it's any consolation, I do know how that feels,' Ainsley said drily. 'I also know from experience that bemoaning one's ignorance and endlessly reassuring oneself that it is both impossible and futile to act is not only fruitless but a self-fulfilling prophecy.'

'You are talking of your marriage.'

She gave his shoulders a final rub, then came round by the side of his chair to stand by the fire. 'Yes, I am. I was afraid to speak up because I thought it would make things worse. I was afraid to act because I thought it would make the situation irretrievable. So I said nothing and I did nothing and—and if John had not died, who knows what would have happened, but one thing is for certain, matters would not have miraculously cured themselves.'

'You're telling me that I'm dithering, and I'm making things worse.'

'I'd have put it a little more tactfully, but yes.'

'You're right,' he said with a sigh, 'I know you are.'

She settled in the chair opposite him. He was staring into the fire, avoiding her gaze. 'It is the not knowing,' he admitted. 'The ignorance. That's the hardest bit. I'm so accustomed to knowing every aspect of my own business, to being the man people turn to when there's a problem. As I said, if something went wrong with the pier, or the new road, I'd know what to do. Or I'd be certain of finding a solution. But here, when it comes to the essence of Strone Bridge, I'm—I'm ashamed. People ask me questions. They look to me for solutions. And I don't have answers. It's—it's— Dammit, Ainsley, I feel like a wee laddie sometimes and I hate it.'

'Did you imagine I would think less of you for admitting to all this?'

Innes rubbed his eyes. 'I think less of myself, truth be told. I don't know what to do, and I don't see how you can possibly help, for you don't know any more of the matter than I do. What's more, though the Rescinding bought me a deal of goodwill, in some ways it's made matters worse, for not only have I raised all sorts of expectations, I've had to write off a load of debt, and the poor, honest souls who have been paying their rent without fail are now resentful of the fact that defaulters have been let off the hook.'

'Oh. I hadn't thought of that.'

'Nor I. How could we have?'

Ainsley wrinkled her brow. 'I don't suppose you

could simply balance the books somehow by writing the other rents off in advance. But no, that wouldn't really balance the books, would it? It would simply mean that you were in more debt.'

'It's not the money that's the problem, but...' Innes sat forward. 'You mean I could give the tenants who are up to date a rent holiday to even matters up?'

'Do you think it would work?'

'It's worth a try. Have you any other genius ideas in that clever wee head of yours?'

Ainsley tried not to feel too pleased. 'It was hardly genius. In fact it was pretty obvious.'

'So obvious it didn't occur to me. Does that mean that you're a genius or that I'm an idiot? And be careful how you answer that, mind,' Innes said, grinning.

'Thank you,' Ainsley said with a prim smile. 'I will opt for genius.'

Waking with a start to the distinctive sound of the heavy front door closing, Ainsley found herself alone. Innes's pillow was cold. She lay for a while going over their conversation this evening. She wished she hadn't lost her temper, but on the other hand, if she had not, she doubted she'd have found the courage to say some of those things to him. She had hurt him, but she had forced him to listen. Then when he had, she had been lucid. She had been articulate. She had not backed down.

She sat up to shake out her pillow, which seemed to be most uncomfortable tonight. And her night-gown, too, seemed to be determined to wrap itself around her legs. She had put it on because it had been laid out at the bottom of the bed, as it was every night. Almost every morning, it ended up on the floor. Some nights, she never even got so far as to wear it.

She pummelled at her pillow again, turning it over to find a cool spot. Where was Innes? Was he angry with her? He hadn't seemed angry. He'd seemed defeated. He was a proud man. Self-made. Independent. All the things she admired about him were also the things that made him the kind of man who found failure impossible to take, and talking about failure even worse. And she had forced him into doing just that. Was he regretting it?

She padded over to the bedroom window, but it looked inland, and there was no sign of Innes, who had most likely headed down to the bay and the workings that would become the pier. Hoping he had more sense than to take a boat out, telling herself he was a grown man who could look after himself and was entitled to his privacy, Ainsley crawled back into bed and screwed her eyes tight.

But it was no good. In overcoming her own reticence, she couldn't help thinking she had forced him to confront a very harsh reality without having any real solutions to offer. Maybe there simply weren't any. She sat up, staring wide-eyed into the gloom of the bedchamber, thinking hard. They were neither of them very good at discussions. She was too busy looking for signs that she was being excluded to listen properly, and Innes was too determined not to discuss at all.

Pushing back the covers, Ainsley knelt upon the window seat, peering forlornly and pointlessly out at the empty landscape. Innes was so determined to solve every problem himself, and it wasn't just because that was what he was used to. He'd admitted it himself, this very night, how small this place made him feel. 'Like a wee laddie,' he'd said. He was ashamed, that was what lay at the root of his inability to ask for help, yet he had not a thing to be ashamed of. There had to be a way to save this place without causing further hardship. There had to be.

Ainsley grabbed what she thought were a pair of stockings. Only as she pulled them on, she saw that they were in fact a pair of the thick woollen ones, which Innes had started to wear with his trews. Though he dressed more formally for dinner, he almost always wore trews and a jumper for his forays out on to the estate these days. Tying her boots around the stockings, she decided that one of those heavy jumpers would provide her with much better insulation against the night air than her own cloak, and pulled it over her head. It smelled of fresh air, and somehow distinctively of Innes. The sleeves were far too long, but they'd keep her hands warm, and the garment came almost to her knees. Smiling fleetingly as she pictured Felicity's face should she ever see her in such an outfit, Ainsley quit the bedchamber and made her way outside.

She found Innes sitting down in the bay, watching the ebbing tide swirl and eddy around the huge timbers that were the beginnings of the new pier. 'I couldn't sleep,' Ainsley said, sitting down beside him on one of the thick planks that lay ready for use, and which had been brought on to the peninsula on an enormous barge that had caused a storm of interest in the village.

He put his arm around her and pulled her close. 'I'm sorry.'

'No, I am.' Tempting as it was to simply leave it at that and give herself over to the simple comfort of his arm on her shoulders, her cheek on his chest, Ainsley sat up. 'I do judge you, Innes. I am too much on the lookout for reasons to judge you to listen to what you're telling me sometimes. I'm sorry.'

'I forget,' he said softly. 'You seem so strong-willed, I forget that there was a time when you did not dare voice your opinions.' He pushed her hair back from her face. 'I know it's not my business. I know you want only to forget, but—did he hurt you, Ainsley?'

'No.' She shook her head vehemently. 'No. Not physically, if that's what you mean.'

'It's what I mean.'

'Then, no.'

'Thank heavens. Not that I mean to belittle...'

'It's fine. At least it was not, but it will be.' Ainsley gave a shaky laugh. The breeze caught the full skirts of her nightgown, lifting them up to expose her legs.

'Are those my stockings you're wearing?'

'I thought they were mine, and then when I put them on they were so warm, I didn't want to take them off.'

'I'm glad you didn't. I had no idea they could look so well. Nor my jumper, for that matter.'

'I must look a sight.'

'For sore eyes.' He leaned over to kiss her softly. 'I'm glad you're here. I know we didn't really quarrel, but it felt as though we were at odds, and I didn't like it.'

The sky was grey-blue, covered by a thin layer of cloud. The distant stars played peekaboo through the gaps, glinting rather than twinkling. The sea shushed quietly, the waves growing smaller as the tide receded. Ainsley leaned closer to Innes, shoulder to shoulder, thigh to thigh, staring out at the water. 'It wasn't that he lifted a hand to me, not once, but I was afraid of him. Partly it was his fault, but partly it was my own. I told you that it was the debts,' she said, 'but it wasn't just that. When you feel worthless, it's difficult to have a say in other things, even when they concern you.'

'Why would you feel worthless?'

She hadn't planned this at all but it seemed right, somehow, to match Innes's vulnerability by exposing her own. 'The obvious reason,' Ainsley whispered. 'I could not give him what he married me for.'

'You mean a child?'

She nodded, forgetting he could not see her. 'Yes.' She was glad of the dark. Such an old story, such an old pain, she had thought it long healed, but it seemed it was not. She could blame her tears on the wind, so she let them fall silently, biting her lip.

His arm hovered at her back. She could feel him, trying to decide whether to pull her closer or let her alone. She was relieved when he let it fall, let her wrap her own arms around herself, hug his jumper to her.

'Ainsley, forgive me, but I know from how you were with me at first. I know that things between you and—and him— They could not have been conducive to your conceiving.'

He did not ever say John's name, she noticed. He did not call him her husband. He was being absurdly delicate. If they had been discussing one of Madame Hera's letters, he would have been much more forthright. If she had been one of Madame Hera's correspondents, how much more of the truth would she have told? Ainsley shuddered.

'When we were first married,' she said, 'things were—were normal between us.' As normal as they were for many of the women who wrote to her, though she was not as fortunate as Mrs J-A, for John's idea of traditional ministering took no account of her pleasure. For some reason, it was important that Innes know this. 'Not as it is between us. He was not a—a *gentleman* in the sense you explained.'

'No,' Innes said gently.

So he had guessed that much, too. Ainsley tried to work out what it was she wanted to tell him. Not all. The memory of Donald McIntosh's curse made it impossible to say it all, for though he had not actually cursed *her*, she felt as though he had. And though she knew it did not really diminish her, her flawed state, still she felt as though it did, and she couldn't bear to reveal herself in that way to Innes.

Ainsley felt for his hand, seeking comfort and strength. 'He was not a cruel man, not really, though some of the things he said and did felt cruel,' she said. 'It was when I first discovered the debts. That's when he accused me of failing him. Until then, I had thought—told myself—hoped— that it was just a matter of time. Then, later, when our relationship deteriorated, he could not— He could not perform.'

It was not easy, but she had the words now; she understood so much more about herself now, and about men, since meeting Innes. 'He blamed me. The worse things got between us— He said I unmanned him, you see. But I knew I had not because I saw him. Alone. I saw he could be aroused, only not by me.'

'I remember now. You asked me about it, whether it was the wife's fault.'

'Yes. Don't be angry. He's dead. If he was not dead I wouldn't be here.'

She felt his reluctant laugh. 'Then I won't be angry, for I'm very glad you're here,' Innes said.

'Are you?'

She turned, trying to read his face in the darkness. It was impossible, but there was no need. He kissed her softly on the mouth. 'I thought it was obvious,' he said, borrowing her own words from earlier.

'We're neither of us very good at seeing that, are we?'

'Not very.' Innes touched her cheek, his fingers tracing a curve to her ear, her jaw, her throat. 'It's true, what you said earlier. There are times when I want to lose myself in you, to forget all the things I can't resolve, but it's you I want.'

'Truly?'

'You must not doubt it. You're thinking that it's another way of doing the same thing, my wanting you, his not. That the end result is you're left out in the cold?'

'Yes. I hadn't— Not until tonight.'

Innes kissed her again. 'Never, ever doubt that I want you for one reason, and one only. Whatever it is between us has been there from the start. I have never met a woman who brings me more pleasure than you.'

'If you carry on kissing me, this thing, as you call it, will be between us again, and I'm trying to be serious.' Ainsley sat up reluctantly, pushing her tangle of hair from her eyes. 'I did not love John. I thought I did, but I did not. I thought he gave me no option but to ignore his—our—problems, but the truth is, I was relieved to be told they were none of my business, and when our marital relations broke down, I was relieved about that, too. What's more, what I've learned from being with you, Innes, has made me realise it wasn't just John who could not perform. I'm afraid my performance was pretty appalling, too. Partly it was because I didn't know any better. Partly it was because I didn't want to know. It was a mess I couldn't fix because there was simply no solution.'

'You can't possibly be sorry that he died.'

'That's what Felicity said. I would never have wished him dead, but I don't wish I was still married to him. You see what I mean?'

'I'm not sure.'

Ainsley laughed drily. 'I know, I've told this in a very convoluted way. I couldn't give John a child, Innes.'

'You don't know that. It may not have been your fault. The chances are...'

Nil, was the answer. 'Slim,' Ainsley said, because she could not say it. 'It's not my fault, but it feels as if it is. Do you see now?'

'You mean my lands.'

'You could not help the fact that you were raised without any knowledge of them. You did not know what your father was doing—or not doing—in your absence.'

'My elected absence. Regardless of who is to blame, they are in a mess.'

'No, you blame yourself for the problem and for failing to fix it.'

'I'm not accustomed to failing.'

Ainsley laughed. 'Then we must make sure that you do not, but I don't think the solution lies with making your lands more fertile. What we need to do is think differently.'

'We?'

'Yes, we,' she said confidently. 'Between your stubbornness and my as-yet-untested objectivity, we shall come up with something. We have to. But right now it's very late, and it's getting very cold. We'll catch a chill if we sit here much longer, and you need to try to get a wee bit of sleep at least.'

Ainsley got resolutely to her feet, but Innes stood in front of her, blocking her path. 'I'm not stubborn.'

'You could have taken one look at the mess of this place and turned around back to your own life, but you have not. You've invested a lot more than money in the future of this place. What would you call that, if not stubborn?'

'Determined? Pig ignorant?' He pulled her into his arms, laughing. 'Have it your way. How do you fancy taking a stubborn man to your bed? Because fetching as you look in that rig-out, what I really want is to take it off you, to lie naked in bed with you.' He kissed her. 'Beside me.' He kissed her again. 'Under me.' And again. 'Or on

top of me.' And again, this time more deeply, his
hands on her bottom through the thin layer of her
nightgown, pulling her up against the unmistak-
able ridge of his erection. 'You see, this is me consulting you. Over, under, beside—the choice,' he
said, 'is yours.'

Chapter Ten

Dear Adventurous Wife,
I must tell you, and other readers of this column, how very refreshing it is to hear of a marriage that is still so happy and so fulfilled after twenty-two years. Instead of being ashamed of your continuing physical desires, you should celebrate them. I applaud your wish to explore new territory, as you call it. No matter how enthralling a favourite, well-thumbed book might be, no matter how satisfying the conclusion, it is human nature to wish to read other volumes, provided that you are prepared to find some of them less—shall we say enthralling? Their conclusions perhaps even less satisfying. What matters, Adventurous Wife, is the journey rather than the destination.

Ainsley laid down her pen, smiling to herself as she remembered some of the journeys she and Innes had taken in the past few weeks. The destination had never been anything other than satisfying, but Madame Hera was a cautious soul, and Ainsley was inclined to think Innes rather more talented than most husbands. Not that she would dream of boasting, though she had indeed, during one particular *adventure* involving a feather and the silk sash from his dressing gown, informed him that he had the cleverest mouth of any man in the world. But that had been under extreme circumstances, and he had returned the compliment when she had employed the same combination of mouth, feather and silken tie on him. She picked up her pen again.

Certain everyday items can, with a little imagination, be employed as secondary aids. Think of these articles as theatrical props. Provided that proper consideration is given as to texture and, it goes without saying, hygiene, and provided, naturally, that both adventurers are content with the selection, then

I think you will find that your journey will be much enhanced.

I wish you *bon voyage*!

Ainsley signed Madame Hera's name with a flourish just as Mhairi entered the room. 'Excellent timing,' she said to the housekeeper. 'I've been wanting to have a word with you while Innes is out. He's with Eoin, so he's bound to be away most of the morning. Do you have a moment for a cup of tea?'

Mhairi smiled. 'I was just about to ask you the same thing. I've the tray ready. It's a lovely day, and we won't get many of those come October, so I thought you might fancy taking it outside.'

'Perfect.' Ainsley tucked Madame Hera's correspondence into the leather portfolio and followed Mhairi on to the terrace that looked out over the bay. The view was not nearly so spectacular as that from the castle terrace, but it was still lovely.

'I could never tire of this,' Ainsley said, taking a seat at the little wooden table.

'It's been a fair summer,' Mhairi said, 'better than the past few.'

'I hope a good omen for Innes's first summer as laird,' Ainsley said, pouring the tea and helping herself to one of Mhairi's scones, still hot from the griddle.

'Better still if the weather holds for the tattie howking in a few weeks, and better yet if there's more than tatties to bring in, for the land is not the only thing being ploughed, if you take my meaning.' Mhairi smiled primly. 'It would be nice if that husband of yours could see some fruits from all his labours.'

'Oh.' Flushing, Ainsley put down the scone, which suddenly tasted of sawdust. 'I see.' She tried for a smile, but her mouth merely wobbled.

Mhairi leaned across the table and patted her hand consolingly. 'It's early days, but it's well-known that the Drummond men carry potent seed.'

Ainsley took a sip of her tea, pleased to see that her hand was perfectly steady, studying the housekeeper over the rim of the cup. Mhairi spoke so matter-of-factly, though her words were shockingly blunt. 'But the old laird had only the two children,' she said.

'Two boys was considered more than enough. 'Tis easy enough to limit your litter if you don't service the sow.' Mhairi buttered herself a scone. 'I've shocked you.'

Unable to think of a polite lie, Ainsley opted for the truth. 'You have.'

'You must not be thinking I hold a grudge against Marjorie Caldwell. Poor soul, she was affianced to the laird when she was in her cradle. She can't have been more than seventeen when she married him and, knowing him as I did, I doubt he made any pretence of affection, not even in the early days. It was all about the getting of sons, that marriage, and once he'd got them—well, she'd served her purpose.'

'Innes said as much,' Ainsley said, frowning over the memory, 'but I thought his views highly coloured.'

'No, Himself has always seen the way things are here clearly enough. The laird thought the sun shone out of Malcolm's behind, as they say. Innes was only ever the spare, just as I was. The difference between us being that I stuck to the role he gave me and your husband went his own road.'

Mhairi stared off into the distance, her scone untouched on her plate. The insistent pounding of mallets on wood told them that the tide was low. The skeleton of the pier emerging beside the old one made the bay look as if it was growing a mouth of new teeth.

Mhairi stirred another cube of sugar into her tea, seemingly forgetting that she'd already put two in, and took a long drink. 'I loved that man, but that does not mean I was blind to his faults, and he had a good many. What my brother, Dodds, said at the Rescinding was true. I was fit to warm the laird's bed, but that was all. He never pretended more, I'll give him that. That annuity, the farm he made over to me, it was his way of making it right. Payment for services rendered,' she concluded grimly.

'But you loved him all the same.'

Mhairi nodded sadly. 'I'd have done anything for him, and he knew it. Until the Rescinding, I thought myself at peace with the one sacrifice I made, but now the laird is dead and buried, and I am too old and it's far too late, I resent it.'

Her fingers were clenched so tightly around the empty china cup that Ainsley feared it might break. Gently, she disentangled them and poured them both fresh tea. Though the late-September sun beat down, hot enough to have chased all the chickens into the cool of the henhouse, she shivered. 'A child,' she said gently, for it was the only explanation. 'That was what you sacrificed.'

Mhairi nodded. 'He would not have stood me

bearing his bairn. Of course, the laird being the laird, it did not occur to him to have a care where he planted his seed. If it took root, that was my problem. He made that clear enough, so I made sure it never took root. I do not practise as my mother did, but I knew enough to do that.'

'The fey wife?' Ainsley's head was reeling. 'Do you mean your mother really could cast spells?'

Mhairi shrugged, but her face was anxious. 'She was a natural healer. Her potions were mostly herbs, but she did have other powers. The curse that Dodds made— Mrs Drummond, I have to tell you it's been on my mind.'

'That the bloodline would fail,' Ainsley said faintly.

'I made sure to bear no child. The old laird's only other child died fourteen years ago. There is only Innes, Mrs Drummond. You will think me daft to believe in such things, but I know how powerful my mother's gift was. You must forgive me for talking about such personal matters, but I can't tell you the good it does me, knowing that the pair of you are so—so enthusiastic about your vows, shall we say. And I was hoping—as I said, I know you'll think it's daft, worrying about a silly curse—but still, I was hoping you could maybe reassure me that we'll be hearing some good news soon. About the harvest I was talking about?'

Ainsley slopped her tea, and felt her face burn dull red. Mhairi was looking at her with an odd mixture of anticipation and concern. She believed in that curse, and as things stood she would be right to. Making a fuss of wiping up her tea with a napkin, Ainsley tried to compose herself. 'Silly me,' she said. 'I'm not usually so clumsy.'

'I've upset you.'

'No.' She smiled brightly. 'Not at all. Why would you— I was merely— Well, it is a rather embarrassing topic of conversation. Though I suppose it is perfectly natural that people are wondering...' She placed the soiled napkin on top of her half-eaten scone. 'Are people wondering? Is an heir really so important?'

Mhairi looked as if she had asked if the land needed rain. 'The estate has been passed from father to son directly for as long as anyone can remember.'

Innes had told her so, back in Edinburgh when they first met. He hadn't cared then, but he had not been to Strone Bridge then, and he had no notion of truly claiming his inheritance. It was different now. She thought back to the pain in his voice a few nights ago, when he had finally admitted how much it meant to him, and how desperately he wanted to make his mark on the place. It would not be long before he realised an heir was a vital element of his restitution.

Ainsley smiled brightly at Mhairi. 'As you said, it is early days.'

Mhairi was not fooled. 'Is there a problem?' she asked sharply. 'Because if there is a problem, I can help.'

Ainsley's poor attempt at a smile faded. 'What do you mean?'

'Just as there are ways to prevent, so there are ways to encourage.'

'Magic?'

'Helping nature, my mother always called it.'

A gust of longing filled her before she could catch it. It was like a punch in the guts, so strong she all but doubled over from it. Impossible not to wonder what difference such a spell would have made all those years ago. A spell! She gave herself a mental shake. She had the word of medical science, and no spell would counteract that. 'If nature needs assistance, it is not natural,' Ainsley said, pleased at how firm she sounded. Magic, white or black, real or imagined, formed no part of her life. She got to her feet and began to stack the tea things on the tray.

The next day Innes left early with Eoin for Rothesay, and then on to Glasgow where they had various meetings with paddle-steamer companies. Though she started missing him the moment he set out, Ainsley was relieved to have some time to spend alone.

She headed out of the Home Farm in the direction of the castle. Sunshine dappled down through the leaves of rowan and oak that bordered the path here. The bracken was high, almost to her waist and already beginning to turn brown, exuding that distinctive smell, a mixture of damp earth and old leather. Autumn was settling in. The sense of time ticking too fast was making her anxious. Though Innes had said nothing of her returning to Edinburgh, Ainsley had a horrible feeling that very soon she would have no option.

Peering down to the bay from her favourite spot on the castle's terrace, she could see Robert Alexander standing with a cluster of men, consulting their plans. The new road would be cut into the cliff. Innes was investigating the possibility of using a steam engine to help with the work. Since that night in the bay, they had spent a great deal of time together poring over maps and account books. She now fully understood his despair.

Crofting was still the tradition here, with each farmer producing enough to meet his own small needs, keeping a few cattle and sheep on the common grounds, and fishing to supplement his family's diet. The crofts were simply too small to grow more, and far too small to meet the huge demands from the growing metropolis of Glasgow, it seemed. The new road, the new pier, the paddle steamers that could berth there, would solve the transport problems, but the crofters of Strone Bridge simply could not produce enough to benefit from these markets. Eoin was encouraging Innes to merge some of the farms, but while many of them had been lying fallow, their former tenants having fled to Canada and America, hardly any of those lands lay together. Innes's farms were dotted about the landscape like patchwork, each a different size and shape. Innes was determined not to take the route that so many of the Highland landlords had done, which was to oust his tenants by fair means of foul, and to turn the lands over to sheep.

Despite the melancholy subject matter, Ainsley had revelled in these hours spent together. It wasn't only that she felt useful, that her opinion was valued, that Innes truly listened to what she said. She had felt included. And there was the problem. She was not part of this place, and never could be, but with every day that passed, that was exactly what she wanted. To belong here. To remain here. With Innes. She was close to letting Strone Bridge into her heart, and even closer, frighteningly close, to allowing her husband in, too.

She could love him. She could very easily love him, but it would be disastrous to allow herself to do so. Gazing out over the Kyles of Bute, watching the dark-grey clouds gather over the Isle of Arran, cloaking it from view, Ainsley forced herself to list all the reasons why it was impossible.

For a start, she was not the stuff that a laird's wife was made of. Not a trace of blue blood. Neither money nor property—quite the contrary. No connections. The Drummonds married for the name and the lands, and Ainsley contributed no good to either. She could not weave or spin or even knit. She knew nothing of animal husbandry, or keeping a house larger than the Home Farm. What she knew of the Drummond traditions Mhairi had taught her. In fact, Mhairi was far better qualified than she was for the role. No one could tell a tale of the castle's history and ghosts the way Mhairi did.

Then there was the fact that Innes didn't actually want a wife. It would be easy to persuade herself he'd changed his mind. He'd managed to overcome his precious need to be the one and only person in control of his life in so many ways. He even confided in her without prompting sometimes, and he made her feel that Madame Hera was every bit as important a venture as Strone Bridge. He had changed, and he had changed her. She was more confident. She was more ambitious. She no longer doubted her femininity, and she knew the satisfaction of pleasure and pleasing. She was cured of John for ever, but the role that had cured her was temporary. She was not a wife. A business partner. A lover. But not a wife. Innes did not want a wife, and Innes would never love her as a wife. She did not think that the mystery woman who had stolen his heart kept it still, but she was fairly certain he would not let it go again. But he would take a real wife because he would realise, very soon, that his commitment to Strone Bridge required him to produce an heir.

Which brought her to the biggest stumbling block of all. The one thing she could not give him. Swallowing the lump that rose in her throat, Ainsley decided to follow the path round to the chapel. It was cool here, in the little copse of trees and rhododendrons. She sat on the moss-covered bench in the lee of the chapel, idly watching a small brown bird wrestling with a large brown worm. She smiled to herself, remembering the woman at the Rescinding who had begged for-giveness for having her husband's dog buried be-side him. His grave must be hereabouts. What was the name? Emerson, that was it. But as she crossed the path to start peering at the gravestones, Ains-ley was distracted by the Drummond Celtic cross.

She read the old laird's name thoughtfully, and then his lady's inscription, too. Marjorie Mary Caldwell had been only twenty-six when she died, and if what Mhairi had said was true, she couldn't have had a very happy life. Caldwell. She remembered now—that was the name of the family who owned the lands that bordered Strone Bridge, somewhere north of here. Innes's near-est gentry neighbours. The ones he'd not wanted invited to the Rescinding, though they must be some sort of relation of his.

The atmosphere in the graveyard was only adding to her melancholy. It was very clear that she had no future here, but she did want to leave a legacy. Furrowing her brow, Ainsley made her way back to the castle. The Great Hall still smelled faintly of whisky fumes and ash. Though it was not yet October, Mhairi was already asking if the traditional Hogmanay party would be held here. It was a room made for great occasions. Parties. Banquets. Ceilidhs. Wedding feasts.

Would their marriage be annulled? Would Innes divorce her? She was fairly certain that the law, which was written by men and for men, would perceive her infertility as ample reason for either. Then some other woman with property and the right pedigree would benefit from the changes in Innes that had cost Ainsley so much. He would not love her, his real wife, but he would respect her, and he would confide in her, make love to her, rely on her to play the role of the laird's lady. And she would give him the son he didn't yet know he needed.

Ainsley dug her knuckles deep into her eyes. No point in crying. In the long drawing room, she gazed out of the French windows at her view. It was a pity more people could not share it, and fall in love with it. Excursionists from the paddle steamers that would be able to dock here within months. They could take tea here in the drawing room. Smiling, she remembered joking about that very thing the day Innes had decided to build the pier. Excursionists who would pay for Mhairi to show them round the castle and tell her ghost stories. Who would buy the local tweed, or the local heather ale.

She stood stock-still. Would they pay to spend the night here? Pay extra to spend the night in one of the haunted bedchambers? Her heart began to race. Innes had told her that the railway between Glasgow and Greenock was due to open next year. He had shares. The journey would be much easier than it was now, a quicker, cheaper escape from the smoke of the city to the delights of the country. There would be more excursionists able to afford the trip, perhaps wanting to take a holiday rather than merely come for the day. And there would be richer people, too, who would be willing to pay a premium to hire the castle for a family occasion. To marry in the chapel and hold their wedding feast in the Great Hall.

She hesitated, remembering the scorn Innes had poured on the idea when she had first, jokingly, suggested it. Ridiculous, he had called it. But that had been weeks ago, before he had decided to stay here. Before the success of the Rescinding, here in this very hall. He must have changed his mind about the castle by now. Certainly he had not suggested knocking it down again. And there would be jobs. The lands would provide enough produce to feed the visitors.

It could work. She just might have been right after all, when she'd said to Innes that they would have to think differently. Strone Bridge Castle Hotel. Ainsley's stomach fluttered with excitement. This would be her legacy.

Innes was gone ten days, during which Ainsley worked on her plan for the castle, determined to surprise him and equally determined not to dwell on the growing sense she had that her time on Strone Bridge was ticking inexorably to a close. He arrived with the morning tide, tired but immensely pleased to see her. Watching his tall, achingly familiar figure stride along the old pier towards her, she forgot all her resolutions and threw herself into his arms.

He held her tightly, burying his face in her hair, exchanging barely a word with Robert Alexander, telling the surveyor brusquely that he had business to attend to before rushing Ainsley back to the Home Farm, leaving old Angus and Eoin to take the cart and deal with the luggage.

They arrived breathless, and headed straight for their bedchamber. 'I feel like I've been gone an age,' Innes said, locking the door firmly behind him. 'I missed you.'

'Did you?' She felt as if she couldn't get enough of looking at him, and stood in the middle of the room, simply drinking him in.

'I missed having breakfast with you,' Innes said, putting his arm around her, steering her towards the bed.

Her heart was beating from the effort of climbing the hill, from the effort of trying not to let him see how very much she had missed him, and from anticipation, too. 'I'm sure you and Eoin had plenty to talk about,' Ainsley said.

Innes smiled. 'We did, but when Eoin smiles at me over his porridge, it doesn't make me want to kiss him.'

'I expect the feeling is entirely mutual,' Ainsley teased.

'Did you miss me?' Innes kissed each corner of her mouth.

'A little.' She kissed him back, her words a whisper on his ear.

'Just a little?' He kissed her again, more fully this time, running his fingers down her body, brushing the side of her breast, her waist, to rest his hand on her thigh.

She shivered. 'Maybe a wee bit more than a little,' she said, imitating his action, her hand stroking down his shoulder, under his coat to his chest, his waist, his thigh. He was hard already, his arousal jutting up through his trousers. She slid her hand up his thigh to curl lightly around him. 'I can see you missed me a good bit more than a little,' she said.

Innes reached under her skirts to cup her sex. 'Do you want to know how much more?' he asked.

He had a finger inside her. She contracted around him. 'Yes,' she said. He started to stroke her. 'Oh, Innes, yes.'

They lost control then. She pulled him roughly to her, her mouth claiming his. He kissed her urgently. Their passion spiralled, focused on the overwhelming, desperate need to be joined. She had to have him inside her. He had to be inside her. There was no finesse to it. Speed, necessity, drove them. Innes struggled out of his trousers enough to free himself. He rolled onto the bed, taking her with him, lifting her to straddle him, her knees on either side of him. She sank onto him, taking him in so high, so quickly, that they both cried out.

Their kisses grew wild. She clung to his shoulders, then braced herself using the headboard, arching back as she drew him in, as he thrust higher, harder, furiously, until the deep-rooted shiver that preceded her climax took her, and he came, too, pulsing, shaking them both to the core, making them forget, in the utter satisfaction of it, that he was still inside her, clinging to her, holding her there, with his arms, with his mouth, though she needed no holding, clinging, too, her harsh breath mingling with is, his heart beating against hers.

She had not planned it, but the connection, having him deep inside her as he came, had been momentous.

A true joining.

A true mistake.

Her body had betrayed her. Ainsley felt as if her world was shattering. She loved him. And even as she felt the truth of it settle itself inside her, she saw his face. Innes looked appalled.

'I'm sorry. Ainsley, I'm sorry. I don't know what— I didn't mean— I'm sorry.'

She shook her head, not quite meeting his eyes as she lifted herself free of him. 'It doesn't matter.' Though it did. It had changed everything.

Innes could not have made his feelings any clearer, but he seemed to want to try. 'It does matter,' he said, hurriedly adjusting his clothing. 'You asked me— I promised I would always be careful. I don't know why I...'

'It wasn't your fault. It was mine.' She would not cry in front of him, but she needed him gone. She gave him what she hoped was a reassuring smile. 'I told you, there is almost certainly nothing to worry about.' He was staring at her, horrified. 'It was simply— We were incautious because we had grown accustomed to more regular release,' Ainsley said, cringing at the words even as she spoke them.

She rolled off the bed. She couldn't look at him now. 'There are a hundred letters waiting for you, and Robert will be wishing to talk to you. Go on downstairs, I will rejoin you shortly.'

Ainsley held open the door, giving him no option but to leave her. Dazed, Innes did as she bade him and made his way downstairs to the sitting room. He sat at the desk, staring at the neat piles of correspondence, feeling as if he'd been punched in the gut.

He cursed long and hard, then poured himself a glass of malt. What had happened? He swallowed the dram in one. It burned fire down his throat and hit his belly too fast. He coughed, then poured himself another. *I'm sorry*, he'd said, but he had not been. That was the worst thing. It had felt so good, spilling himself inside her. He hadn't thought of the consequences. He hadn't been thinking of anything at all, save for his need to be with her. In all honesty, he couldn't have cared less about the consequences. But Ainsley had. Her face. *Stricken*, that was the word. She'd tried to cover it up, but he was not fooled.

Innes finished his second glass of whisky, feeling as if he'd just been given a death sentence. All he'd been able to think about these past few days was coming home to Strone Bridge and to Ainsley.

Home. Ainsley. The two words had somehow become connected, and as if determined to make sure his mind made the connection, too, his body had made it impossible for him to ignore. Which left him where, exactly?

He swore again, bitterly. Terrified and confused as hell, was where it left him. He could no longer trust himself, and Ainsley would no longer trust him. Things had changed fundamentally, yet some things would never change. He still carried the burden of the past with him. Whatever he felt for Ainsley, he had no right to let it flourish.

This was a warning, a very timely one. The truth would see to the outcome. He felt sick at the thought of it, but he didn't doubt it was the right thing to do. The only thing. He cared enough to want her to understand, which was a lot more than he'd ever cared for any woman since that first one. He cared too much. Far too much.

Checking the clock on the mantel, Innes saw that half an hour had elapsed. With a heavy heart but with his mind resolute, he set out to find her.

Ainsley was seated in front of the mirror, staring at her reflection as if it was another person entirely. She loved him. Did she really love him? How could she be so foolish as to have allowed herself to fall in love with him? Had she forgotten how miserable she'd been, married to John?

No. She had not loved John. Innes was not John. This marriage was not at all like her first. 'Because it is not real,' she hissed at her reflection. 'Not real, Ainsley, and you have to remember that. This is not your life, it's a part you're playing, and that is all, so there is no point in hoping or wishing or dreaming that it will continue.'

Yet for a blissful few moments, that was exactly what she allowed herself to do. She was in love, and for those few moments, that was all that mattered. For those few moments, she allowed herself to believe that love would conquer all the barriers she had so painstakingly examined and deemed immovable. She was so overwhelmed with love, surely anything was possible. She loved Innes so much, he could not fail to love her back. They could not fail to have a future together, because the idea of a future without him was incomprehensible.

The knock on the door made her jump. Innes looked as if he was carrying the weight of the world on his shoulders. 'We need to talk,' he said, and not even her newly discovered love could persuade Ainsley that the words were anything other than ominous.

Fleetingly, she considered pretending that nothing momentous had happened, but looking at the expression on Innes's face, she just as quickly dismissed the notion. Feeling quite as sick now as he looked, Ainsley got to her feet and followed him out of the door.

To her surprise, he led them outside, along the path towards the castle. At the terrace they paused automatically to drink in the view. 'I went through to Edinburgh when I was away,' Innes told her. 'There were matters to tie up with the lawyers. I was going to call on Miss Blair. I know you'd have wanted me to let her know that you were well, but—you'll never believe this.'

'What?'

'Eoin,' Innes said, shaking his head. 'I wondered why he insisted on coming through to Edinburgh with me when the man never wants to leave Strone Bridge. It turns out that he and your Miss Blair have been corresponding, if you please. He went off to take tea with her and made it very clear I was not wanted. He was away most of the day, what's more, and not a word could I get out of him after, save that he was to pass her love on to you. What do you make of that?'

'I don't know what to make of it at all. I had no

idea—she certainly has not mentioned this correspondence to me.'

'Do you think they'll make a match of it?'

'Oh, no.' Ainsley shook her head adamantly. 'That will never happen.'

'You seem very sure. I thought you'd be pleased. You would have been neighbours.'

'Innes, I will not be...'

'No, don't say it,' he said hurriedly.

'You don't know what I was about to say.'

'I do. I do, Ainsley.' His smile was tinged with sadness. 'Poor Eoin. But I didn't bring you here to talk about Eoin. I can see you're bursting to talk, but let me speak first. Then perhaps I will have spared you the need.'

Chapter Eleven

Ainsley had assumed they were going to the chapel, but when they got there Innes left the well-trodden path to push through a gap in the high rhododendron bushes in the nook forming the elbow of the graveyard, which she had not noticed before. The grass here was high, the path narrow, forcing them to walk single file. It led through the tunnel of the overgrown shrubs, emerging on a remote part of the cliff top looking not over the bay where the pier was being constructed, but over the far end of the Kyles, and the northern tip of the Isle of Bute.

'That's Loch Riddon you can see,' Innes said, putting his arm around her shoulder, 'and over there in the distance is Loch Striven.'

'It's lovely.'

'It was Malcolm's favourite view.' Innes took

her hand, leading her to the farthest edge of the path. Here, the grass was fresh mown around a small mound, on top of which was a cross. A Celtic cross, a miniature of the Drummond one. And on it, one name. 'My brother,' Innes said.

Ainsley stared at the birthdate recorded on the stone in consternation. 'He was your twin! Oh, Innes, I had no idea.'

He was frowning deeply. She could see his throat working, his fingers clenching and un-clenching as he stared down at the stone. She was not sure if he was going to punch the stone or break down in front of it. She was afraid to touch him, and aching to. 'It's a very beautiful spot,' Ainsley said rather desperately.

'Aye. And it was his favourite view, but all the same he would not have chosen to spend eter-nity here. Malcolm...' Innes swallowed compul-sively. 'I've said before, Malcolm— It wasn't just that he was raised to be the heir, Ainsley, he lived and breathed this place. The traditions meant as much to him as they did to my father. He would have wanted to be buried with the rest of them. Except they would not let that happen. No matter how much I tried to persuade them, they would not allow it.'

'Why not?' Ainsley asked, though she had a horrible premonition as to the answer.

'Consecrated ground,' Innes said. 'My brother killed himself.'

Shock kept her silent for long moments. Then came a wrenching pain as she tried to imagine the agonies Innes must have suffered. Must still be suffering. 'No wonder you left,' she said, the first coherent thought she had. Tears came then, though she tried to stop them, feeling she had no right, but his face, so pale, so stiff, the tension in the muscles of his throat, working and working for control were too much for her. 'Oh, Innes, I am so, so sorry.'

Seeking only to comfort, wordless, distraught, she wrapped her arms around his waist. He stood rigid for a moment, then his arms enfolded her. 'I'm sorry,' Ainsley said, over and over, rocking her body against him, and he held her, saying nothing, but holding on to her, his chest heaving, his hands clasping tighter and tighter around her waist, as if he was trying to hold himself together.

Gradually, his breathing calmed. Her tears dried. His hand relaxed its hold on her shoulder. 'I had no idea,' Ainsley said, scrubbing at her tear-stained cheeks.

'Why should you?' Innes replied gruffly. 'I made sure not to tell you anything. While I was away from here, I could pretend it had not happened.'

'That's why you never came back?'

'One of the reasons.' He heaved a deep sigh, tracing the inscription on the cross, before turning away. 'Come, there's a rock over there that makes a fairly comfortable seat. It's time you knew the whole of it.' He touched her cheek, then dipped his head to kiss her. A fleeting kiss, tinged with sadness. 'After this morning, we both know we can't carry on as we have been.'

She knew, but only when he said it did she realise that she still had not accepted it. She'd hoped. Despite all, she had hoped. Sitting down beside him on the huge chair-shaped boulder, her heart sank. Whatever Innes was about to tell her would destroy that hope for ever.

Innes was staring out at the sea, where the turning tide was making ripples on the summer blue of the surface. 'You know how things were with me here, when I was growing up,' he said. 'I can't remember a time when I didn't want to leave, but to leave without my father's permission would undoubtedly have caused a breach between myself and my twin. It would be an exile for me, unless I returned under the whip, and one that Malcolm would feel obliged to uphold. You must remember, in those days, my father was not so old. An enforced separation from my twin for years, maybe even decades, was not something I wanted to have to deal with.'

'And yet you left,' Ainsley said.

'I had planned to wait until after I came into an inheritance from my mother. I had persuaded myself that it would make a difference, my having independent means, that my father would not see it as a flaunting of his authority. As it turned out, I didn't have to put it to the test. Events— events took over.'

Ainsley's hand sought his. She braced herself.

'There was a woman,' Innes said.

He was still staring out to sea, his eyes almost the exact colour of the waters below. She loved him so much. A sigh escaped her, and he turned that beloved face towards her.

'You guessed?' he asked.

She stared at him blankly, her mind still trying to come to terms with what her heart had been trying to tell her for days now. Weeks? How long had she loved him?

'I suppose it was obvious,' Innes said. 'My being so dead-set against marriage—I always wondered what you made of that.'

'I thought...' What? What! She gazed at him, such longing in her heart, letting it flood her for just a moment. Just a moment. She loved him so much.

'Ainsley? You thought...' Innes prompted.

He must not guess she loved him, that was what she thought. Because if he guessed, he would send her away immediately, and she needed a few more weeks. Just a few more. 'I thought there must have been,' she said. 'A woman. I thought that's what it must have been.'

'Well, you were right.'

She waited, trying not to show what she was feeling. Was she looking at him differently? Innes was staring out to sea again, his throat working. Whatever was coming next, he was struggling with it. She didn't want to hear him talking about another woman, but he obviously needed to tell her. Ainsley ruthlessly thrust her own storm of feelings to one side. 'Go on,' she said. 'There was a woman. And of course she was lovely.'

'She was. She was very lovely.'

She hadn't meant him to agree with her. Now, perversely, she wanted to twist the knife, as if knowing how very different she was from his one true love would stop her loving him. 'No doubt she was graced with a fortune, too,' Ainsley said.

'She was rich. An orphan and an only child, she was brought to live at Glen Vadie when she was just a bairn.'

'Glen Vadie. That is the Caldwell estate?'

Innes nodded. 'Aye, she was a distant relative of my mother's. We grew up together.'

It was beginning to sound horribly like a fairy story, though without the happy ending, Ainsley thought. She already hated this rich, charming, well-born, beautiful woman.

Innes heaved a sigh. 'I'm sorry, I'm not being very articulate. The truth is, I can hardly bear to think of it, for even after all this time I'm ashamed, and I don't know what you'll think of me.'

'Innes, I could never think ill of you.'

He shifted uncomfortably on the stone and then got to his feet. 'Ainsley, you will.' His expression was deeply troubled, his eyes stormy. 'I could let you go without telling you. I considered it, but I did not want this all to end on a lie.'

'End?' He had said it. She had known he was going to say it, but she wished he had not.

'It was always going to end, Ainsley. We both knew that. It was what we agreed. You made it very clear you did not want anything else.'

Felled. Could a person be felled? She was felled. 'And you?'

She hadn't meant it to sound like a question. She couldn't bear the way he answered her with such finality. 'And me, too,' Innes said gently. 'Your being here, it was only meant to be for a wee while, to help me decide what to do with the place.'

'But you haven't decided,' Ainsley said, unable to disguise the desperation in her voice. She was clutching at straws, she knew that, and knew, too, that it was pointless, but she couldn't help herself.

'I've decided that I'm going to stay,' Innes said. 'Besides, you know that's not the point.' He was flushed, but his mouth set firm, and when he spoke, though the words were said softly enough, the tone was resolute. 'This morning I realised how much I have come to care for you, Ainsley. It's not only that it breaks the terms of our agreement that makes my feelings for you wrong, nor that I know you don't *want* the complication of any feelings at all, it's that I can't. It has to stop before either of us gets in too deep, for I will not allow myself to love you, Ainsley. I won't.'

It hurt even more than she'd expected. She bit her lip hard, dug her nails into her palms, telling herself that she was glad he had not guessed her own feelings.

'You'll think me arrogant,' he said, 'telling you I won't love you when you have no thought in your head of loving me.' He sat down beside her again and took her hand, which she quickly unfurled from its fist. 'This morning, we both got carried away. I could see from the look on your face afterwards that it—it shocked you as much as me. I don't know what it is between us, maybe it's spending so much time together that's…I don't know, intensified it, made it seem more than it is?' He shrugged. 'I do know that we neither of us want it, though. I do know that if I wasn't telling you that it's over, you'd be saying it to me, wouldn't you?'

She ached to tell him just how far off the mark he had been in his interpretation of her reaction, but she was not so foolish. It was not pride that stopped her telling him how wrong he was, but love. Heartsick, she could only nod.

'Aye.' Innes nodded slowly. 'I thought about letting you go without telling you, but I couldn't. I want you to know, you see, not only because I owe it to you but because I—I can't afford to allow myself to hope. This morning was like a glimpse of heaven and glimpse of hell at the same time.' He stopped, running a shaky hand through his hair, and drew her a very ragged smile. 'That's why I brought you here. To remind me why it can't go any further, and by showing you the worst of me, I'll be making sure that even if I kept on wanting what I am not entitled to, I could never have it.'

As he looked over his shoulder at the cross, beneath which lay his brother's mortal remains, goosebumps made Ainsley shudder. Her heart was clinging to Innes's confession of how much he had come to care for her, wanting to believe it would be enough to turn the situation around, to persuade him that he could care more. Hope, that treacherous thing she could not seem to extinguish, blew this tiny flame to determined life. All she had to do was tell him that she loved him. That was all it would take.

But her head was having none of this. Innes did not want her love. Innes *would not* love. Innes did not feel entitled to love. It was a strange word to use, but as he turned back to her, his face bleak, the question died on her lips.

'Her name was Blanche,' he said.

It was, as Ainsley anticipated, horribly like a fairy tale. Blanche, Malcolm and Innes, like brothers and sister at first, until Blanche changed, seemingly overnight, blossoming into a beauty. The brothers no longer felt at all filial towards her. Desire, lust, and with it competition, had entered into their Garden of Eden.

'But Blanche preferred you?' Ainsley said, because of course she would, and who would not?

Innes looked genuinely puzzled. 'How did you guess?' Fortunately, he did not wait for an answer. 'We tried to ignore it,' he said. 'How pathetic that sounds.'

'You were very young.'

'Old enough to know better.'

'But if you were old enough—and you and she— If you were in love, then why— I don't understand what the problem was.'

'The problem,' Innes said grimly, 'was that Blanche was betrothed to my brother.'

Ainsley put her hand to her mouth, caught Innes watching and made a conscious effort to wipe the shock from her face. 'But you were twins. Surely if Malcolm knew how you felt…'

'He did not. We made sure he did not. At least, I thought we did,' Innes told her, his mouth curled with disgust. 'Besides, you're forgetting that this is Strone Bridge. My father and Caldwell of Glen Vadie had signed the betrothal papers. A younger son would be no substitute for the heir.'

'But if Blanche was in love with you…'

'But Malcolm was in love with Blanche. And since Malcolm was my twin, I persuaded myself that I would be doing the honourable thing in giving her up, then I set about persuading Blanche that marrying Malcolm would not be so very different to marrying me. She and I enacted a most touching little scene, worthy of Shakespeare.' Innes's voice dripped sarcasm. 'The lovers renouncing each other. There were tears and kisses aplenty, though needless to say, there were more kisses than tears.'

He couldn't look at her. His hands were dug deep in his pockets as he stood before her, gazing over her shoulder at the cross on the grassy mound. 'Blanche refused to go along with it at first, but I was determined. Carried away with my own sense of honour, I thought I was,' Innes continued in a voice that poured scorn on his own youthful self. 'I pushed her. I was determined, and Blanche was in the end a pliant and a dutiful wee thing, so she agreed, and the betrothal was formalised at a party in the Great Hall. I thought myself heartbroken, needless to say, but I told myself that I'd done the right thing by my brother and I told myself that what she felt— Well, I told myself that I knew best and she'd come to realise it. I told myself a lot of things, all of them utter drivel. I was that sure I was right, it didn't even occur to me to ask what anyone else thought. What a fool I was.'

Ainsley made a sound of protest. Innes shook his head. 'No, I really was, and arrogant with it. If you give me a minute, I'm nearly done. I just need a minute.'

He took a deep breath, then another, obviously steeling himself. Ainsley had no option but to wait, feeling quite sick at what he told her, and at what the telling of it was doing to him.

With a little nod, as if in answer to some internal dialogue, Innes continued brusquely, 'Blanche wrote to Malcolm. It hadn't occurred to me that she'd do that, that she'd want to try to explain herself—and me, too, in the process. She had the

letter delivered after she'd fled. She had relatives
in London. They were happy to take her and her
fortune, I assume. I don't know. She ran, and Malcolm got her letter, and when he showed it to me, I
am ashamed to say what I felt was anger. I'd done
my best to make all right, and she'd thwarted me.
I didn't think of her feelings or even his at first,
only mine.'

Innes was speaking quickly now, the words
tumbling out, as if they'd been packed deep inside him all these years. 'So I was angry with her.
I think I even went so far as to tell Malcolm I'd
get her back for him, persuade her to marry him.
The arrogance of me! It was that word I used,
persuade, that betrayed me. Malcolm had suspected of course, but he had not been sure. "What
do you mean, persuade her?" he asked me, and
you should have seen the look on his face. Even
now I can picture it. "How could you persuade
her? Why should you?" I felt sick. Then, when the
accusations finally came, I tried to lie to him, but
we could never lie to each other, Malcolm and I,
I should have remembered that from the first. So
finally I told him, trying to sound as noble as I
thought I'd been, only in the face of it, seeing his
face, seeing his hopes, his dreams, crushed—for

he had loved her truly, you see. Unlike me. He really had loved Blanche. "I'd have given her up," he told me. "I only ever wanted her to be happy. How could you think I would marry her, knowing that she wanted you?"'

Ainsley sat as still as stone, her attention riveted on Innes, but he kept his eyes on the cross. His voice was cold now, as stripped of emotion, as his face was stripped of colour. Listening to him, she felt chilled.

'I told him it all,' he was saying, 'and Malcolm—Malcolm got quieter and quieter. When I asked him if he forgave me, he said there was nothing to forgive, but that he wanted to be left alone, and I was so racked with guilt that I wanted nothing more than to leave him. Then he said that I should go after her. That I should make her happy. He said again that all he ever wanted was for us to be happy, and then he closed the door on me, and—and those were the last words he ever spoke to me.'

Ainsley was lost for words, but Innes was not finished tearing himself apart. 'So you see,' he said, with a painful crack in his voice, finally meeting her eyes, 'my brother took his own life, but it was me who killed him. And now I have his lands, too,' he said with a bitter laugh. 'I have all of it, and I deserve none of it.'

'You do not have Blanche,' Ainsley whispered. 'You gave her up, though you loved her.' It was dreadful, but that was the thing that hurt the most.

'Don't go thinking there was anything noble about that,' Innes said with a sneer, 'because there was not. I didn't love her. That's why it was so easy to try to hand her back to Malcolm like an unwanted parcel, only I was so carried away with my own lofty gesture that I didn't notice that until later.' He rubbed his knuckles into his eyes, looking deeply weary. 'When it came down to it, what I really wanted was to give my brother a reason to side with me against our father. If Malcolm was beholden to me for the love of his life, then he'd take my part, he'd help force my father to let me leave Strone Bridge on my terms. Do you see, Ainsley?' Innes said earnestly, clasping her hands in his. 'I was selfish at every step of the way. It cost my brother his life. I owe it to Malcolm to restore the heritage I deprived him of. I can atone here for what I've done, but I don't deserve to be happy. This morning, I caught a glimpse of what that might be like. A timely reminder of what I deprived my brother of. I don't deserve it, but you do. Do you understand now, why I told you?'

Sadly, Ainsley understood only too well. He thought to drive her away. He thought to disgust her. She felt only unutterably sad, for his tragic confession changed everything and nothing. 'I understand that I can't make you happy,' she said, 'but if what you intended was to make me despise you, then you have failed. You were all so very young.'

'That is no excuse.'

His tone made it clear he would not be swayed. Only a few months ago, Ainsley would have accepted this. 'It is,' she said. 'We all make mistakes through lack of experience. If I had loved John as much as I thought I did, perhaps he would not have died.'

'That's ridiculous. You know—'

'I know *now* how much my own lack of confidence contributed to the—the deterioration of our marriage, but I did not know then,' Ainsley said heatedly. 'I know *now*, thanks to your encouragement, that I'm neither useless nor unattractive.'

'Ainsley, he did that to you—'

'No,' she interrupted him determinedly. 'I am not saying John was without fault, but nor was he entirely to blame. We were a—a fatal combination, but, Innes, how were we to know that?' She clutched tightly at his fingers, pulling him towards her. 'I have learned so much since I came here. I still feel guilty, and I still have regrets, but I am no longer eaten up with them. John is dead, and there's nothing I can do about it, save make sure I don't make the same mistakes again. You can do the same. Would not Malcolm want you to be happy?'

He held her gaze for a long moment, then flung her away, getting to his feet. 'That's not the point. I understand that you're trying to make me feel better, but you can't. You don't understand.'

'I do.' She got slowly to her feet, feeling quite leaden. 'You have made up your mind that I must go, and that is the one thing upon which we agree. I ask only that you allow me to remain here until I can— There are some things that I…'

'Of course. Obviously we must wait to ensure that there were no consequences from this morning.'

It took her a moment to understand his meaning, and when she did, another moment to control the tears that welled suddenly into her eyes. Ainsley turned towards the sea, hoping to blame the breeze. 'A few weeks,' she said, thinking that would suffice to both torture her and accustom her.

'The end of the year,' Innes said. 'An ending and a beginning.'

She whirled round, thinking for an awful moment that he was making fun of her, but his expression was as bleak as she felt. The thought that he was finding this almost as difficult as she was, however, was no comfort at all. 'Until the end of the year,' she agreed.

They made their way back past the chapel in silence, each wrapped up in their own tortuous thoughts. It was not until they reached the terrace again, and both stopped of their own accord, that Ainsley remembered her plans for the castle, but immediately abandoned any notion of sharing them with Innes right now. Instead, she asked one of the two unanswered questions. 'What about Blanche? What happened to her?'

Innes stared at her blankly. 'I have no idea.' Did he care too little or too much? It seemed impossible that he should not know, for the Glen Vadie estate was less than twenty miles from here. 'She never returned to Scotland,' he added, presumably in response to her sceptical look.

'Don't you want to know if she's happy?'

Innes shrugged dismissively. 'I never sought her out, and she has never, to my knowledge, tried to get in touch with me for the same reason. Guilt,' he clarified. 'She will not wish to be reminded of those times any more than I do, and I have done enough damage, without dragging it all up for her. I know you think that's hard, Ainsley, but it's best left alone.'

'You are very sure of that,' she said.

'Yes. That's not arrogance. I've had fourteen years to make sure.' He pushed his hair back from his face and smiled very wearily. 'You do understand, Ainsley, this is how it has to be? I won't—I won't— I will sleep in my own bedchamber from now on.'

'Yes,' she whispered.

He took a step towards her, then stopped. 'I must go and speak to Robert. Don't wait dinner for me.'

He turned away, but she caught his arm. 'Innes, I— Thank you for telling me. I won't— I promise I won't make it difficult for you.'

He enveloped her in a fierce hug. 'I never thought you would. I only want— I'm sorry.'

She watched him go, hurtling down the scar in

the cliff that would be the new road, allowing the tears to run down her cheeks now that he could no longer see her. She stood for a long time, staring out at the Kyles of Bute, her mind numb, her heart aching. Then she scrubbed at her eyes with her sleeve and drew a shaky breath. Innes had done so much to help free her from the burden of her past. She had until the end of the year to do what she could to return the favour. Which meant she had better make haste if she was going to track down Blanche Caldwell.

Chapter Twelve

Dear 'Anna',

Your letter touched my heart. The love you feel for this man shines like a beacon from the page. I do not doubt that, as you say, you have in him found your soul mate. It therefore pains me all the more to tell you that I can see no way for you to have a future with him that could be anything other than troubled. Were you a woman of fewer principles, if you loved this man less, then I would gladly tell you what you so desperately want to hear, that love can triumph over all. But, my dear, this can only happen when that love is equally given and received, and sadly, in your case, it is not. This widower, you have made clear, loves his three children before all else, and these children have made their unequivocal opposition to his proposed marriage to you abundantly clear over a prolonged period. You have done all you can to win them round. Their opposition has increased rather than decreased over time, and now encompasses their dead mother's family, too. Frankly, if this man loved you as much as you love him, he would have made a stand by now. He will never put you first. The rights and wrongs of this make no difference, 'Anna', because you love him too much to endanger his happiness, and if you truly believed that this was with you at the potential cost of his relationship with his children, you would have acted accordingly. That you have turned to me for advice tells its own story, don't you think?

It is therefore with profound regret that I am forced to advise you this: you must leave him, for he will never let you go, but nor will he marry you while the situation remains as it is. I hope you will take strength from doing what is right for you. I pray, as I am sure all our readers will, too, that you will find the future happiness that you deserve.

With my very best wishes,

Madame Hera

Ainsley put down her pen and dabbed at her cheeks with her handkerchief. This was one letter that she would not show to Innes. It was now the beginning of December. Having bared his soul, he had retreated like a wounded animal, making it clear that he wanted neither comfort nor further discussion on the subject of Blanche and Malcolm. Or the date of Ainsley's departure from Strone Bridge, set for the first week in January.

She had been through the wringer of emotions, from shock to horror, from pity to compassion, sorrow and sadness, jealousy, anger, dejection, but she had not once doubted, since that day at Malcolm's graveside, that she must leave. Reading over Madame Hera's advice to 'Anna', Ainsley was confronted with how fundamentally her own feelings had changed in the face of Innes's determination not to allow himself to be reconciled to his past. She had not given up hope of contacting Blanche to help with this, but having had no response to her letter, and with only a few weeks left till the end of the year when she must leave Strone Bridge, Ainsley was not optimistic.

In one sense, it made no difference. Like 'Anna', she had found her soul mate, but unlike 'Anna', Ainsley could now see very clearly that her soul mate was not free to love her as she deserved to be loved, and also unlike 'Anna', Ainsley had grown to believe that she would settle for nothing less. It was strange and surprising, too, how much less important her inability to bear children had become. It grieved her deeply, but in a sense, she had been forced to acknowledge, she had been hiding behind it, pretending to herself that it was this that prevented her from declaring her love, telling herself that she was making a noble sacrifice in removing herself from Innes's life when in fact she must have known that it would have made no difference. He would not love her. He would not allow himself to love her. And Ainsley, having experienced second best, was not about to accept it again.

Lying wide awake and aching with longing at night, she could not decide which was worse: knowing that Innes wanted her so much, or knowing that he did not want her enough. She loved him, but in her time here she had come to love the person she had become, too. She knew he still wanted her, she no longer questioned her own desirability, but she would not use it to push them both into temporarily satisfying a passion that would ultimately make it harder for her to leave.

She longed more than anything to force Innes
to see his past more clearly, but she could not,
and the woman who could do so remained in-
communicado. So Ainsley concentrated on the
one thing she could do to help, her plans for the
castle, which today she had decided were finally
in an advanced enough state for her to share with
Innes. Putting Madame Hera's correspondence
to one side, she hurried to her room to check her
toilette. Her dress was of taffeta, printed in autumn colours. The bodice was fitted tightly to her
waist, and came to a deep point. The fashionable
oval neckline was trimmed with shirring of the
same material, and the long sleeves, like the bodice, ended in a sharp point.

Though it was early December, the sun had a
hint of unseasonable warmth as she made her way
to the pier in search of Innes. He was in his shirt-
sleeves. He had lost weight since coming to Strone
Bridge. Days spent in the fields and out here in the
bay had sculpted his muscles. He would smell of
sweat and the sea and the peaty air, and of himself. There was a spot, just where his ribs met,
where she liked to rest her cheek and listen to

his heartbeat and where she always imagined she could breathe in the essence of him.

'Ainsley? Did you want me?'

'Yes.' Too late, she heard the longing in her voice. It was no consolation to see it reflected momentarily in his eyes, too. 'I mean, I was hoping to speak to you,' she amended hastily. 'I have something I'd like to discuss with you.' Innes nodded, pulling his heavy fisherman's jumper over his shirt. 'I thought we could go up to the castle,' she said when he looked at her expectantly. 'That way we won't be interrupted.'

The climb back up helped calm her flutter of nerves. She had worked so hard on her plans, but though she had been sure that it would be a pleasant surprise for Innes, it occurred to her belatedly that she had, by keeping her work a secret, contradicted her own hard-won wish to be consulted.

She opened the heavy front door with her keys and led the way through to the Great Hall. 'Do you remember,' she asked nervously, 'that I said the solution to Strone Bridge's economy would prove to be something other than modernising the crofts? In fact, you came up with the idea yourself, that first day you showed me round this place.'

Innes shook his head, frowning in puzzlement. 'I'm not sure I'm following you.'

'Napier did it a few years ago—the Loch Eck tour,' Ainsley said. 'I've been reading about it. He built the pier for the steamer and arranged the onward connections to places of interest. Do you not remember joking about it—a tea room, a gift shop for the tweed?'

'Vaguely, but I'm not sure…'

'And you told me yourself that the railway will run all the way from Glasgow to Greenock soon, so that there will be any number of people able to make the trip.'

'Excursionists. Is that what you're talking about?'

'More than that.' Ainsley smiled, excitement taking over from her nerves as she led him over to the table where she had laid everything out so carefully. 'Welcome to Strone Bridge Castle Hotel,' she said with a flourish.

Innes stared down at the plans, the drawings she and Mr Alexander had pulled together, the sketch she herself had made of the railway poster. He picked up the draft of the guidebook, leafing through it, and then the pages of costings she had so painstakingly worked on. 'You did all this?' he asked.

'I should have told you,' she said. 'I know I ought to have consulted you, but I wanted to surprise you.'

'You have.' He wandered round the table, picking up papers and putting them down again, the frown deepening on his face. 'Do you really believe people will pay to stay here?'

'Innes, I can't imagine anyone *not* wanting to spend the night here. I know you hate the place, but it's a real castle, for goodness' sake, with real turrets, and all these huge big rooms, and lots of pomp and splendour, and the views and— Yes, I really do think there would be any number of people willing to spend the night here. Or several. As you can see, I've even considered the possibility of leasing it out for weddings and the like. You can charge different prices, depending on which of the bedchambers people occupy, and more for the ones with ghosts in them.'

He was staring down at the railway poster. She had no idea what he was thinking. 'I thought that Mhairi would be the perfect candidate to run the place,' Ainsley continued. 'I thought it was the sort of restitution that would appeal to you, to have her installed as a chatelaine here.'

Now he did smile, albeit fleetingly. 'You were right about that. My father would be furious.'

'More important, there isn't anyone who could do a better job,' Ainsley rushed on. 'And there will be employment for any number of people here. Staff for the hotel, groundsmen. There's room for about forty or fifty guests at least, I'd say. And then there will be the food that can be provided direct from the crofts, and the tweed to sell, and— and it will mean that people don't have to emigrate to find a new life, Innes.' She laced her hands together tightly. 'What do you think?'

'I don't know.' He ran his hand through his hair. 'I can't believe you've done all this yourself.'

'Not myself. Robert has been helping, though I've sworn him to secrecy, for I did not want anyone else to know before you.' Still, Innes gave her no clue as to what he was thinking. 'You're worried it still won't be enough,' Ainsley rushed on. 'I wondered that myself, and also I was thinking that even fifty well-paying guests would not turn enough profit to justify the renovations for several years—you can see the rough figures—very rough, I'm no expert. So I thought— Well, actually it would be better if I showed you.'

'Showed me what?'

She led them through the Great Hall out into the atrium and produced the key that opened the hidden door. 'Wait till you see. I've got it all thought out, I…'

'Where are you going?' Innes stopped dead in front of the doorway.

'The tower. The view is magnificent, and it is easier to show you what I'm proposing from there.'

'You've been up there?' He had his hands dug deep into his pockets. 'I told you not to go up there.'

He looked angry. 'It's perfectly safe, if that's what you're worried about,' Ainsley said. 'I had Mr Alexander look at it, and he said that it was structurally sound. I had him look over all of the castle, and in fact he said…'

'I'm not interested in Robert's opinion. I thought I'd made it very clear that this tower was off limits.'

'No, you didn't. You said the key was lost, and that it was unsafe, and since neither have proved to be the case—' She broke off, at a loss to understand his reaction. 'It's the cottages,' she said. 'The tied cottages that have been empty for several years. I was thinking we could renovate them and let them out to families who cannot afford to holiday in the hotel, and who—'

'Enough!'

Ainsley flinched at the fury in his voice. 'What is wrong?'

'I told you,' Innes roared. 'I said to you not to go up there.'

'You didn't. You're being quite unreasonable. You said…'

'Did you not ask yourself why the place was locked? For God's sake, did not Mhairi say anything?'

'Mhairi doesn't know anything of what I'm doing. No one does, save Mr Alexander. I— It was meant to be a surprise. Is it because I didn't tell you, Innes? Is that what's wrong?'

He gazed at her for a long moment, his eyes dark, his lips thinned. 'My brother died by throwing himself from that tower, that's what's wrong, and that's why all your plans must come to nothing.'

Innes turned the key in the lock of the hidden door, then detached it from the rest of the bunch and pocketed it. 'I'm sorry for all the hard work you've put into this, but you've wasted your time,' he said curtly before turning on his heel and walking away without a backward glance.

Chapter Thirteen

Innes did not return to the Home Farm until late that night, and he was gone for the rest of the next day. It was late and Ainsley had been lying wide awake for several hours, torn between fretting and anger, when she heard his footsteps in the corridor. They did not stop outside his room, but carried on to hers. She scrambled up in bed as the door was flung open. 'You couldn't leave it, could you?'

'I don't know what you mean.'

'This!' He strode over to the bed, waving a piece of paper at her. 'Don't pretend it wasn't your doing, for she mentions you herself, and even if she had not, I recognise some of your handiwork—or should I say Madame Hera's! "Take the opportunity to put the past to rest." That's one of yours,' Innes quoted, his voice heavy with sarcasm, 'and then there's "free to make a fresh start." One thing hasn't changed. Blanche's letters leave no room for misinterpretation.'

'Blanche?' Ainsley repeated. 'You mean Blanche wrote to you?'

'At your behest.'

'Yes, but— No, I thought she would write to me, but—Innes, what does she say?'

'That fourteen years is enough time to realise that love should conquer all and it's time we surrendered to the happiness Malcolm sacrificed himself to give us,' he said mockingly. 'Wouldn't your Madame Hera just love it if she did? Isn't that exactly what you hoped for when you interfered?'

His words were like whiplashes, deliberately and painfully cruel. The old Ainsley would have been intimidated, frightened, silent. The new Ainsley was hurt, but also furious. 'I hoped that you'd take the opportunity to at least listen to whatever she had to say,' she said through clenched teeth. 'What you call interfering was actually done through a genuine concern for your happiness, which, contrary to what you believe, I think you deserve. I hoped that you would credit me with actually caring about you, Innes, enough to risk meddling. Obviously I was wrong, and you are for reasons known only to yourself absolutely set on making the rest of your life as miserable as you can, though why you think that will make any sort of restitution when... Och, what the hell does it matter now what I thought! If you won't listen to Blanche, why would I think you'd listen to me?'

Innes crunched the letter into a ball and threw it at the grate. 'Dammit, Ainsley, it's you who won't listen! Why must you— I told you, I don't want you to care for me. I told you...'

She had had enough. Pushing back the blankets, Ainsley got out of bed and stood before him, hands on her hips. 'Do you think I could forget for a moment what you told me when it almost broke my heart!' she exclaimed. 'For goodness' sake, Innes, just because you want something to be so doesn't make it so! There are some things you can't control, and how I feel is one of them.'

'You think you're so damn clever! Can you not see, you annoying, interfering woman, that how I feel is another?' he said, yanking her into his arms.

He gave her no chance to respond, but covered her mouth with his. His kiss was passionate, dark and desperate. Exactly how she felt. Ainsley kissed him back with an abandon that left no room for thought. They staggered together, kissing, tearing at each other's clothes, kissing. Her back was pressed against the wall. His hands were on her breasts, her waist, her bottom. She wrapped one leg around him to steady herself. He pulled his jumper over his head and tore at the opening of her nightgown, groaning as he took her nipple into his mouth and sucked hard, making her moan, arch against him, thrust herself shamelessly against the thick bulge of his arousal.

She clutched at his behind, her fingers digging into the taut muscles of his buttocks. His mouth enveloped her other breast now, tugging at her nipple, making her ache and thrust and moan. Her fingers fumbled with the opening of his breeches. Her hands slid in, wrapping around the satin-soft length of him, sliding up to the hot, wet tip, and back down. 'Innes,' she said, the strain in her voice making her sound as if she'd run a mile.

'Ainsley,' he said raggedly, 'I need to be inside you.'

'Yes.' There was no hesitation in her agreement. She knew without a doubt that this was no beginning but an end, but she wanted him, needed to be part of him, this one last time. 'Yes,' she said, and when he hesitated, she arched against him. 'Yes, Innes, now.'

His face was dark, colour slashing his cheeks, his eyes deep pools. He lifted her onto the edge of the bed, pulling up the skirts of her nightgown. She wrapped her legs around his flanks, bracing herself on the mattress. He kissed her. He lifted her. He entered her. She started to come as he slid inside her. Tension, unstoppable, winding tighter and tighter as she thrust, pulsing around him as he thrust for the second time, her cries harsh, loud, demanding more and harder and more. Not enough, she didn't want it to stop, but she wanted him to have what she had. 'Come now,' she said. 'Innes, come with me.'

He did just as she asked, though he did not spend himself inside her, and panting, spiralling out of control, clinging, she did not regret that, because she knew he would, and this had to be it, the last time, the perfect time. She kissed him deeply, her lips clinging to his, her tongue touching his, touching, clinging, kissing, telling him with her mouth what she could not speak. There were tears lurking, but she would not shed those. Only she kissed him again. His mouth. His jaw. His neck. Nuzzling her face into the hollow of his shoulder, closing her eyes and trying to etch it all in her mind, as his heart thundered under her and his chest heaved, and his hands held her so tight, as if he would not let her go, though she knew he would.

Ainsley knew, even as they lay there, breathing heavily in the aftermath of their union, that it was completely and irrevocably over. Innes cared for her, but it tormented him. He had lost himself in her to stop that torment, and she had lost herself in him because she could not resist him. But she could not carry on this way, and she would not allow herself to be the means by which he escaped his past.

'I'm sorry.'

She dragged her eyes open as Innes rolled away from her, his expression troubled. 'What for?' she asked.

'Not this, but the way it happened. You meant well—the idea for the hotel, writing to—to her. You meant well, I know that. I shouldn't have lost my temper.'

But he wasn't going to change his mind. Ainsley got to her feet and pulled on her wrapper. 'I should have consulted you,' she said, turning her back to him to tend the fire.

'It would certainly have saved you a lot of effort.'

The final confirmation, as if she needed it. He was standing behind her now. 'You must be tired,' she said. 'You should get some sleep.'

'Ainsley, I really am sorry.'

He looked quite wretched. She surrendered to the temptation to comfort him one last time and went to him, wrapping her arms around his waist, resting her cheek on his chest. He pulled her tight, almost crushing the breath from her. 'You do understand,' he said.

'I do, Innes.' She looked up, brushing his hair from his eyes, and kissed him gently on the lips. 'I understand perfectly,' she said. 'Now go and get some sleep.'

He went. He would have stayed if she had asked him, but she did not. Instead, she set about making her preparations to leave, packing a few necessities in a bandbox, leaving the rest to be sent on. She found Blanche's balled-up letter lying under the nightstand and smoothed it out. Her own words, quoted in the other woman's elegant hand, leaped out of the page at her, and at the end, a plaintive request from Blanche for a meeting. Nothing more. It was signed with a flourish, the first name only.

Innes had been joking when he suggested marrying Blanche would make all right, but there was still a chance it would. Blanche was his first love. His only one? How easy would it be for him to fall in love with her again if he could be persuaded his dead brother sanctioned the match? Blanche had always been intended to be the wife of the laird of Strone Bridge. She had been groomed for it. She had birth and money and beauty. She would be a laird's wife worth her salt. A woman who belonged here. A woman blessed by the last laird. No usurper. A woman who was perfect in just about every way, including, no doubt, her ability to pop out any number of the requisite heirs.

Feeling slightly sick, Ainsley folded the letter carefully. Pulling Innes's discarded jumper on over her nightclothes, she made her way softly down the stairs. Outside, the air was sharp with the first hint of frost. The stars were mere pinpricks, the moon a waning crescent, but she knew her way now, without looking. Up to the castle, along the path, to the terrace and her view. That was how she thought of it, though it would not be hers after today. Gazing out at the black shape that was the Isle of Bute, longing gripped her, tinged with anger. All her hard work had come to naught. When she was gone from here, there would be nothing of her left. Perhaps that was what Innes wanted, to forget all about her, and to immolate himself on the altar of the past. Tragic as it was, Ainsley was becoming impatient with his determination to earn a martyrdom. She loved him with all her heart, and more than anything, she wanted him to be happy, even if he did decide to marry Blanche. He had lived with guilt and regret for so long, she would not add to that with tears, with long goodbyes, with dragging out her time here.

Eyes straining into the inky blackness, she sought to capture the view in her mind for all time. Then she turned away and headed back to the Home Farm to complete her preparations. Before dawn broke she was tapping on the front door of Eoin's croft, her luggage already left waiting down in the bay.

Dearest Innes,
I am writing this as myself, and not Madame Hera, though the truth is, in my time at Strone

Bridge, I believe we have become more or less one and the same thing. No doubt reading this as Madame's advice will make it easier for you to ignore. I expect you will. I wish with all my heart that you will not.

As you can see, I have rescued Blanche's letter. I hope you forgive me when I confess to having read it. Innes, please do as she asks and meet her. If you cannot put your own de-mons of guilt to bed, then perhaps you can help her. The poor woman was but a child when these tragic events that have shaped both your lives took place—as indeed were you, though I know you do not agree with me on that score. You are in the unique position of being able to help each other. I beg you to try to do so.

As to the rest. Robert Alexander can answer any questions about my proposal for Strone Bridge's future, which my documentation leaves unanswered. It is not pride—well, only a little!—that leads me to ask you to consider this, but a genuine belief that it will help save your estates and the people who live there. I'd like to think I've left something of value behind. I hope it's obvious how much I have come to love the place and the people.

I leave it to you to manage the termination of our agreement in whatever way you think best. I leave Strone Bridge a much stronger person than the poor wee soul you met at the lawyer's office all those months ago. I leave it ready to do battle with whatever the future holds, and confident that I can. You have helped me in too many ways to list. I do not regret a second spent with you. With all my heart I wish you happiness, because you're wrong, Innes, it is something you well and truly deserve.

A.

Innes finished reading the letter, then started all over again, as if a second reading would change the content. He looked up from the breakfast table to discover Mhairi was still there, watching him with such an expression of compassion on her face that he knew there was no point in pretending.

'Do you know when—or how—she left?' Innes asked.

'Eoin took her at first light. She left me a note asking to have the rest of her things sent on.'

'Where to?'

'It is a carrier's address in Edinburgh.'

Innes looked at the housekeeper helplessly. 'I don't even know if she's got any money. She has her allowance, but—I'll need to— I'll have to arrange to— She'll need a place to stay. I…'

'I think Mrs Drummond's more than capable of sorting that out for herself, if you don't mind my saying,' Mhairi interrupted drily. 'It seems to me that you'd better concentrate on sorting yourself out.'

'What do you mean?'

'Blanche Caldwell is back at Glen Vadie, did you know?'

Innes tore his eyes away from a third, fruitless reading of Ainsley's missive. 'At Glen Vadie? No, I didn't know. She wrote me a letter, though.'

'Does Mrs Drummond know?'

'About the letter?'

'About Blanche, Innes,' Mhairi spoke sharply. 'If that good woman has gone haring back to Edinburgh to leave the way clear for you to pick up where you never should have started with that Caldwell woman…'

'Dear God, do you think that's it?' For a moment, his heart leaped. If that was all it was, he could fetch her back. But for what purpose, and for how long? Innes slumped back miserably in his chair. 'What are you waiting for?' he demanded, seeing Mhairi, arms akimbo, was still there. 'She's gone, and she's made it very clear she won't be coming back, so go and pack her things and leave me in peace.'

But peace was not something Innes could find over the next few days. On the one hand, he was tracking Ainsley's journey in his mind, wondering where she was, who she was with, whether she was thinking of him, whether she was missing him as he ached for her. On the other, he was determinedly trying to put her firmly out of his mind and refusing to allow himself to think about what was staring him in the face—or, more accurately, fighting to be heard from his heart.

He did love her. He had, despite all his best efforts, fallen completely in love with her. He loved her in a way he had never loved Blanche, as if she were part of himself. Without her, he felt as if that part was missing. It did not help that every corner of Strone Bridge reminded him of her. It did not help, lying in her bed, the scent of her on the pillow. It did not help, avoiding her favourite view, any more than it helped forcing himself to stare at it. Mhairi's tight-lipped disapproval didn't help any more than her misguided attempts to comfort him, or Eoin's insistence that when he left her on the Isle of Bute, Ainsley had been 'very well', whatever that meant. Innes hoped she was very well. It was wrong of him to hope that she was as miserable as he, wrong of him to hope that she missed him as much, ached for him as much, loved him as much.

She had never said the words, but he was standing on the castle terrace looking out at the Kyles of Bute when he realised that she did love him, and it hit him then, how much he was wilfully throwing away. What was wrong with him? Looking up at the tower, he remembered exactly what was wrong with him. Standing in front of Malcolm's grave a while later confirmed it. Guilt. The demons of the past. Ainsley was right.

Something glinted in the browning grass by the stone. Stooping to pick it up, Innes found a brooch. A simple thing of silver, with a name etched into it. He recognised it, for she had always worn it. So she had been here. He wondered how she'd managed it without his knowing, but it wasn't much of a puzzle. Mhairi or Eoin, or both.

Finally, Innes allowed himself to consider the advice Ainsley had left him in her letter. Heading back to the Home Farm, he read it again. And again. He found the keys on the desk where Ainsley had left them. The tower key, he still had in his coat pocket. In the Great Hall, all Ainsley's plans were still there as she had laid them out for him. So much work. He couldn't believe how stupid he'd been not to see the love that had gone into it. He felt sick to the back teeth thinking of how ungrateful he'd sounded, how much it must have hurt her to have it all thrown back in her face.

He lit a lamp and picked it up. At the doorway, goosebumps prickled on his arms. Mhairi always said there was no mistaking what she called a presence. It grew cold, she said, as if you'd walked into an icehouse, and you got a sense of it, like a breath of wind over your shoulder. Innes whirled round, but there was nothing there.

The lock turned easily. He climbed the stairs slowly, his feet remembering the twists and turns as if it had been yesterday, and not fourteen years since last he was there. Past the first-floor landing and then the second. The door at the top was closed. Heart pounding, he took a deep breath, pushed it open and stepped inside.

Nothing. Standing on the threshold, lamp held high, he felt absolutely nothing of his brother's presence. Mouth dry, he made his way over to the window. The view, in the gloaming, was as Ainsley had always said: spectacular. He opened the casement and forced himself to look down. The ground rose up to meet him, dizzying. Innes drew back hurriedly, looking over his shoulder, feeling like an idiot but unable to stop himself.

No Malcolm. Instead, he saw the table, so carefully set out. The scale model that Robert must have made of the castle and its grounds, the tied cottages, the newly landscaped gardens. Setting the lamp down, Innes pulled up a chair, picked up the sheaf of papers covered in Ainsley's distinctive scrawl and began to read.

Edinburgh, two weeks later

Ainsley put down the book she thought she'd been reading when she realised she'd been turning pages for the past half hour and could remember not a single word. Getting up from the nest of cushions and blankets she'd made for herself on Felicity's worn but comfortable sofa, she wandered over to the window. Outside, the streets of Edinburgh's New Town were quiet, for it was the

Sunday after Christmas, and the church bells of St Andrew's and St George's were silent, the morning services well underway.

Felicity was spending the week with her family, so Ainsley had the flat to herself. While Felicity had been here, she'd forced herself to pin a smile onto her face and get on. With Felicity absent, Ainsley had allowed herself a few days to mope. Not that she was regretting what she had done, but she needed time to make sure it had sunk in. Innes hadn't been in touch. Though her luggage had arrived at the carrier, it had contained no note from him. Not that she'd been expecting it. She certainly hadn't been expecting him to rush after her, and even if he had it wouldn't have changed anything, so there was no point in wishing for such a stupid waste of effort.

Sighing, bored with the circles her mind was running round, she pressed her forehead to the windowpane. Next week, the first of the New Year, she would start to look for a room. Even if she'd remained at Strone Bridge as agreed, that time would now be over. She wondered how Innes would see in the New Year. Ainsley—or Madame Hera—had been invited to a party hosted by the

Scottish Ladies Companion. She knew she ought to go.

Outside, a post chaise pulled up on the cobbled street. Her heart did a daft wee flip, then sank as the door opened and a maidservant descended, followed by a young woman. Ainsley watched listlessly as the baggage was unloaded. Farther along the crescent, a man had appeared. Tall, dressed in black, he was making his way slowly along, checking the numbers on each of the doors.

It wasn't him. Why should it be him? All the same, Ainsley gazed down in dismay at her crumpled gown, put a hand to her hair, which was falling down from the loose knot she'd put it up in this morning. She dare not leave the window to consult the mirror over the fireplace. Not that it could possibly be Innes. Even though he did walk like Innes.

It *was* him. Her heart stopped and then began to race as she looked down into his face. Such blue eyes. He raised his hand in recognition. She couldn't move. He disappeared up the steps. The bell clanged. Still partly inclined to believe he was a figment of her imagination, Ainsley went down to open the door.

'It is you.' He looked tired. He looked—nervous? Afraid? 'Has something happened?' Ainsley asked, panicking. 'Is someone— Is everyone…?'

'Fine. They're all fine.'

'And you?'

Innes shrugged. He smiled, or he seemed to be trying to smile. 'I don't know. I'm hoping to find out. Can I come in?'

'How did you know I'd be here?'

'Eoin finally gave me Miss Blair's address.'

'She's not here. She's gone to her parents for New Year.'

'Ainsley, can I come in?'

She opened the door wider and Innes stepped through, following her up the stairs to the living room. She closed this door behind her, then simply leaned against it, unsure what to say, refusing to allow herself to think about what this might mean. It had been hard enough to leave him the first time. 'What is it?' she asked, and her voice sounded sharper than she meant, but it couldn't be helped.

Innes took off his greatcoat and put it over one of the chairs. His hat went on the table, and his gloves. He stood in front of the fire, hands clasped behind his back. Then he went over to the window, where she had been standing a few moments ago. Then he joined her at the door. 'I don't know where to start,' he said. 'I had a speech, but I can't remember it now.' He waited, but she could think of nothing to say. 'I've seen Blanche,' he said.

Ainsley's heart plummeted, even as she told herself firmly that this was good news. 'Good,' she said, as if saying out loud would make it so.

Innes nodded. 'Yes, yes, it was.' He took another turn round the room, to the fireplace, to the window, back to her. 'You were right. Or Madame Hera was,' he said with another of those lopsided smiles.

'Good,' Ainsley said again, this time with a firm nod. 'I'm glad.' She didn't sound glad. She sounded as if she were being strangled. 'Did it help?'

Innes ran his hand through his hair. He had had it cut. Suddenly she couldn't bear that he'd had it cut and she hadn't been there. She blinked furiously, but a tear escaped and ran down her cheek. She brushed it away quickly, but another fell.

'Ainsley…'

'It's nothing. I'm fine.' She pushed him away and went to sit on the sofa, pulling the comforting woollen blanket over her, not caring how she looked or what he thought. 'Just tell me, Innes, and get it over with.'

'I thought you'd be pleased.'

'I am! I will be,' she said through gritted teeth. 'Would you just tell me?'

He stared at her in astonishment, and then he laughed. 'Don't tell me Mhairi was right.'

When she had nothing to say to this strange remark, Innes came to sit beside her. He was smiling, this time in a way that made her heart, which had become as wayward as her voice, start to do what felt peculiarly like a dance. 'Ainsley, you can't possibly be thinking that I would want Blanche?'

She shrugged, though the gesture was somewhat obscured by the blanket covering her. 'You did before,' she said, and though she sounded like a petulant child now, she couldn't help adding, 'You told me yourself that she is beautiful, rich, well born.'

'But I'm married to you.'

'Not really. I told you in my letter that I would cooperate with however you saw fit to end it.'

'And in the meantime, you don't mind if I'm bedding my first love, is that it?'

'No!' Though he had not raised his voice, he

sounded angry. Ainsley pushed back the blanket and got to her feet. 'You should not use a word like that in reference to your— To someone— To Blanche,' she said, picking up the poker and applying it furiously to the coals.

'Ainsley, I'm not bedding Blanche. I've no intentions of bedding her or even of making love to her. I can't believe you would think that. I'm married to you.'

'Not for much longer.'

The poker was wrested from her fingers. She was yanked to her feet, and held very tightly in an embrace. 'I came here in the hope of persuading you to make it for life. Please tell me I'm not wasting my time, Ainsley.'

Now her heart felt as though it was about to jump out of her mouth. The way he was looking at her, as if his life depended on her. But it did not. Surely it did not. She shook her head. 'I don't know what you're doing here.'

'I'm trying, in a very, very roundabout and long-winded way, to tell you that I love you. My only excuse for doing it so badly is that I've not said it before. Not like this. I've never meant it like this, and if you mention Blanche one more time...'

'It was you who mentioned her.'

He laughed. 'I was trying to show you that I'd understood. That I'd done what you advised. That I'd taken the opportunity to "put the past to rest", to quote Madame Hera.'

'That was me, actually.'

'But, as you pointed out to *me*, they are become one and the same person.' Innes pushed her hair back from her face. 'I thought I had to prove myself worthy before I told you, but I think I did it the wrong way round. I love you, Ainsley. I love you with all my heart, and though I can live without you, I can get by with my guilt and my demons persuading myself that it's all I deserve, I don't want to. I want to be happy, and the only thing that will make me truly happy is you.'

She had never believed there was such a thing, but she could have sworn what she saw in his face was the light of love. She had so many questions, but right now all that mattered was that. 'I love you,' Ainsley said, 'I love you every bit as much, and I could do as you said, too, I could live without you, but, Innes, I really don't want to.'

'You don't have to. Dearest, darling Ainsley, you don't have to.'

He kissed her in a way he'd never kissed her before. Gently. Tenderly. Tentatively. He kissed her as if he was afraid she would not kiss him back. He kissed her as if he was begging that she would. 'Ainsley, I know it's all back to front, but I love you so much,' he said. And then he kissed her again, and she told him, with her hands and her lips, how very, very much his love was returned.

Later, Innes thought, kissing her. There would be all the time in the world for explanations later. What mattered now was that he loved her, and she loved him, and she was in his arms and he could finally admit just how much he had missed her and how close he had come to losing her. He kissed her, whispering her name over, whispering the words over, kissing her, touching her, pulling her so close there was no space between them. He never wanted to let her go. He wanted to make love to her right now. Make real love. Make love that he'd never made before. 'I love you,' he said. 'I can't believe how much I love you. I can't believe how daft I've been not to realise.'

He kissed her again. She laughed. She kissed him. She laughed. She kissed him. They fell, kissing, laughing with happiness, on to the sofa. And there, they made love. Laughter giving way to sighs, and then seamlessly to bliss. Love. Who would have thought it? Love.

* * *

'I meant to do this the other way round,' Innes said afterwards, lying splayed on the couch, with Ainsley draped languorously on top of him.

She giggled. 'Is this a new variation in the palace of pleasures you haven't told me about?'

'Hussy!' He grinned. 'I meant that I planned to tell you what's been happening since I read your parting letter before declaring myself, but if it's variations you're interested in, my wanton wife, then I am sure I can come up with something.'

'Really? Already?' Ainsley wriggled against him, her smile teasing. 'Are you trying to live up to the Drummond reputation for potency?'

Her face fell at her own silly words. Though she tried to hide it, he saw the flash of pain there as she moved away from him. 'Listen to me a moment,' Innes said urgently, pulling her right back to where she had been, lying over him. 'I love you exactly as you are. You need to believe me.' He touched her face gently. 'Strone Bridge is our legacy. It's all the legacy we need, and your love is all I need. I don't need you to prove it any other way than by being by my side, for better or for worse. I don't need a bairn, and I don't want you to go down the track of thinking that, or of thinking that you've somehow failed me if it doesn't happen. I need you to promise me that you believe me.'

A tear rolled down her cheek. 'Innes, you need to understand, I've been told by a doctor it's simply not possible.'

'And you need to understand that I mean what I say. I want you. That's all that matters to me. If it turned out I could not have a child, would you walk away?'

'Of course not!'

'Well, then, is this not a case of what's good for the goose being good for the gander?'

'Shouldn't it be the other way round?'

'Ainsley, I'm serious. I want you to be my wife. My real wife. My forever wife. My only love. I won't have this become an issue between us. I want us to have a fresh start in everything. I want us to be married. Will you marry me, my darling?'

'Again?'

'If that's what it takes.'

'Love me, that's all that it takes, and I promise, I won't let anything come between us.'

She kissed him softly on the mouth. Then she smiled at him, and Innes thought that maybe it was true what they said, that hearts could melt. He hugged her tightly, then he sat up, pulling her into the crook of his arm, wrapping the blanket around them. 'Now,' he said, 'I think I owe you a story. It's a long one, but I'll give you the gist of it now.'

He frowned, thinking back on all that had happened over the past two weeks. 'It wasn't finding the brooch that made me get in touch with her, or even her letter, but yours,' he concluded some time later, smiling fleetingly down at Ainsley. 'Your leaving like that brought to me my senses about how I felt for you. I'd always thought Strone Bridge was haunted by the ghosts of the past, but that was nothing compared to how it felt without you there. I kept expecting to see you at every turn. Especially at that view of the Kyles. Then there was Mhairi. And Eoin. And Robert—my goodness, that man went on and on about you. Everyone, asking me where you'd gone, when you'd be back.'

'Really?'

He laughed. 'You've no idea how much people have taken you to their hearts. It's not just me. You're part of the place, Ainsley.'

She kissed his hand, her eyes shining. 'It's

part of me, too. I missed it nearly as much as I missed you.'

'Who'd have thought it?' He kissed the top of her head. 'It was when I was away the last time with Eoin I realised I'd come to think of it as home, and to think of you there, too. It scared the living daylights out of me.'

'That's when you told me about Malcolm?'

'Aye, there are no flies on you.' Innes kissed her again. 'That letter you left me—you said I deserved to be happy. That was the biggest problem, for I just couldn't see that I did. But then I was standing there in the tower looking at all the hard work you'd put into those plans, and I realised it wasn't just about me, but you, too. And Blanche—that point in your letter hit home, too. Was I actually glorying in my guilt, or so used to it that I couldn't see a way of escaping it? That turret room, I thought it held the bogeyman, but it was just a room with a view. You were right about that. It was there I began to think maybe you could have been right about other things. So I went to see her at Glen Vadie.'

Ainsley scrambled upright. 'And?'

'And it turns out things were not quite as I'd imagined,' Innes said wryly. 'Blanche ran away because she couldn't bring herself to marry Malcolm, as I told you. She wrote the letter to him, thinking that it was the right thing to do, to tell him, though she could not find the courage to do so to his face. She didn't think what it would do to him, because she didn't really think about what she'd said. That she didn't love him. That she couldn't marry him. She didn't say that she wanted to marry me, because she didn't.'

'What?'

'I know. It's farcical. Or it would be if it weren't so tragic. I'm not the only one who's been tying themselves in knots of guilt for the past fourteen years, nor am I the only one who swore off love, either.' Innes shook his head. 'I still can't believe it. She's been living in London unmarried all these years, until she met her man Murchison and fell head over heels at the age of thirty-two. So when your letter found her, out of the blue, she was delighted at the chance to finally come clean.'

Ainsley's jaw dropped. 'Blanche never wanted to marry you?'

'I know, love, it's unbelievable,' Innes said, grinning.

She slapped him playfully. 'You know what I mean.'

'I do.' He sobered. 'She said the same thing as you about Malcolm—that he'd have wanted us both to be happy. He thought, in his tragic, misguided way, that was what he was doing, clearing the way to make us so. It finally clicked with me, after you'd gone, that paying him back by making myself miserable was a stupid thing to do.'

'And Blanche?'

'Realised the same thing, not so very long ago, but all she did was confirm what you'd been telling me, Ainsley.'

'So she's as lovely on the inside as she is on the outside.'

He laughed. 'I expect she is, but there is no one as lovely as you for me. I thought I'd just proved that.'

'I hope you'll prove it again very soon.'

'Now, if you like.'

She smiled at him, the smile that sent the blood rushing to his groin, the smile he'd thought he would never see again. He kissed her on those delicious lips that were made for kissing. 'Now, and always,' he said, 'and for ever, too.'

Epilogue

Strone Bridge, New Year's Eve, 1840

Ainsley's gown for the first Hogmanay party to
be held at Strone Bridge by the new laird and
his lady, was of ivory silk. Cut very plainly, both
the *décolleté* and the bodice were her favourite
V-shape, showing her waist and her modest cleav-
age to advantage. The sleeves were short, puffed
and trimmed with the same black lace that bordered the hem, and was formed into little flowers
at the end of the ruched silk that ran in vertical
stripes down the skirt, like waves on the sand.

The party was to be held in the Great Hall. She
and Innes had arrived from Edinburgh only the
day before, but it seemed Innes had left matters
in Mhairi's capable hands beforehand. 'What if
you had not found me? What if I had refused to

come back?' Ainsley had asked him on the paddle steamer. Failure, he'd told her, was not an option. The look he'd given her then, aglow with love, made her want to kiss him then and there, on the blustery and freezing-cold deck of the *Rothesay Castle*.

It had begun snowing when they'd arrived at Strone Bridge, and it was snowing still. The last day of the year was spent making sure that the Home Farm was spotless, hanging rowan in the doorways for luck, and hazel to stop the bad spirits who'd been swept out getting back in again. Mhairi's advice, of course, but Ainsley had become so accustomed to pandering to good faeries and warding off bad that she'd almost started to believe in them.

She was making a final check in the mirror when the door opened and Innes entered the bedchamber. He was in the full Highland regalia he'd worn for the Rescinding. Her pulses leaped when he smiled at her. His hair was black as night. His eyes were the blue of the sea. She loved him so much.

'May I tell you, wife, that you look absolutely ravishing?'

'You may.' She dropped him a curtsy. 'May

I tell you, husband, that you look absolutely ravishable?'

He laughed. 'I'm not sure that's a word, but I like it.'

'I think it's an excellent word, and I intend that Madame Hera makes it a popular one.'

'To keep a happy marriage, make sure your husband is ravishable at all times.'

'You see, it's perfect.' She put her arms around him and stood on her tiptoes to kiss him.

'Shall I prove how perfect?' he whispered.

She chuckled. 'Maybe next year. We have a ceilidh to attend.'

'A whole six hours, you're making me wait!'

'I'll make it worth your while, I promise,' Ainsley said with a meaningful look.

'I shall hold you to that,' Innes said with one of his devilish smiles. 'Did I tell you about the tradition of Reaffirming?'

'Is this another one of your invented customs?'

'It is.' He reached under the pillow and pulled out a leather box. 'I had this done in Edinburgh. Open it.'

Her fingers shaking, she did as she was bid. The rose-tinted diamond was the same, perfectly cut stone as before, but the setting was completely different. The diamond sat flat inside a very modern-looking circlet of gold, and the white diamonds that had encircled it were now also sunk inside the gold band. 'I've never seen anything like it,' Ainsley said. 'It's breathtaking.'

Innes slid the ring onto her finger, not where she had worn it for the Rescinding, on the middle finger of her right hand, but on her left hand, above her wedding band. 'A symbol of the passing of the old and the birth of the new,' he said. 'A reaffirming of what we promised, and a promise of so much more. I love you, Ainsley. I plan on loving you a little bit more every day.'

'A Reaffirming.' Her eyes were wet with tears, but she had never felt so happy. 'I think that might be my favourite custom yet.'

She had not thought she could be any happier, but as she stood by her husband's side in the Great Hall awaiting the bells that would herald the New Year, Ainsley thought she might burst with it. Looking around her at the faces, bright with the exertions of the reels and jigs, she couldn't help but compare it with the last time she had been here in this hall, a virtual stranger among them. Now she knew every person here by name. She knew which of the huddle of bairns at the far end of the hall belonged to which family and which croft.

But tonight, it was not only the people of Strone Bridge who were here to celebrate the New Year. There were new faces, too, from as far afield as Arran and Bute. The laird of Glen Vadie was here, and so, too, was his ward. Blanche Murchison, née Caldwell, was every bit as beautiful as Ainsley had imagined. Her hair was golden blonde. Her eyes were cornflower blue. Her brows were perfect arches. Her lips were a perfect Cupid's bow. The gown she wore was of silk the same colour as those big eyes of hers, and the diamonds on her necklace were obviously not paste. She was slight, several inches smaller than Ainsley, and she was most infuriatingly curvaceous. She had a smile to melt a man's heart, and she had one of those bell-like voices into the bargain. Were she not so obviously besotted by the man whose name she bore, Ainsley might have been worried. Then she turned to her own husband, who had made the introductions, and saw the way Innes smiled at her, felt the pressure of his hand on hers and looked down at the diamond glinting on her hand, and she decided that she had no need to be worried about a single thing.

The bells rang for midnight. On cue at the last chime came a thumping at the door, and the first foot arrived, chosen for his coal-black hair, sheepishly bearing a bottle of whisky and a black bun cake. Glasses were filled, and the call for a toast went up.

Innes put his arm around Ainsley's waist and called for silence. 'I'll keep this short and sweet,' he said, 'for you've better things to do than to listen to me. At the Rescinding, we put the past to bed. Tonight, this first day of 1841, I want to talk about the future. The future my wife and I have planned here at Strone Bridge. The future I hope you will all share with us. Robert?'

He nodded over at the surveyor, who, with the help of several men, brought a long table into the centre of the room. 'This, I am proud to tell you, is all my lovely wife's idea,' Innes said. 'This is our promise to you. A Reaffirming,' he said, giving Ainsley a glowing look. 'A symbol of the passing of the old, and the birth of the new.

Ladies and gentlemen, lads and lassies, I'd like you to raise your glasses to Strone Bridge Castle Hotel. *Sláinte.*'

* * * * *

MILLS & BOON®

Why shop at millsandboon.co.uk?

Each year, thousands of romance readers find their perfect read at millsandboon.co.uk. That's because we're passionate about bringing you the very best romantic fiction. Here are some of the advantages of shopping at www.millsandboon.co.uk:

* **Get new books first**—you'll be able to buy your favourite books one month before they hit the shops

* **Get exclusive discounts**—you'll also be able to buy our specially created monthly collections, with up to 50% off the RRP

* **Find your favourite authors**—latest news, interviews and new releases for all your favourite authors and series on our website, plus ideas for what to try next

* **Join in**—once you've bought your favourite books, don't forget to register with us to rate, review and join in the discussions

Visit **www.millsandboon.co.uk**
for all this and more today!